RED CREEK
RAVENS

2

BROKEN
PUCK

L. ANN
CLAIRE MARTA

BROKEN PUCK

Cover design by Honey & Sin Designs

Cover Model - Eric Taylor Guilmette

Cover Photographer - Christopher John

Interior Formatting by Crow Fiction Designs

Edited by Teresa Smith

Back Matter Blurb by Tami Thomason

First Edition: August 2023

ISBN: 9798856220789

Dear Reader

What happens when a bad boy realises he's lost his way?
When he discovers that the one thing he tried to break was the
only thing keeping him sane?
When their whole world has fallen apart, can he repair the
damage?

Red Creek Ravens contains scenes of:-
Bullying, knife play, hunter and hunted, primal play, dub con.

If domestic violence, alcohol abuse, suicide, gun violence,
mental and physical abuse, panic attacks and PTSD are triggers for
you, please take care when you step inside our world.

Playlist

MIDDLE FINGER - BOHNES

SCARS - BOY EPIC

PROTECTOR - CITY WOLF

CHALK OUTLINES - REN

RECKLESS - JAXSON GAMBLE

COMPLICATED - AVRIL LAVIGNE

PRETTY LIES - WRITTEN BY WOLVES

DIRTY LITTLE SECRET - ALL AMERICAN REJECTS

KISS ME A THOUSAND TIMES- RAIGN

DON'T LOOK BACK IN ANGER - OASIS

Dedication

Back for more, Book Bitches?
The Zamboni has scraped the surface, and we can see the grooves
that's been scored into the ice by the skates and sticks.
Thank you for all for coming to our game.
Take your seats. We're about to begin.

PART ONE

L. ANN & CLAIRE MARTA

I swallow a mouthful of vodka, my eyes on the pile of pills on the table.

How will it feel? Will I just go to sleep and never wake up again? Will my parents be waiting for me, or will it just be eternal emptiness? What if your mom isn't there? Don't they say that suicide is a sin?

I pause mid-reach for the pills. I'm not religious, not by any stretch of the imagination, but if that's right then I won't see her or Dad ever again.

You're not going to see them ever again, anyway.

Grief cascades over me, almost crushing me under its weight.

I can't do this anymore. I can't live like this.

I reach for the pills.

What about your friends? The team?

What about them? They'll move on without me.

You don't think they'll miss you? Grieve for you the way you are

3

for your parents? The devil on my shoulder isn't backing down on making its opinion known.

It's not the same. They'll get over it.

What about Bailey? You don't think she'll wonder if it's her fault? That she drove you to this?

Pain stabs through my chest.

She won't care. I've destroyed any feelings she's ever had for me.

Do you want to destroy her life as well? You question whether it's your fault your mom killed herself. You think she won't ask herself the same thing? You're being selfish and cowardly. Face your mistakes.

My hand shakes, hovering over the pills.

Is this really the answer? You're the captain of the Red Creek Ravens. Do you really want this to be how they remember you? Covered in shit and vomit.

At least it'll represent the mess I've made of my life. I snatch up the pills. *I've ruined everything else, so why not?*

A loud thump sends some of the pills scattering when I jump.

"What the fuck is that?"

The banging starts up again, coming from the front door.

Frowning, I stare at it. *Who would be knocking at this time of night?*

"Rush?" A male voice. An *unexpected* male voice.

Dropping the pills back onto the table, I stand and cross the floor, check the security chain is on, then crack open the door.

Hank Hicks is standing on the steps, one hand raised.

"What?"

"Open the door, kid." He doesn't bother to whisper and his smoke-roughened voice echoes around the silent trailer park.

"Why?"

"Because I can see what you're doing through the window. Open the door, or I'll break it open."

"You can see—" I twist around and, sure enough, the side window close to where I was sitting faces out toward his trailer.

"I was having a smoke and happened to glance over this way. Open the door."

"I'm not—"

His hand slaps against the flimsy plastic door, snapping the security chain taut. "Boy, don't make me tell you again."

Silently, I push the door closed and slide the chain off, then reopen it. He's inside less than a second later, and immediately strides across to the table to sweep up the pills into one large hand.

"Boy, nothing is worth this."

"My name is Rush, and you have no fucking idea."

"I know what your name is." He picks up the bottle of vodka and moves past me.

"What are you doing?"

He doesn't reply, but I get my answer a few seconds later when he tips the pills into the toilet, pours the vodka over the top, and flushes. When he's done, he tosses the vodka bottle in the trash then turns to face me.

"I've been watching you for a while now."

"Well, that's not at all fucking creepy," I mutter.

He folds his arms. "You had your grandma fooled, and you might have everyone else around you convinced that you're okay, but you're not. I can see it, clear as day."

"How the fuck would you know?"

"Because I've been where you are, boy."

"My *name* is fucking Rush." The words are snapped through gritted teeth.

He ignores me. "I know you miss your momma, but alcohol and pills ain't the answer, kid."

"If you know all the fucking answers, tell me what is."

"I don't claim to know all the answers, boy. But I know what I know. And I know that you need help. Your grandma should never have left you alone, but you hoodwinked her good 'n' proper. How do you think she would feel, if she got a call saying you had done the same thing as your momma? Do you think she'd survive that?"

The words are like a slap in the face, and I physically rock back. I've been so focused on me, and what I've done, that I didn't stop to think about my grandmother. I scrub a hand down my face.

"Fuck."

Hank nods. "Fuck, indeed. Sit your ass down, I have something to say to you."

More than the truth bombs he's already hit me with?

I drop to the couch, sinking my head into my hands. "I've fucked up so bad."

"There's nothin' in this world that can't be fixed with hard work."

"Speaking from experience?"

"You've heard the rumors about me, so you already know the answer to that question."

"Are any of them true?"

He shrugs. "I haven't heard them all, so I can't say. Maybe one day we can sit and go through them all. That's not why I'm here right now, though."

"I don't know what to do." There's a pleading note to my voice that I can't hide.

The couch creaks as Hank lowers himself onto it beside me. He pats my back.

"Getting sober is the first step. The path you're on right now is a dark one, boy. One I've traveled. Believe me, it's not a journey you want to go on."

"I don't know how to stop," I whisper. "It's the only thing that makes getting through the day easier."

"Then you need to find something else. Something *better* to focus on."

My laugh is bitter. "I've fucked up the one thing that was better."

"Why don't I make us some coffee, and then you can tell me all about it?" He rises to his feet.

He's halfway across the trailer when there's another thud against the door.

"Did you invite company to witness my fuck up?"

He shakes his head.

"*Police.* Open up."

My gaze jumps to the door. "Police? Did you call the police?"

"Not me, son." Hank changes direction, slides the security chain back into place, then opens the door. "Can I help you, Officers?"

"Rush Carter?"

"No. He's inside. What do you want with him?"

"We're here to take him down to the station for questioning."

"For what?" I lurch to my feet.

"For the assault and rape of Miss Bailey Linnett."

2
Bailey

"Oh my god, Bailey." The familiar voice penetrates the darkness for a second.

"—Seven, call an ambulance—"

A hand touches my shoulder, and I whimper. I can't open my eyes. They feel glued shut.

"Rush." I try to move my head, but pain explodes through me, and I cry out.

Voices talk around me, fading in and out.

"—It's going to be okay—"

"—kill Carter when I find him—"

"—Cooper found her right before me and Dom—"

"—Jamie, calm the fuck down—"

"—the fuck up, Seven—"

"—no, Nicky. We shouldn't—"

"Rush." I whimper. "Rush?"

My throat tightens as full awareness briefly trickles in. Everything hurts. I'm cold. I can't stop shivering. Then darkness sweeps over me one final time, and everything goes silent.

***

I draw in a slow, painful breath. My ribs ache and the pain in my head makes me nauseous. Unconsciousness loosens its grip and awareness comes back to me in stages. I force my eyelids up, but only one eye opens fully, but not for long. The bright harsh light makes it water and I snap it shut. I try again, ready for the light this time. My vision wobbles, flickers and dances at the edges.

"Take it easy, sweetheart." A woman's concerned face leans over me.

"W-where am I?" My face aches.

"How are you feeling?"

"Everything hurts."

"You took quite a beating." The nurse's voice is soft. "I'm going to get the doctor. I'll be right back."

When she leaves, memories surface—broken pieces that dissipate as quickly as they form.

School. The diner. Talking to Cooper at the party. Rush's cruel words.

My lips tremble. My eyes burn.

"I'm Doctor Ferris and I'd like to ask you a few questions."

The nurse is back, with a tall dark-haired male doctor.

He gives me a kind smile. "Can you tell me your full name?"

I swallow around the thickness in my throat and scrub a hand over my eyes, flinching at the bolt of pain when I touch the right one.

"Bailey Linnett."

"Do you know what day it is?"

"Saturday? I think."

"Do you know where you are?" He moves deeper into the room, stopping to take the notes at the end of the bed and flicking through them.

"The hospital, I guess."

"Do you remember what happened to you?"

"No."

He nods, and perches on the edge of the bed. "Bailey, there's something we need to talk about." His voice softens. "When we brought you in, there were signs of ... more than just a physical assault. Do you remember anything about that?"

I shake my head, and regret the action immediately. I squeeze my eyes closed, fighting against nausea.

He reaches out and covers my hand, where it lies limply on the sheet. "Bailey, we'd like to do a rape kit test. We need your consent for that. I know you're hurting, but there's a time factor in this."

"R-rape?" Tears turn everything blurry. "I was raped?"

The nurse moves around the bed to take my hand. "We don't know, so we'd rather be sure." She gives me a small smile. " It's just a precaution, sweetheart."

A sob breaks free. "Okay."

"Nurse Steele will explain everything to you and take you through every step," the doctor continues. "If you need anything, she'll help you." And with that he leaves the room.

Head on the pillow, I fight to contain the panic rising in my throat.

I was raped?

No, they said it was a precaution.

But they wouldn't do it, if they didn't think it happened.

Nurse Steele touches my hand. "Honey, listen to me. I know this is a lot to deal with, but the first seventy-two hours after a potential attack is the time most likely to give accurate results. Your parents have been called, but they're out of town so we're not sure how long it will be until they return. Is there anyone else who you'd like to sit with you?"

I laugh, the sound slightly hysterical. *Who? Who would want to sit with someone being tested for rape?*

"No, no one. W-what do I have to do?"

"There are two parts to the exam. I'm going to need to ask you a lot of questions. They're going to be very personal, Bailey, and I'm sorry about that. But the more honest you are, the better it will be. After that, I need to do a head-to-toe examination. It's important to be honest in the answers to your questions as the things I'll need to check will be based on your answers. I'll need to do a full body examination, especially given the bites and marks I can see. I'll also need to take blood and urine samples, and swabs.

"I'm not going to sugarcoat this, honey. The exam *is* invasive. I'm going to need to take photographs of your body, and the damage done. I'll also have your clothes tested for any DNA of the perpetrator."

I stare at her, the horror of what she's suggesting pressing down on me like a heavy weight.

I can't breathe past the lump in my throat. Can't see through the tears spilling down my cheeks.

"I don't … I can't …"

"We can go as slow as you like, sweetheart. I'll be with you every step of the way."

***

I'm wrung out, exhausted, ashamed and embarrassed. The rape kit took hours. The questions Nurse Steele asked left me mortified and crying.

I thought that was the worst of it.

I was wrong.

The examination that followed broke me into pieces, and by the time it was over, all I wanted to do was turn off the lights, crawl beneath the sheets and hide from the world.

"Miss Linnett?" A new voice shatters the silence of my hospital room.

Two detectives are standing by the door, matching somber expressions on their faces

"I'm Detective Silver, and this is Detective Russo." The older-looking one tells me. "We'd like to ask you some questions about what happened."

I frown. "Russo? Are you related to Nicky?"

The younger man nods. "She's my cousin. Small town. Big family."

They move further into the room and take up a position at the end of the bed.

"Would you be comfortable answering some questions for us, Miss Linnett?"

"I … I guess." Anything was better than reliving the past couple of hours.

Detective Silver pulls out a notepad and a pen. "What do you remember from this evening?"

I pluck nervously at the edge of the blanket that covers me. "My brother threw a party at our house."

"Witnesses say you had a fight with a boy called Rush Carter. Is that true?"

"Yes." *That* I remember. In vivid detail.

"Would you mind telling me what it was about?"

"He was angry because I was dancing with someone else."

"You fought, and then witnesses say he left. Do you know where he went afterward?"

"No."

"Why did you go outside, Bailey?" Detective Russo asks.

I run my tongue over my lips. "I … I needed some air. The house was crowded. I was angry after my fight with Rush. I just needed to get out of the house."

"Do you have any idea who attacked you?" His voice is soft.

The image of a figure looming over me builds in my head, but it's faceless, *featureless.*

"It … it was dark. They wore a hoodie, I think."

"Was it the boy you argued with? Rush Carter?" Detective Silver's voice is hard.

Did Rush do this to me?

I think back to every time he held a knife to my throat or threatened to hurt me. And then the angry words he'd thrown at me when we last had sex come back to me.

He'd never mark you the way I do, Little Rose. Inside and out. He wouldn't know how to get you off. You need the pain, the anger, don't you?

No. I can't believe that. I *don't* believe it. Rush wouldn't do that to me. Tears blur my vision.

"I didn't see their face. I don't know who it was."

3
Rush

THEY DON'T CUFF me and, honestly, I'm too confused to argue. I let the two detectives lead me outside to where a patrol car with two uniformed officers inside is waiting, and climb into the back.

"Is he under arrest?" Hank's voice is loud, shattering the silence of the mostly-sleeping trailer park.

"We just want to talk to him. No arrests have been made yet."

"Rush, ask for a lawyer. Don't say anything without one present. I'll call your grandmother and let her know what's happening."

One of the detectives turns to me. "I don't recommend taking the word of an ex-con," he says, then slams the door, sealing me inside.

We make the drive to the station in silence, neither officer in the front speaking to me or each other. My mind is racing.

What has happened to Bailey? Did she claim I forced her to have sex with me? Why? Why would she do that?

Because you shamed her, embarrassed her, and hurt her, you fucking idiot. That devil on my shoulder is back.

When we arrive at the station, they lead me through the building and into a small room. Inside is a table, two chairs, and a two-way mirror on the wall. I look toward it and then away again.

"How many people are watching us?"

"No one is in there. Sit down, Rush. I can call you Rush, can't I?"

"Sure."

The taller of the two detectives pulls out a chair and sits down. The other doesn't come inside, remaining near the doorway.

"Would you like a drink?"

I shake my head.

"I'll get you a can of soda just in case." He disappears through the door, closing it firmly behind him before I can reply.

"Sit down, Rush. I need to ask you some questions."

I lower myself into the chair opposite him. As soon as I'm seated, he places a notepad, closed paper file, and a recorder onto the table between us, which he switches it on.

"My name is Detective Silver. I'm in interrogation room five with Rush Carter. The time is one twenty-five a.m. ..."

I tune out the rest of the details, until he mentions his partner's name. "Sorry, can you repeat that?"

"My partner, who has gone for your soda, is Detective Russo."

"Russo? Any relation to Nicky and Trent?"

"You know them?"

I shrug. "They're in my year."

"Did you see them earlier tonight?"

"I don't think so. No, wait, I saw Nicky. She was with Dom."

"So, you *were* at the party?"

"I wasn't at first. Then Dom sent me a text."

"That would be Dominic James?"

I nod.

"And why did he text you?"

"Because—" *Fuck.* If I tell him that it was because Cooper was making moves on Bailey, that's going to make this situation even worse than it already is.

"That's alright, you don't have to tell me, I already know. It was because Cooper Dawson was dancing with Bailey Linnett, and according to witnesses at the scene, you didn't like it. Is that right?"

"Everyone knew we were together."

"Together? As if she's your girlfriend?" His pen hits the folder in front of him in a rhythmic beat.

"I gave her my jersey, yeah."

"Your jersey? Oh … that's a hockey thing, right?" His tone makes his thoughts about hockey clear. He isn't a fan.

"That's right. We only give the girl we're serious about a jersey with our name and number on to wear."

"And you're serious about Miss Linnett?"

"It's complicated."

"Okay, we'll come back to that. Why don't you tell me what happened tonight? Have you been drinking?"

I lean back on my seat. "Am I being charged for something?"

"Not right now. This is just an informal chat. You can refuse to talk, of course, but you should be aware that doing so will make you look even more guilty than you do already."

L. ANN & CLAIRE MARTA

4
Bailey

Is THIS MY fault? None of this would have happened if I'd stayed inside the house. Inside my room, and stayed away from the party like I'd first planned.

My eyes feel gritty and sore every time I blink. One side of my face is swollen and throbbing. After the detectives left, the nurse helped me into the adjoining bathroom, where I stared at my reflection in the mirror for what felt like years, but was probably no more than ten minutes.

A bandage covers a cut on my forehead. Nurse Steele said it had needed stitches—fifteen of them—and they did that while I was still unconscious. My eye below it is swollen almost shut. My ribs are badly bruised but she assured me that none of them are broken.

I feel disconnected, as though it's all happened to someone else.

"Bee?"

I look at the girl sitting beside the bed.

Nicky's eyes are red-rimmed, but she tries to smile at me. "Your mom and dad should be here soon."

Her words don't bring me comfort.

"Do you need anything?" Dom asks quietly from somewhere behind her.

My gaze rises to search him out. He's standing near the window, with Jamie and Cooper. The nurse had allowed them in earlier, after checking with me to make sure I was happy to have visitors. She told me they refused to go home, waiting for me to wake up, so they could make sure I was okay. The relief I'd felt at knowing that *someone* cared what had happened to me had agreement spilling from my lips without really thinking about it.

I regret it now. I hate the pity in their eyes.

"The cops will find out who did it." Cooper speaks with the assurance only people with money have. In his world, the police always bent over backward to fix things.

"Yeah, they will." Dom turns on him. "It's weird how Seven and I found you crouched over her."

"It wasn't me."

"I'm just saying it looks fucking suspicious from where I'm standing."

Cooper's face turns red. "It could have been *anyone*."

"Stop it! She doesn't need to listen to you two arguing." Nicky shoves to her feet and plants herself in front of Cooper, hands on hips. "Why are you here, anyway?"

"Bailey was my friend long before she was yours." He stares her down.

The door bursts open just as I'm about to scream at them *all* to get out, and my parents walk inside.

"Mom. Dad." I burst into tears at the sight of them.

Mom freezes as she stares at me, a horrified expression settling over her features.

Dad dashes across the room to my side to take my hand. "My poor baby. What happened?"

My answer is an anguished sob.

Jamie straightens away from the wall where he's been leaning. "It was Rush Carter."

Mom's head snaps around. "*What?*"

"He attacked her."

"You don't know that," Dom interjects, glaring at my brother.

My dad's eyes narrow on him. "Who the hell are you?"

"He's one of Carter's friends," Jamie says before I can introduce him.

"He's Nicky's boyfriend." My words are lost in the angry shout of my mom.

"Get the hell out!" Mom takes two steps toward him, her fingers curled into fists. "Don't you dare come anywhere near my daughter again. Do you *hear* me? Or I swear to God, I'll have you arrested!"

Nicky rises from her chair and catches Dom's arm. "Come on, let's go." She leans down and kisses my cheek—the least bruised one. "Text me when you want me to come and see you."

Cooper follows them out, and I'm left alone with my family. Dad sits on the edge of the mattress, and I crawl into his arms so I can burrow into the warmth of his chest. It hurts to move but having his arms around me, feeling the security of his embrace, is worth it.

"It's okay. You're safe now. You're safe now, my Little Bumblebee."

The name he used to call me when I was small makes me sob harder. He hasn't used it in forever.

"How could you have thrown a party?" Mom's voice is loud and harsh. "Jamie Linnett, you have a lot of explaining to do!"

"It was just supposed to be some fun." Jamie's tone is defensive.

"Does it *look* like it was fun to your sister? How can you be so irresponsible? We trusted you to watch out for each other."

"It's not like she's the only one who got hurt. Some asshole stole some of my sneakers out of my room. They were limited fucking edition ones, as well. And I'm pretty sure Carter is the one who smashed up my windshield."

"I knew that boy was trouble the second I laid eyes on him."

My dad's hand strokes my hair. "How could you let this happen to her?"

"*Me?*" Jamie scoffs. "She's been seeing him for weeks, even after you told her not to."

I stiffen in my dad's embrace, my emotions raw and fragile. A tense silence descends over the room. My eyes are closed, so I can't see their faces, but I prepare myself for their anger.

"We'll discuss that at another time." Dad's voice is quiet. "We need to get Bee home. God only knows how much this is going to cost us."

I peek at my brother. His hands are shoved in the pockets of his jeans, and a muscle flexes in his jaw. His expression is closed, his eyes dark. My gaze locks with his for a second, before I tear it away.

I want to go home and pretend none of this has happened.

I want to bury myself under the blankets in my room, where nothing can touch me.

I know when everything settles, I'm going to have to face what happened, but right now, all I crave is a place to hide.

L. ANN & CLAIRE MARTA

5
Rush

I'M NOT SURE how much time has passed. There's no clock in the room and they've taken my cell. It could be hours, it could be days.

I don't *think* it's been days. I'm pretty sure they can't keep me here indefinitely without actually charging me with something. They keep insisting I can leave if I want to, but it'll look bad for me if I do … and so I stay. I answer their questions. I repeat over and over again the events of the evening.

I die a little inside each time I have to recount the insults I threw at Bailey after we were done. The way I left her bedroom door wide open so anyone could see her half-naked just-fucked body sprawled on the bed.

Detective Silver tells me it doesn't look good for me. I have nothing to say in response to that.

What *can* I say? I did what I did, but the sex was consensual.

It was angry, and violent, sure. But it *was* consensual. That I won't back down on.

When the detective tries to insinuate that I missed the signs, that she wasn't as eager to fuck as I was, I shut him down.

Not once did she tell me to stop, or say no. Nor did I think for a single second that she wasn't as into it as I was.

"Did you bite her?"

"Yes. Her throat, her breasts, wherever my mouth could reach."

"Did she cry?"

"No." I snap the word.

"Would you have stopped if she did?"

"Of course I would. But she didn't."

"Have you bitten her before?"

"Yes."

"Other students at the party said you fought with her."

"We fight all the time. It's foreplay."

"Did *she* know you viewed it like that?"

"Yes."

But did she? Am I wrong? Did I misread her responses? I give a mental headshake. *I'm not wrong.*

"After you had sex and left, where did you go?"

"Back to the trailer."

"What about the clash you had with Jamie Linnett?"

I think back. "He was by the door when I left. We had words. He hit me. I left."

"According to the report of other students, you were taken outside by Seven Brannagh."

"That's right. He wanted to make sure I didn't ride my bike back home."

"Did you?"

I shake my head. "I left it outside the house and walked."

"And your so-called friend just let you walk home alone?"

I can't stop a small laugh from escaping. "If I know Seven, he'll have shadowed me back, but he won't have walked with me. I wasn't in a good mood. We'd have ended up fighting."

"You weren't in a good mood because of what happened with Miss Linnett?"

"No, I was annoyed with her brother."

"What time did you get back to the trailer park?"

"I'm not sure. I don't know what time I left the party. It takes about fifteen minutes to walk there."

"And you didn't stop or go back to the party?"

"No."

"Do you have anyone who can confirm that?"

"I don't know. I didn't see anyone on the way. If Seven followed me, he can confirm it. Tamara Rees saw me when I got back. She had a letter for me. And then Hank Hicks came over." I scrub a hand down my face. "Look, I don't know what happened after I left."

The thought that someone hurt Bailey gnaws at me. I need to know she's okay. That someone *didn't* take advantage after I left. That this was a big fucking mistake or a drug and alcohol-fueled nightmare.

"I've answered all your questions. Will you please answer mine? What happened to Bailey?"

THE LATE OCTOBER sunlight is bright, but the wind is cold as the rental car parks up outside the house. I'm exhausted after another restless night at the hospital. The doctors insisted on keeping me there for two nights.

"Slowly now." My dad's hand steadies me as he helps me out of the passenger seat of the car.

I ease myself onto my feet and wince at the way my entire body aches. "I'm okay."

Mom is already at the front of the house with the door open. "Let's get you upstairs to bed."

They fuss over me as we move through the hallway and up the stairs. Jamie is waiting for us at the top. I limp past him and stop outside my open door, attention focusing on the damage.

"What happened to my lock?"

Jamie shrugs. "Guess someone broke it during the party."

Dad touches my shoulder. "We'll worry about that later. Come on, into bed with you."

I cross the room and sink down onto the bed, with a tired sigh. My parents help me take off my sneakers.

"We need to go to the store." Dad puts my sneakers under my chair by the desk. "I'll call into the diner and tell them you won't be coming back. I spoke to school this morning."

I struggle to my feet. "No! I can't let Darla down."

"You need to rest."

"But we can't afford—"

"*Bailey Linnett*, you will stay right where you are until I tell you otherwise." My mom growls fiercely.

I gape at her, then settle back down. "Okay."

"Now, do you want anything to drink?" She tucks the blanket up around my chin. "Juice?"

"Juice would be nice, thanks."

"I'll get it before we head out." She pats my hand and rises from the edge of the bed.

Jamie smiles at her. "Juice sounds good."

She levels him with an icy stare. "You are quite capable of getting your own."

"But mom—"

"No." She sweeps out of the bedroom before he can reply.

Dad ignores both of them. "Is there anything you want from the store?"

"No thanks."

"We won't be long. If you need anything, tell Jamie."

My brother huffs, his smile gone. "Great, I get to play nurse."

Dad spins around. "Bailey's done it for you plenty of times without complaint." There's an angry bite to his voice.

I close my eyes, only to pop them open again at the sensation of being stared at. "You don't have to stand there like a creeper. I'm not going anywhere."

Jamie eyes me from his position in the doorway. "Dad said I had to keep an eye on you."

"I don't think he meant you literally have to stand there staring at me the entire time they're out."

There's a ping from my phone. I reach for it. It must have been on my nightstand since the party. There's a bunch of messages and missed calls from my friends.

Zoey: Kellan told me what happened. Whose skull do I need to break?

Kendall: Bee, are you okay? Text me when you can.

Zuri: I miss you. Please be okay!

Faith: What happened? Zoey said something happened to you, and Kendall has been freaking out.

Zuri: There's a rumor that the Red Creek hockey team captain is responsible. Bee, did that bastard hurt you?

Zoey: Who do we need to hunt down and kick in the balls?

Jamie moves further into the room. "Who's the message from?"

"Zoey and my friends."

"Are you going to talk to them?"

"Later, maybe. I'm tired " I drop the cell phone on the mattress beside me.

"You know it was Carter, right?"

I take in the serious look on my brother's face. "I never saw who it was."

"But it *had* to be him. Everyone heard you fighting."

Everything still feels open and raw, the events of that evening are jumbled together in my head, but there's a little voice at the back of my head questioning Rush's part in what happened to me. "I don't know."

"That fucker is capable of violence. You know he is."

"I don't want to talk about it."

Mom appears in the doorway, a glass of orange juice in her hand. "Here we go, Darling."

"Thanks, Mom." I smile.

"Out! Let her have a nap." She shoos Jamie out of the room and closes the door behind her.

Silence settles over me, but doesn't relax me the way I'd hoped it would. Alone, my mind replays everything I can recall.

Rush's hands on my body. His teeth and lips on my skin. Memories of the cruel words he threw at me are like spikes of barbed wire ripping through my heart.

I'm not sure what to think anymore.

My mind, body, and soul hurt.

I press my face into the pillow. I wish I could wake up. That this was all a bad dream. I'll wake up, and everything will be better.

But even as I make the wish, I know it won't happen.

***

"Detectives Silver and Russo are here to see you."

My gaze bounces from the TV screen to my mom where she stands in my bedroom doorway.

Carefully, I sit up from where I'm slumped against the pillows on my bed. "Do they have some news?"

"They just want to talk to you again."

Conscious of the bruises on my arms and face, I snatch up my old Churchill Bradley hoodie and tug it on. I draw the hood up when we walk down the stairs, its comforting weight is a shield I can hide behind. Dad is with the two men in the living room.

"Miss Linnett." Detective Silver inclines his head at me. "How are you feeling?"

I shrug. "Okay, I guess."

Dad motions for me to sit down. "Take a seat, sweetheart. They just have a few things to go over."

My stomach twists, and I perch on the edge of the couch. Mom and Dad sit either side of me, while the officers take the two armchairs.

"Have you remembered anything else about Friday night?" Detective Silver asks, his notepad and pen in his hands.

"Some things, yeah."

Detective Russo's dark eyes are fixed steadily on my face. "We have a few questions that we need to ask, Bailey. *Personal* ones. Are you comfortable answering them with your parents here? Or would you prefer to do this alone?"

"No, no. They can stay. I have nothing to hide from them."

"Are you sure?" His voice is insistent.

I nod.

"Did you have sex with Rush Carter that night?" Silver asks.

Shit. Maybe I should have asked them to leave. My gaze darts to my dad. He gives me an encouraging nod.

"It's okay, honey. Tell the detective the truth."

I lick my lips and look down at the floor. "Yes," I whisper.

"Did he rape you?"

My spine snaps taut. "No!"

"You're saying that the sex was consensual?"

"Yes," I repeat.

Shame washes over me, and I fight to keep my composure. I can feel the weight of my parents' eyes on me. I wish the ground would open up and swallow me down. I shouldn't feel this way. I have *nothing* to be ashamed of, but the memory of the photographs the nurse took during her examination are burned into my mind. Rush's fingerprints, his teeth marks. I know how it looks, what people think of girls who like rough sex.

"Are you *sure*, Bailey?" Detective Russo continues. "We saw the bitemarks and bruises. If you're scared, we can protect you."

I curl my fingers into my palms until I feel the sting of my nails. "Rush didn't force me to do anything I wasn't comfortable with."

Mom wraps her arm around my shoulders. "Are you confused, honey? You don't have to be frightened of that boy."

I release a shaky breath. "I'm telling the truth."

"The sex might have been consensual, but he *still* assaulted my daughter."

Detective Silver sighs. "Ma'am, we have no witness, and your daughter didn't see who attacked her. We can't be sure that it's him."

"He's caused us nothing but trouble since we moved here."

"Your husband informed us about his family being the previous tenants in this place."

Detective Russo sits forward in his chair, forearms resting on his knees. "Is there anything else you can remember Bailey? Anything you remember that might help us?"

"I ... My attacker wore sneakers. There was a logo ... a lightning bolt, I think. I'm not sure."

"That's good. Anything else?"

I shake my head. "No, I'm sorry."

Detective Russo nods. "That's a popular brand of sneakers. Unfortunately, a lot of kids buy the knock-off ones that don't cost as much. Most of the boys at the high school more than likely own a pair of the fake ones."

"Your son also reported the theft of three pairs of sneakers. Limited edition ones." Detective Silver scribbles something in his notepad.

"Do you think the thief and her attacker are the same person?"

He glances up at my dad's question. "It's a possibility."

They don't know who did it.

The words sound hollow in my head.

My stomach twists, but surprising myself, anger is the strongest emotion that fills me.

If I can piece together more information, maybe I'll come up with the answer. A name or a face.

Whoever it is, I'm not going to rest until they pay for what they did to me.

L. ANN & CLAIRE MARTA

7
Rush

I'M EXHAUSTED. MY head is throbbing. I'm hungry and probably dehydrated. I haven't left this room in god knows how fucking long. It's been at least half a day since they escorted me into the restroom to pee. I'd caught a quick glimpse of Hank standing talking to a man in a rumpled suit, but was hustled back into the interrogation room before either of us could speak.

"I'd like you to go through the evening for me again."

I lift my head from where it's resting on top of my arms and look at the detective seated opposite me. Detective Finnagan raises an eyebrow. He's replaced Detective Silver, who is off doing … whatever it is he does.

"What's the point?"

"You might have forgotten something."

"I haven't."

"You've admitted that you were drunk. You were angry with

Miss Linnett for dancing with Cooper Dawson. You dragged her up to her room—"

"No, I *followed* her to her room."

"Because she was running from you."

"Because she was annoyed with me." I rub at my forehead, the throbbing has moved to behind my eyes.

"And because you were angry, you trapped her inside and raped her."

"That's not what happened."

"Then afterward, not content with raping her, you waited until she was outside, possibly looking for her brother to tell him what you did, and then attacked her."

"No."

"You didn't want her to tell anyone about the rape. As the captain of our school hockey team, you used your position and power to take advantage of a girl who is new to the school and doesn't have many friends."

"That's not true."

"Just admit it, Rush. Once you do that, we can move on. You can have something to eat, maybe get some sleep. But first you need to tell me the truth."

I lurch to my feet, hands slamming down onto the table top. "I *am* telling you the fucking truth. I didn't do *anything* to Bailey that she didn't want me to do."

"And yet she's lying in a hospital bed covered in bites and bruises, with your DNA all over her!" Detective Finnagan roars back at me. "Do you want to see what you did to her, Rush?" He flips open the folder on the table and slides a photograph across to me.

Bailey stares up at me out of those incredible eyes. But they're lacking the fire and fight that I'm used to seeing. They're dull, with no spark at all. Bruises mar her face. I stroke a finger along her jaw.

"I didn't do it." My voice is soft. I would never mark her like that. *Never.*

"Did you do these?" He tosses another photograph at me.

This one is of her throat and torso. My teeth marks are clear over her throat, collarbone, and breast above the bra covering her modesty. But there are other bruises and marks, ones I *didn't* do.

"I did these ones." I point to the ones I know I did. "But not the rest."

"I don't believe you. I think you did them all, Rush. I think after you raped her, you realized she was going to tell someone, so you tried to silence her."

"No, I—"

The door swings open to reveal Detective Russo. He jerks his chin at Finnagan, who stands.

"We'll continue in a minute. Look through the rest of the photographs, Rush, and when I come back, you can tell me the truth."

I do as he says, not because I did what he's accusing me of, but because I want to know what was done to her, so I know what *I* need to do to the bastard responsible when I catch up to them.

The detective isn't gone for long, and when he returns, there's a strange expression on his face.

"You're free to go."

It takes a moment for the words to sink in, and when they do, I *still* don't move.

"Come on, kid." Another voice speaks and my gaze jerks past the detective to where Hank is standing just behind him.

"I can go?" I frown. That doesn't seem right.

"Miss Linnett has confirmed that the sex between you was rough, but consensual. Two neighbors at the trailer park also came forward and confirmed your whereabouts for the rest of the evening," the detective explains.

"That's it? Just like that ... I can leave?"

"Your grandmother is waiting for you." Hank pushes past the detective. "Let's get you out of here."

"But—"

He wraps an arm around my shoulders and guides me out of the door. I'm enveloped in my grandma's arms the second I step outside.

"Oh my god, Rush! Let me look at you!" She peppers my face with kisses, then cups my face between her palms. "What have you been doing while I was gone? Why didn't you tell me what was happening?"

"I don't—" I'm so fucking confused. One minute I'm facing a rape charge, and then next I'm thrown out of the room.

"It doesn't matter. Not now. We're going home, and then you're coming with me."

"With you?" I can't focus properly, can't think straight, can't keep up with what she's saying.

"He's in shock." The voice seems to come from far away.

I blink, trying to focus but there's a buzzing in my ears, and my vision is wavering in and out. There's a shout, and then I'm falling. Hands catch me before I hit the floor and, while I don't completely pass out or faint, it takes me a second or two to get my brain and eyes to work properly.

"Eat this." A candy bar is shoved under my nose. "You've been stuck in here for almost forty-eight hours."

"Two days?" It feels longer. A month maybe. I take the candy and peel off the wrapper so I can take a bite out of it. "I need to see Bailey."

"That's the last person you need to see right now," my gran snaps. "That family has caused nothing but trouble for you. It ends now."

I'm not sure what stirs me from sleep, but when I move my head, the right side of my face aches. The painkillers I took last night must have worn off. My eyes adjust to the early morning sunlight that filters in through my window, and it takes my sluggish brain a moment to register that it's open. I push myself up in shock, expecting to see a familiar face in the room, but there's no sign of Rush.

The thought that he might have been here while I slept leaves me shaken, but before my mind can spiral with possibilities, my bedroom door swings open.

Jamie hovers on the threshold. "I thought I heard a noise. Are you okay?"

I hesitate for a second, my gaze darting to the open window.

His expression twists into a scowl. "Was Carter here?"

"I don't know. It was open when I woke up." I huddle under my blanket. I'm shaking.

From relief I'm alone or from disappointment?

"Son of a bitch." He stalks across the room and slams the window shut. "I heard the cops let him go."

Does that prove he's not the one who hurt me? Or just that there isn't enough evidence? Maybe they've released him because I said sex was consensual. Are they still looking for who did it? He's said more than once that he wanted to hurt me. He admitted it in his letters to me.

Should I have shown the detectives the letters?

"—and mom has gone to work at the store."

I blink and focus on my brother. "Huh?"

"I said Dad is asleep," he repeats slowly. "He has a shift at the factory tonight, and Mom has gone to work at the store."

"She got a *job*?"

"Started this morning."

"*Mom?*"

He nods.

Is it because of the medical bills I now owe?

"What time is it?" I can't reach my cell from where I'm lying.

"Ten."

"Why aren't you at school?"

Jamie walks toward the door. "Someone has to stay at home and look after you."

"You just want to avoid all the classes, don't you?"

"Mom thought it was a good idea." He doesn't answer my question. "I'll be right back."

I listen to the thump of his footsteps as he runs down the stairs. While he's gone, I get out of bed and limp across the room to the bathroom. The door clicks shut behind me, sealing me inside. I switch on the light, and do what I need to do, then walk over to the sink to wash my hands.

My reflection greets me. I've been avoiding it since I was brought home. Purple blooms across my pale skin, merging in places with black. The cut on my head is still covered by a bandage, and I can't even imagine what the scar and stitches will look like. The doctor had told me I might have a permanent scar.

I huff out a breath. My hands shake as I wash them.

The bruises on my skin may heal, the scars the attack has left on my soul will be there forever.

Jamie is standing by my window when I shuffle back into the room.

I pause, eyebrows raised. "What are you doing?"

"What does it look like?" He hits the window frame with a hammer.

"Why are you nailing my window shut?"

"To stop Carter and anyone else from getting in."

I move closer. "You could just go to the hardware store and get a new lock."

"This is quicker." He brings the hammer down onto another nail.

"But I won't be able to open it." I sit on the end of my bed. "What if there's a fire, and I need to get out?"

"Then you run through the bathroom and use *my* window."

It takes Jamie a while to seal the whole thing, but when he's finished he steps back and smiles.

"There."

I roll my eyes. "You can take them out again when I get a new lock."

"A thank you would be nice." The words are barely out of his mouth when a ping comes from his pocket. He pulls out his cell. "Cooper keeps asking about you."

That dislodges a memory from the hospital. "He's the one that found me, right?"

"Yeah," Jamie frowns. "Then Dom and Seven showed up."

"Did he see anything?"

"No. He said he went out for a smoke and you were on the ground near my car."

He types a message, while he talks to me. "Carter must have made a run for it before he saw them."

"You're dead set on it being Rush who hurt me."

"Everyone heard your fight." His eyes lift to meet mine, and he grins. "Guess who's just been made center of the Red Creek Ravens?"

I'm not sure why the news surprises me. "*You?* What about Rush?"

Jamie makes a derisive sound. "Carter isn't at school. From what I've just been told, he's not even in *town* anymore."

BROKEN PUCK

PART TWO

TWO WEEKS LATER

L. ANN & CLAIRE MARTA

9
Rush

"RUSH, ARE YOU ready?" Gran taps on the bedroom door.

I roll off the bed. "Coming."

Grabbing my hoodie off the top of the dresser on the way past, I pull it over my head and throw open the door. My grandma is standing just beyond it.

"I'm going to take you in, and then do some shopping for an hour. Is that okay, or would you prefer me to stay with you?"

I shake my head. "No, it's fine. You go do some retail therapy. Is Mrs. Rafferty going with you?"

Mrs. Rafferty is the friend my grandma came to stay with. After the call from Hank to tell her I'd been taken by the police for questioning, she agreed to let me come and stay here as well. She's nice enough, and in the two weeks I've been here, she's made use of my—as she puts it—strong young body to get some long-needed

DIY done around the house.

I can't complain. It's kept me busy and my mind focused on things other than the fuck up of a life I've left behind. But my gran thinks that's a problem, so she arranged for me to see someone. She thinks I need to talk about what's happened over the past year because she believes that my recent behavior is due to bottling everything up.

I could tell her it's not, but I don't think she'll listen. And, anyway, I've given her enough to worry about, so I will do it … just this once, and then I can tell her it doesn't work.

"No, honey. She's given me a list though." My gran's voice pulls me out of my thoughts.

We walk down the stairs toward the front door together. There's a car waiting outside. I don't think it'll matter how long I'm here, I'll never get used to needing to call a cab or an Uber to get around.

I open the passenger door for my gran, then slide in beside her. She tells the driver where to take us and it pulls into traffic. My cell chimes in my pocket. I pull it out and check the notifications.

Seven: Thanks for the card.

Me: Happy birthday. Wish I could be there. Are you doing anything to celebrate?

Seven: The team wants to go out after practice tonight. Not sure whether I'll bother.

Me: You should go.

Seven: I'll think about it. Are you going to that appointment today?

Me: On my way there now.

Seven: Call me afterward and tell me how it went.

Me: Will do.

"Who are you talking to?"

I glance over at my gran. "Seven. It's his eighteenth today."

She pats my hand. "I'm sorry, honey. You must want to be there."

"It's fine."

"We're here." The driver says as the car pulls up outside what appears to be a house.

"Thank you, dear." My gran reaches forward to pay for the ride.

I open the door to climb out, then help her out.

"Are you sure this is the place?" I eye the black door.

She smiles, and tugs on my sleeve. "Positive. Come along." She walks up the two steps to the door, then pushes on the buzzer to the left.

The intercom crackles to life. "Hello?"

"We have an appointment at eleven. Rush Carter."

"Come in. Straight along the hallway, then take the third door on your right." A click precedes the door swinging open.

Inside, it's apparent that this is an office building and not a home. The door we were instructed to take opens onto a reception area. There's an older woman behind the desk, and she smiles when we enter.

"If you'll take a seat, Dr. Michaels will be with you shortly."

I sink into the seat nearest the door.

"Are you sure you don't want me to stay?"

"It's best if I see Rush alone." A new voice answers before I can.

I look up and my gran turns toward the man standing in the doorway just behind the desk. He strides forward, one hand outstretched.

"Dr. Michaels. You must be Rush." He smiles at Gran. "And you must be Delancy Carter."

"That's right. We talked on the phone a couple of days ago," she says.

Dr. Michaels nods. "I remember. You can stay out here, if you like. Martha will make you a drink."

"No, I have some shopping to do. I just wasn't sure if—"

"Gran, I'm *fine*. Go and enjoy yourself." I stand and dip my head to kiss her cheek. "I'll call you when I'm done, okay?"

"If you're sure ..." she hesitates for a second longer.

"I'm sure."

"Come through, Rush ... Is it okay if I call you Rush, or would you prefer something else?"

"Rush is fine." I follow the doctor into his office.

"Would you rather sit by the desk or over on the couch?"

I shrug. "Don't care."

He smiles. "Alright, why don't we take the couch. It's more comfortable than the office chairs." He waves a hand to the corner of the room where a circular gray couch has been positioned beneath the window. There's a matching chair beside it.

"Your grandmother tells me that you've dealt with a lot of grief over the past year," he says once we're both seated.

"My parents died six months apart."

"That must have been difficult."

"It wasn't easy." I pick at an invisible thread on my jeans. My parents' deaths aren't really something I want to talk about.

"Are you uncomfortable?"

I lift my eyes to meet his gaze. "A little bit."

"Why do you think that is?"

I shrug again.

"Do you think you could share what happened when your dad died?"

I chew on my bottom lip for a second before replying. "I'm not sure what you want me to tell you. He went to work as normal. I saw him at breakfast. He was fine. I went to school. I was eating lunch when Mom called to say he'd had a heart attack, and was being taken to the hospital. By the time I got there, he was dead."

10

Bailey

"IT'S HEALED NICELY." Doctor Ferris probes gently at the scar on my forehead.

I wince but keep my head still. The stitches were removed a week ago, but the area is still sensitive and the scar that's been left behind is red and ugly.

Leaning back in his chair, he tugs off his surgical gloves. "I think we can discharge you. The skin around the original wound is nice and pink, and the angry redness of the scar should fade over time."

I slide off the stool.

With a smile, he picks up a sucker and offers it to me. "For being so brave."

I take it from him and shove it into the pocket of my hoodie. "Thanks."

Mom and Dad are waiting for me when I slip out into the hallway.

They stand when I exit and we make our way into the parking lot. Tension thickens the air once we're in the rental car. Money my dad had to spend because Jamie's car still has a broken windshield. Guilt niggles at me, but I push it down and try to ignore it.

Mom fastens her seatbelt. "You're lucky you survived with just the one set of stitches. Thank God you weren't raped."

When I'd got the results back from the rape kit, showing that only Rush's DNA was on me, I'd cried with relief. The confirmation that he was the only person I'd had sex with has lifted some of the crushing weight on my shoulders.

Some ... but not all.

Dad twists in the driver's seat to face me. "We need to talk about what happened."

Shoulders hunched, I fold my arms. "I told you that I had nothing to do with Jamie's party."

"I'm talking about the fact you were having sex with that *boy*."

"Those marks he left over you." Mom's voice drips with disgust. "How could you let him do that to you?"

"His name is Rush." I reply tightly, wishing I was somewhere else with every atom of my being.

She refuses to say his name. It's as though just the thought of it fills her with revulsion.

"Sweetheart, that's not how a man is supposed to treat you," Dad says, his voice gentle. "Maybe you found it exciting, but it's not right. He left bruises on your skin like an animal."

"I can't believe you continued seeing him after we told you not to. You let him make you his *whore*."

"Jesus, Shawna, that's enough!"

"Oh, come on, Kelvin," she snaps back at him. "You saw what he did to her, consensual or not. None of this would have happened if she'd done as she was told."

Does she really think this is all my fault?

"We both know that's a lie. If you hadn't gone to the trailer to demand money—"

Mom's laugh lacks humor. "*Me? You're* the one that kicked them out of the house in the first place."

"Because we needed somewhere to live!"

"Because *you* lost all our money. This is all your fault."

Dad's hand slams down on the steering wheel hard. "Maybe we would have been able to save some if you hadn't blown your way through so much with your expensive bags and lunches out with your friends."

I pull up the hood of my hoodie and close my eyes. Their angry voices rise and fall as the argument continues. I wish I had headphones with me to drown it out, but I don't so I make do with staring out of the window as we drive toward school.

It's a relief when we finally pull up outside.

Dad's gaze meets mine in the rear-view mirror. "Straight home after you finish."

"I know." I climb out of the car and head for the front of the building.

Classes have already started, and the hallways are silent as I walk along them. Everyone glances my way when I enter the classroom.

Miss Chappell pauses, her pen on the whiteboard. "Take your seat, Miss Linnett."

I hurry toward my desk. Dom tries to catch my eye as I pass him, but I turn my face away. Sofia leans across to one of her friends and whispers in her ear. Both girls giggle.

"What's so funny, Miss Colson?"

"Nothing, Miss Chappell." She smiles.

I take out my math books, conscious of the scar on my forehead. My hair is the only thing that hides it. The mottled bruises on my face are still visible. I don't want to be here, I want to be at home. Away from the curious eyes, the whispers that start up every time I leave a room or walk along the hallway.

I start work at the diner again tomorrow night, and I can't help but wonder if it'll be just as bad there.

I want to continue hiding at home, but I can't do it. We need my paycheck.

When the bell rings, I shove my things into my bag, and turn toward Dom's table.

"Here. Give this to Rush if he ever comes back." I dump the jersey in front of him.

He flips it over so the word 'Carter' shows. "You should give it back to him."

"I don't want to see him."

"He didn't do it."

Anger tightens my throat. "Just make sure he gets it."

Dom pushes it back toward me. "Keep it until he takes it back. You need to talk to him."

I don't pick it up.

"He said more than enough last time I saw him. I'm a *Puck Bunny* now, remember?" My lips twist. "Puck bunnies don't get a player's jersey. He can give it to Sofia."

Before he can reply, I walk away.

11

Rush

"IN OUR LAST session, we talked about the different stages of grief and how it's not a linear process."

I settle onto the couch, nodding. "You said that although they're listed in a specific order, sometimes you can jump around, and return to a stage or stay in it for longer. I remember."

"Okay, good. Well, I think it's safe to say that you've spent a lot of time in the anger stage of grief, and every time you moved to a different one, anger dragged you back because it took you immediately into denial again."

"I know where you're going with this."

Dr. Michaels laughs. "I would have been more surprised if you didn't. You're a quick study, Rush. But allow me to continue. To combat the other stages—denial, bargaining, and acceptance … *especially* acceptance—you stayed firmly in anger. To do otherwise would mean eventually reaching the point where you had to face the facts. But because you still hadn't finished grieving for your father, although anyone would have thought you had because you were excelling at school and with hockey, when you lost your mom, all those unresolved grief emotions came back, twice as hard. But this time you had an outlet, a focus, something to blame."

"Bailey." My throat tightens as I say her name.

"That's right. It was easy to focus on Bailey, and her family instead of how you were really feeling. It was much simpler to embrace the anger and say it was caused by her."

I lower my head, staring down at my sneakers.

"It was easy to lash out at her, because the person I wanted to yell at wasn't there." I force the admission out. "I still think that if her parents hadn't forced us out of the house, my mom might still be here, but that wasn't the only thing that drove her to do ... what she did."

"I spoke to your grandmother about your mom. She said that your mother had been sick for a long time. It started long before your dad died, but once she lost him, it got harder for her to control her demons."

"Yeah." My voice is soft. "I wasn't enough to keep her here."

"You know that's not true. She loved you more than anything. Mental illness, the likes of which your mom battled with ...it makes it difficult to believe that things will be better if they stay. She was convinced you would be much better without her, her love for you wanted you to have the best things in life, and her illness twisted that to make her believe that you would only achieve it without her presence."

My smile is small. "And that brings us to guilt, right?"

"It does. Guilt because you think it's your fault; guilt because you think you weren't enough; and guilt because you couldn't stop it from happening." He leans back on his seat. "But, and this is important, Rush, *nothing* you could have said or done would have changed the outcome. What she did had absolutely nothing to do with you, and everything to do with her mental health."

"I know that." I tap the side of my head. "Up here. I think I've always known that she was fragile. My dad used to say she was his fragile little rose." *Little Rose.* My eyes close briefly. "She's never going to forgive me."

"Who?"

I frown. *Did I say that out loud? Fuck. I did.*

"Bailey. Not that I deserve her forgiveness."

"Have you spoken to her since you left town?"

I shake my head. "I'm probably the last person she wants to hear from. My gran doesn't want me to contact her."

"Have you heard of the Twelve Step Program?"

"You mean for alcoholics?"

"Yes. One of the steps is called Integrity. One of the hardest things in life is to be honest about why you've done what you've done. The vulnerability of opening yourself up is something that's very hard to do. But, if you can speak your truth, lay it all out there in its pure unfiltered form, it can help you to accept and acknowledge what has happened."

I stare at him, my heart pounding a rapid beat against my ribs.

"You think I should write her a letter?"

12

Bailey

JAMIE KEEPS PACE with my strides as we walk along the sidewalk. I'm grateful for his presence beside me. My confidence in the fifteen-minute walk from the house to the diner is absent. I can't shake the sickening sense of dread I feel every time night falls. It brings back memories of the night I was attacked. Combine those with the nightmares I've been experiencing and it leaves me in a constant state of near panic.

The parking lot outside the diner is busy. A quick glance through the window confirms that most of the tables are crowded with people. Jamie halts before we reach the door.

"I'll be here for you at eleven."

I toy with the strap of my bag. "It might be a few minutes after. We have to clear up once the diner closes."

"Whatever. Just don't take too long, and don't come out until you see me."

"Okay. See you later." I don't wait to see him leave and head into the diner.

I wonder if he'll search my room for more money I might have hidden while I'm out. Not that he'll find it. I opened a bank account the day before I went back to school, and deposited Rush's three thousand dollars in it. I still need to find some way to get it back to him. Giving it to Dom isn't an option, and I don't want to mail it. It makes more sense to put it somewhere no one but me could access it. A place I can also save my tip money without the fear of it going missing again.

A few of the diners glance up at me as I walk through. I keep my gaze trained on the floor, not wanting to field any questions about my appearance. My hair is loose around my shoulders. The elastic band I use to tie it back on my wrist.

"Bee!" Sara races around the counter toward me.

Hank and Dennis appear from the kitchen and Darla steps away from the cash register. They crowd around me.

Dennis' gaze sweeps over me. "Sweet baby Jesus."

"Leave the girl be." Darla takes my arm. "Come on, honey, we'll talk in the kitchen."

Is she going to fire me?

She guides me past the counter and through the door.

"I'm sorry I took so long to come back. I didn't want to—"

"It's fine. We had to do some juggling of shifts, but it worked out." Her eyes roam over my face, and she sighs. "You can't serve the customers looking like that."

"Please don't fire me. I really need the money." I can't hide the desperation in my voice. "I'll take extra shifts. I'll do anything you need. Cover for anyone who needs it."

Darla's eyebrows rise up to her hairline. "I'm not about to fire one of my best waitresses." Turning, she raises her voice. "Dennis, Bailey is on washing up duty. You can work upfront with Sara."

It takes a moment for her words to register. Tears threaten to spill, but I blink them back. "Thank you. Thank you so much."

"Just take it slow tonight, okay?"

I nod, the warmth of her concern choking me up a little. "You got it."

"And if you need help, yell," Dennis says on his way past.

"I will, I promise."

Darla smiles. "Go on now, put your things away."

I hurry out of the kitchen to the storage room. Once my coat and bag are hung up, I close my eyes and release a long sigh. Emotions threaten to break through the numbness I've surrounded myself with, but I force them back.

I've still got my job. I might not make much but I can help pay something toward the medical bills with my tip money. It will be one less thing for Mom and Dad to fight over.

I tug the elastic band off my wrist and use it to secure my hair up into a ponytail. I'm conscious of the scar on my forehead as I walk back into the kitchen. Hank glances toward me from his position in front of the stove. He doesn't say a word.

Crossing to the dirty dishes stacked on the counter, I pull on the rubber gloves. Dennis has already filled the sink with water. I place a handful of silverware in and then start to clean them. The task is repetitive and gives me a sense of control. Scrub, rinse, stack, and repeat. I lose myself in the rhythm of the work. It empties my mind, and leaves me calm enough to focus on the lyrics of the song that plays quietly from the radio. The words speak of heartbreak and pain.

My vision blurs with tears, thickness clogs my throat. Everything hurts so much.

"Bee?" Hanks's voice sounds from nearby.

"I'm okay." A tear slips free from the corner of my eye, and I swipe it away with my forearm.

It's a lie. Nothing is okay.

I try to swallow down my sob but fail. My chin drops to my chest as I cry, shoulders shaking.

A hand touches my shoulder, and then a large white handkerchief is pressed into my hand. "It's okay to cry when you need to." He says quietly. "We can't always be strong all the time. Let it all go."

My sobs grow louder, chaotic. I take the handkerchief and bury my face into it, and cry.

I cry for what I went through. All the fear, pain, and the knowledge that the person who hurt me is still out there somewhere.

And I cry for Rush. The boy who had been my friend before all that had been lost.

13
Rush

~~Hi Bug,~~

~~Hey,~~

~~It's me,~~

I STARE DOWN at the various opening lines I've tried. None of them feel right, so I screw up the sheet of paper and toss it in the trash can by the door with the rest of them. The cellphone by my elbow lights up with an incoming call. I check the caller I.D. before connecting it and hitting the speaker icon.

"Hey, Dom."

"When are you coming back?" He gets straight to the point.

"Not sure. Gran doesn't want me to be there alone, and Mrs. Rafferty isn't well enough to be left yet."

"Bailey came back to school a couple of days ago."

Tension zips through me at her name. "How is she?"

"Angry. I have your jersey."

I expected that, but it still makes my stomach twist.

"I didn't do it, Dom."

"I know. We all do."

My laugh is bitter. "Sure."

"Okay, yeah there are a few who aren't convinced, not after the shit you pulled at the party, but everyone who knows you *knows* you wouldn't hurt her. Not like *that*, anyway. There will always be some doubt. Unless she knows who did it and is keeping quiet."

"I don't think she'd do that."

Even with everything I put her through, I am sure that she wouldn't accuse me of something if she was certain I hadn't done it.

I look down at the notepad.

"Jamie has taken your position on the team."

"Seven told me."

"You need to get your ass back here and take it back. The team doesn't work as well without you on it."

I don't think I'll be back on the team when I return anyway, but I don't tell him that.

"I have to go. As soon as I know what's happening, I'll update you." I cut the call before he can say anything more.

Bending my head, I start to write.

Dear Bailey,

I know that the probability of you opening this, seeing it's from me, and tearing it up without reading is high, and I have no right to ask you to reconsider. But on the off-chance that you don't throw it in the trash unread, I'm going to carry on writing.

I'm sorry.

I'm sorry for using you as an outlet for my anger.

I'm sorry for blaming you for things you had no control over.

I'm sorry for everything I've done to you.

I'm not going to make excuses for any of it.

I didn't deserve the amount of times you tried to reach me. And you didn't deserve the way I treated you.

I spoke to Dom, who told me you gave him my jersey to return. I understand.

~~My biggest regret is that I made you feel less than~~

My biggest regret is telling you that you were nothing but a Puck Bunny. You were never a Puck Bunny. You are so much more, have always been so much more.

You were my Little Rose.

You were my Bug.

You have always been my girl.

I'm sorry.

~R~

L. ANN & CLAIRE MARTA

14

Bailey

I GLANCE UP and down the hallway, but there's no sign of my brother. School has ended, and the majority of students have already headed home.

Sighing, I unlock my phone and type a message.

Me: Where are you?

Minutes pass while I stare down at the cracked screen waiting for a reply that doesn't come. I clench my teeth, fingers tapping out another text.

Me: I'm going home.

It's been a long day, and all I want to do is go home. Sofia and her little minions have snickered at me all day long, but she has kept her distance. I know that's not going to last, though.

I slide my phone into the back pocket of my jeans and walk toward the door. Whatever Jamie is up to, I'm in no mood to wait around for him. The wind is cold as I step outside, and I pull up the collar of my jacket to protect my face from its icy bite. A few groups of students are huddled on the sidewalk outside the school. I tuck my head down and I ignore them as I set off in the direction of the house.

I'm tired.

Drained.

I have been since I broke down in the diner the other evening. The storm of tears left me empty and cold inside. They hadn't washed away my sorrow. There has been no rainbow after the storm. If anything, it left me feeling even more miserable.

I'm not sure the broken part of my heart works anymore.

"Hey freak." A hand shoves me forward.

I stumble but catch myself before I fall.

"Nowhere to run now, bitch." Sofia moves around in front of me, and her friends form a circle around us both. "You still think you're better than us?"

"Just leave me alone." I move to my left but they block me.

Sofia steps closer, her finger jabbing my chest.

"Listen to me, you little skank. Stay away from the hockey players, or I'll carve up the rest of your face so bad that not even your brother will want to take you to prom."

I inhale sharply, and my hand twitches with the desperate need to cover the scar on my forehead.

Is she for real?

"What the fuck do you think you're doing?" Dom's voice rings out.

Sofia pastes a smile on her lips. "Nothing. Just having a little chat with Bailey."

He pushes through the girls and puts his arm around my shoulders. "Sure, you were. Come on, Bailey. I'll walk you home."

I don't argue with him, and let him guide me away. When I glance over my shoulder, Sofia's eyes are burning with hate

"You got lucky this time, slut," she mouths at me.

I'm not with Rush anymore, so what's her problem?

I turn my attention to Dom. "Thanks."

"Where's your brother?"

"I don't know."

"He's your constant shadow now. I thought he went everywhere with you? School, the diner ..."

"How do you know that?"

Dom drops his arm. "I've seen him with you."

"Oh."

"Have you remembered anything from the evening you got attacked at all?"

My pace slows. "What?"

"Do you remember who hurt you?"

"No."

Dom opens his mouth to say something else, but footsteps pound up behind us on the sidewalk and he shakes his head.

"Bailey!" Jamie runs toward us, his face red and eyes narrowed on the boy walking beside me. When he reaches us, he puts himself between me and Dom. "What are you doing with him?"

"Sofia Colson was giving her some trouble." Dom says before I can answer. "I stepped in."

"She doesn't need your help."

"Relax, man."

Jamie lifts his chin. "Fuck off."

Dom's gaze meets mine. "See you around, Bailey."

My brother grabs my arm as he walks away. "Why the fuck didn't you wait for me like you were supposed to?"

"You left me hanging for thirty minutes." I snap and shake myself free of his grasp. "I sent you a text, but you didn't answer."

"I was talking to some of the guys on the team. Coach says there will be a couple of talent scouts at the next game. All I need is for them to see me play. It's my ticket out of here."

I roll my eyes and drown out his voice as he drones on about how he's going to become a famous hockey player. My thoughts are elsewhere.

The walk home feels like it takes forever, and when we finally get there, it's to a quiet house. Mom is working at the store, and Dad is still asleep.

Jamie bounces past me into the kitchen. "Mom said she was making enchiladas for dinner tonight. She better have bought extra cheese."

I deposit my bag on the kitchen table. "Please don't complain if she hasn't."

He opens the refrigerator. "I can't eat them any other way."

I shake my head, and pick up the pile of letters on the countertop. The one on top has my name and address on it written in neat familiar handwriting.

Rush.

My heart skips a beat.

Jamie is still talking, his head buried in the refrigerator, but I barely hear him through the roaring in my ears. When he turns toward me, I stuff the envelope into my bag.

"—the sour cream Aunt Carol used to make."

My cheeks are hot. "I'm sure she'll make it."

Jamie tilts his head to the side. "Are you okay? Your face is red."

"I felt a little woozy. I think I'm going to lie down until dinner."

Grabbing my bag, I walk out of the kitchen, and hurry up the stairs. With every step, my heart jumps, expecting the letter to fall out and someone to see it.

Why is he writing to me? Why here at the house and not my mailbox?

I close the bedroom door and pull it out.

Did he send it here to cause more trouble? Are the pages dripping with hate? Maybe he's angry that the police took him in for questioning. He probably blames me for that.

My hands are shaking.

I can't open it. I don't want to know what he says.

Crossing the room, I open my sock drawer and hide the letter at the bottom.

Whatever he has to say, I'm not ready to hear it. Not now. Maybe not ever.

Especially when the stitches in my heart are barely holding it together.

L. ANN & CLAIRE MARTA

"THE GAME TODAY was a fucking shit show. Jamie is not the center, you are." Seven's voice is an angry growl down the line.

I roll onto my stomach and prop my chin up on one hand.

"Did you lose?"

"We were fucking annihilated. It was a bloodbath. We need you back here."

"Gran is talking about coming home this week sometime. School has been in touch and they've said they don't want me missing too many days with it being our last year. They gave me a two-week approved absence because of the *incident*." I roll my eyes, even though he can't see me. "But now they're telling her that I either need to go back, or she has to make arrangements for me to attend another school."

"Do you *want* to come back?"

There is no easy answer to that question. "I don't want to go to a new school. The problem is Mrs. Rafferty still isn't ready to be left alone, so Gran isn't sure what to do."

"You're eighteen, you don't have to stay there if you don't want to."

"I know." It's something I've thought about, but I've fucked up enough things over the past couple of months. "I'm going to wait and see what she decides. Living alone hasn't worked out well for me so far."

"What if we promised to check in on you daily?"

I laugh. "Not sure that'll convince Gran."

"What if we come and kidnap you?"

"I think that'll get me into more shit than I am already."

"True."

There's a small moment of silence.

"Have you seen Bailey at all?" Inside, I berate myself. I swore I wouldn't ask after her. She hasn't replied to my letter, so I have to assume that was ripped up the second she received it. But I can't help myself. I want to know how she's doing.

"She's in some of my classes, so yeah, I've seen her."

"Seven." I sigh.

"Rush, the girl has caused you nothing but fucking grief since the day she arrived in town. You're hundreds of miles away because of her."

"She hasn't caused me anything."

"You know what I mean."

"Just check on her, okay?"

"You gave her your jersey, you know we'll be watching over her."

***

Hey Bug,

I'm sending this letter to your box instead of the house.

I know I shouldn't write to you again, but I can't shake the whole 'what if' thing. What if the last letter I sent didn't arrive? What if it wasn't handed to you? What if you haven't just ignored it?

This is the last one, I swear. If you don't reply to this one, then I know for certain that it's a decision you've made.

Really though, I wanted to let you know I'm coming home next week. I don't want you to see me and be blindsided by it. So, this is me telling you that I'll be back at school soon. Hank has offered to be my supervision until Gran comes home. I've spoken to him a couple of times since coming out here. He's really helped me to put some things into perspective. I've also been seeing a therapist. It was his idea to write to you in the first place. Well, kind of. Gran has arranged for me to continue seeing someone when I'm back home.

Anyway, I just wanted to let you know what's happening and to make you a promise that I won't try to speak to you, or disrupt your day. I'll stay out of your way as much as I can.

~R~

I fold the letter, pop it into an envelope and seal it. The address of her PO Box is imprinted into my brain, so I scrawl it across the front, and shove it into my back pocket. If I get it posted today, it should be there before the weekend. Which, if she reads it, will give her a couple of days' warning before I arrive at school.

"Hey Gran, I'm going for a run."

I don't tell her about the letter. She's still angry over me being questioned by the police. I don't think she'll appreciate hearing that I'm reaching out to the very person who may have caused them to believe that I was suspect number one. I assume Bailey told them it wasn't me and they believed her.

Or maybe Tamara and Hank's witness statements saying they'd seen me at the trailer park around the time Bailey was attacked did the trick.

I don't know what the reason is that they let me go, I'm just thankful they did.

16

Bailey

I JERK AWAKE, heart pounding and my skin slick with sweat. It takes a few minutes for the images of the nightmare to recede, and panic to loosen its grip. The room is shrouded in darkness, other than the soft glow of my cell's screen which informs me that it's three a.m.

I reach out to switch on my bedside lamp, but its low light isn't quite enough to chase the lingering cobwebs of my nightmare away.

I heave a ragged breath and toss the blanket off my legs. I'm feeling anxious, out of sorts, full of a nervous anticipation and I don't know why. I stand up and grab my hoodie, pulling it on, and walk out of the room.

The house is in silence. My fingers grip the banister tightly as I descend the stairs. Light spills out through the kitchen doorway, but I don't hear any noise. Tiptoeing into the room. I spy Dad sitting at the table. Arms folded on the surface, he's slumped over them, his cheek resting on top, his eyes closed.

He must have just got back from his shift at the factory. My gaze moves from his face to the papers spread out on the table. *More bills?* My stomach clenches at the thought. I step closer, and the first thing I make out is the name of the hospital on top of one of the sheets.

Cautiously, trying not to wake him, I use one finger to slide the sheet out so I can look at it. The five-figure number near the bottom catches my attention, and I stare at it.

"Thirty-five thousand dollars?" I blurt the words out. "They can't be serious!"

Dad stirs at the sound of my voice. "Bumblebee? What are you doing awake?"

"I couldn't sleep." I pick up the invoice. "Is this really how much my time at the hospital cost?"

He scrubs a hand over his face and nods. "No, that's just what *we* have to pay toward it. I didn't want to tell you, but you have a right to know. Our insurance doesn't cover the whole thing."

I sink down into the chair beside him, nausea roiling in my stomach. "There's no way my tips will pay off all of this. It's going to take years."

"We'll figure something out, sweetheart"

I drop the letter to the table. "I'm so sorry, Dad."

He pats my arm. "It wasn't your fault."

"I should have stayed inside—"

"Bee, look at me. This was *not* your fault."

"But—"

"Your mom was right." He swallows hard, pain rippling over his expression. "We should never have moved back here. Maybe we should have sold the house and found somewhere else. All this is *my* fault."

"This was home when I was little. It made sense to come back here."

Seeing him so defeated breaks something inside me. I've always seen him as invincible. The one to come to when I had a problem. My cheerleader and defender. My light when I couldn't see the path in front of me.

A smile touches his lips. "I noticed the marks on the living room door frame yesterday, where we used to mark your height."

"You used to cut a new one into the wood every time we got a little taller."

"Then there was that day you brought that stray cat home."

"Sir Lancelot." The memory of the cat warms me.

"He was the meanest, ugliest one-eyed beast I'd ever seen, but you adored him."

"Mom wouldn't let him in the house."

He chuckles quietly. "Yeah, I remember. He made a home in the garden, and you used to sneak out cans of tuna for him."

I don't tell him that the cat used to climb in through my window and spend the night on my bed. Or that Rush buried him in the backyard when he passed away.

"We made some good memories here."

"We did, Bumblebee." His smile fades. "Go on, get yourself back up to bed. You have to be up in a couple of hours for school."

I rise from my seat and drop a kiss on his cheek. "I love you, Dad."

"Love you too, sweetheart." His gaze moves to the letter on the table. "Don't worry about the bill."

I don't reply, but I'm already thinking about what I can do to help. There's no way I can let him pay it off alone. Whatever spare hours Darla has, I'll take. If it means working over Thanksgiving and Christmas, I'll do it.

I creep back up the stairs to my room, memories of when I was little running through my head.

It's as though when we moved back into the house, the universe decided to make us pay for ruining another family's happiness. There's none of the laughter that I remember filling the rooms, none of the happiness.

Maybe I'm just remembering it through rose-tinted glasses. The recollection of a child with no fears or worries.

I close the door behind me and move toward my bed.

I've got some bad news. Sir Lancelot died last night. Mom says he was old when we met him, and it was his time. He went peacefully in his sleep, curled up in the box with a blanket I made him under the window. I dug a hole and buried him in the backyard. There's a big stone under the tree at the back of the yard marking where he is. I'm going to miss the fur ball. I know you loved him. We did too.

The words from Rush's letter echo through my head. One more thing we'd shared. He cut me deeper with his words than he ever could have done with any knife. I thought our bond as Bug and R was unbreakable, yet I'd been so wrong.

The sharp bite of anger replaces the sadness I've been wrapped in.

Why not just rip off the band-aid and be done with it?

I'm standing in front of my dresser before I fully think it through.

Rush's letter is buried under all my socks. I take it out, rip it open, and brace myself for his cruel words.

Dear Bailey,

He used my name, not Bug. Seeing it there on the paper is strange and unreal. It makes me pause for a second. I read it again.

Dear Bailey,

I know that the probability of you opening this, seeing it's from me, and tearing it up without reading is high, and I have no right to ask you to reconsider. But on the off-chance that you don't throw it in the trash unread, I'm going to carry on writing.

I'm sorry.

My fingers clutch the sides of the letter, as I try to swallow around the lump of emotion in my throat.

I'm sorry for using you as an outlet for my anger.

I'm sorry for blaming you for things you had no control over.

I'm sorry for everything I've done to you.

I'm not going to make excuses for any of it.

I didn't deserve the amount of times you tried to reach me. And you didn't deserve the way I treated you.

I spoke to Dom, who told me you gave him my jersey to return. I understand.

I blink fast to dispel the tears that blind me for a second.

~~My biggest regret is that I made you feel less than~~

My biggest regret is telling you that you were nothing but a Puck Bunny. You were never a Puck Bunny. You are so much more, have always been so much more.

You were my Little Rose.

You were my Bug.

You have always been my girl.

I'm sorry.

~R~

His girl?

I sink slowly down onto the side of the bed. The need to believe him hurts, but I can't. I can't trust his words … can I? Does he really regret what he did to me, or is there a darker motive behind this?

I don't know what to think anymore. But I do know one thing. I'm going to write back to him. It's a driving force inside me that I can't ignore.

I leave his letter on the mattress and find paper and a pen.

Rush,
You used me to get back at my brother.
~~You broke my heart.~~
All I wanted to do was help you.
~~I love you so much and you ripped that all apart.~~
Be your friend.
I should have told you I was Bug, and I regret I never got the chance. You've been part of my life for so long.

You were my sunshine on the days I only had rain. I was there to comfort you when all you had was pain.

I wish we could go back to that.

~~I wish we'd never met at all.~~

A boy and girl with nothing between them but the words they write.

You knew the real me. I was the one person in the entire world I bared my soul too.

~~You destroyed me.~~

You hurt me.

You turned into my enemy because of something I didn't do.

It's easy for you to say you're sorry but it doesn't fix things.

Bug.

BAILEY'S LETTER IS burning a hole in my pocket. It arrived ten minutes before I left the house to travel back to Red Creek. A ten minute delay because I couldn't find my hoodie. If not for that, I wouldn't have been there to receive it.

It's a sign … right?

I haven't opened it yet. I haven't had time. I don't want to open it while I'm traveling. I want to be alone before I read the words she's written to me. I'm aware that they might be nothing more than her telling me to fuck off, but it doesn't matter. She took the time to write *something* and that gives me hope.

I spend the entire journey back to Red Creek reading 'Beauties: Hockey's Greatest Untold Stories' by James Duthie. It keeps my mind occupied and stops people from talking to me. Hank meets me at the other end when I get off the train. He takes my bag silently and stows it in the back of his pickup.

"How do you want to do this?" he asks once he's in the driver's seat.

"What do you mean?"

"You can stay with me, or you can stay at your own place and I'll check in on you daily. Or would you like me to stay with you?"

"Check-ins might be easier. I'm going to be at school all day, then hopefully practice with the team, if Coach allows me back. You have your shifts at the diner. I need to speak to the manager at Paladin's and see if my job is still there. If it is, I can swing by the diner after my shift is done. Will Gran be okay with that?"

"I'll speak to her. She wants me to call her once a day and keep her updated on how you're doing."

I nod. "She wants me to do the same."

"Good. Okay, that's that settled." He turns into the trailer park and parks outside his home. "Your gran has asked me to regularly check for alcohol."

"Really?"

"You were drinking heavily, Rush."

"I haven't had a single drink while I was staying with Gran."

"But now you're going to be on your own again."

"I guess."

"You don't think you were drinking too much?"

I laugh. "Oh, I *know* I was drinking too much. But I haven't wanted a drink for weeks."

Hank reaches across to pat my shoulder, then unclips his seatbelt. "That's because you've had no pressure or stress. All that will change once you're back at school." He climbs out of the pickup.

I do the same, grab my bag and walk up to the trailer I left almost a month ago. The closer I get to the front door, the quicker my heart beats. I don't know why I'm so nervous about going inside. No one is going to be there. Everything will be exactly how it was when I left.

And *that's* the problem.

I unlock the door, open it, then step inside. My gaze moves around the interior. Everything is neat and tidy. There's no sign of the beer or vodka bottles I'd left scattered around. I turn and frown at Hank, who's standing at the bottom of the steps.

"I cleaned up before you came home. I also did a grocery shop. Your gran sent me a list of food and drinks you like."

"Thanks." My gaze shifts to the bedroom my mom used to share with my gran.

"I didn't go in there. Just cleared this room, and your room. I got rid of any alcohol I found. Now's the time to tell me if you have any stashed."

"No, I don't think I do. I just bought it as I wanted it."

"Listen to me, Rush. You might not think you had a problem, but once you're back in the school environment and dealing with all the same stress, you're going to want a drink. I need you to tell me if that happens, so I can help you."

"Talking from experience?"

"I wish I could say no, but yes. I've been where you are. I let my anger over a situation I couldn't control drive me. I tried to drown my pain in alcohol and when that didn't work I turned to drugs. Unlike you, I didn't have people around me who wanted to help, and I lost ten years of my life paying for the bad choices I made. I don't want to see the same thing happen to you."

I move deeper into the trailer. "What did you go to prison for?"

"Armed robbery. I held up a gas station. I had a drug habit and no money to fund it."

"Did you hurt anyone?"

"No. But I had a terrible lawyer."

"That sucks."

"You have no idea."

18
Bailey

"Seven, Riley, and Dom haven't stopped bitching about me to Coach," Jamie complains as we walk toward the school. "If they actually played hockey properly, we wouldn't have lost the last game."

"From what Nicky told me, the team hasn't played this bad before." I stifle a yawn behind my fist. The extra evening shifts at the diner are catching up with me. I feel like I've barely slept at all when my alarm goes off in the morning.

"I think Dom wants to take my place as center." Jamie scowls. "Or they just want to make me look bad."

"I think you're being paranoid." I didn't go to the game, and I stayed far away from the ice rink. I didn't want the reminder of the day I gave Rush my virginity.

Rush …

It's been a few days since I sent my reply to his letter.

Do I regret sending it? *No.*

Maybe it will give me some closure. The shoe box of old letters is stuffed at the back of my closet, and that's where it's going to stay.

"You're working tonight, right?" Jamie's abrupt topic-change makes me frown.

"I've already told you I have a shift every night this week."

"You did?"

"I told you yesterday, then again this morning at breakfast. I'm so glad to see you were paying attention."

"I just want to know how much longer I've got to babysit you back and forth."

"Babysit me?"

"I have a life and things to do with my evenings, that don't involve running you to and from work."

"Wow, and here I was thinking you cared."

"It's been a month since the party."

"And?"

"It doesn't take *that* long to get over what happened. You're just playing on it now for attention."

I gape at him. "Are you for real?"

He shrugs.

"You are such a jerk!" I pick up my pace and walk away.

"Hey, slow down!"

I enter the school with the rest of the students. My teeth are clenched, my body almost vibrating with anger over my brother's words. He doesn't seem to understand that what happened is still fresh in my mind. The bruises might have faded, but the shadow the assault left still marks my soul. He has no idea of how I feel at night. The anxiousness at being alone in the dark. How, at every single sound, my mind screams at me that the person who attacked me has come back to finish the job.

The detectives came by a day or two ago to inform me that they still have no leads on who did it. I overheard them talking to my parents about there being a chance that the case would remain unsolved, due to lack of evidence to follow.

That means whoever it was is still out there, they could be watching me, *waiting* to strike again, and *that's* the most terrifying thing of all.

Jamie catches up with me just as I reach my locker. "Why did you run off like that?"

"Do you really have to ask?"

He rests his shoulder against the locker next to mine. "Oh, come on, Bee. I wasn't going to hold your hand forever."

"Whatever."

"Okay, fine! I'll walk you to and from work for one more week. Then you really need to sort yourself out."

"Please don't go out of your way on my account."

"You're not a fucking child. You can look after yourself. It's not like you were actually raped, is it?"

I stare at him. He rolls his eyes.

"I have things to do."

"You mean lay around, order pizza and watch TV?"

"I have to study."

I laugh, the sound brittle. "*You*? Study? Yeah, right."

"Mom is going to kill me if I don't graduate, and I want to try for Harvard and Yale."

"That's a joke, right?" Slowly I turn to face him. "I don't know what planet you live on but Mom and Dad can't afford the tuition fees for Harvard or Yale."

He shrugs. "That's where I want to go."

Movement just beyond him stops any reply I was going to make. There, at the other end of the hallway, is Rush, surrounded by his friends.

Shock, panic, and uncertainty bombard me, but it's the vulnerability and a strange sense of elation that washes over me that catches me off guard.

Almost in slow motion, his head turns. His eyes find mine and pause. It's a quick glance that lasts less than a heartbeat in length before he looks away. There's nothing on his expression. No emotion. It's a blank mask. I continue to stare at him, tracking over the way he's standing, the clothes he's wearing, the messy hair flopping forward into his eyes. How can someone who's hurt me so much look so good?

"What the fuck is he doing back?" Jamie's angry voice snaps me out of my staring.

I ignore his question and open my locker. Out of the corner of my eye, the group of friends move. They make their way toward us, Rush in the center. I wait until they're almost opposite me to turn my head, and follow their path with my eyes. Rush keeps his attention forward, and doesn't look in my direction once.

I ignore the stab of pain that twists right through me, and force my attention back to my locker.

Rush Carter is back at school, and he's just made it perfectly clear I don't exist.

It should make me happy.

So why do I want to cry?

19

Rush

I HAVEN'T TOLD anyone I'm back. Well, no one other than Bailey. But she doesn't count, because I don't know if she's read my second letter or not. I know Seven and Dom will give me shit when they find out I've been home all weekend, but I'm just not ready to face them. It's different talking to them on the phone, and the whole way home I was excited to see them. I felt good, positive about the future … until Hank left for his shift at the diner, and I was on my own in the trailer.

For the first couple of hours, I find things to do. I make something to eat, watch some television, take a shower, and unpack clothes. But then I run out of distractions. I go to bed, toss and turn, while a little voice in my head tells me that I shouldn't be here. That everyone, including my friends, believe I'm the one who beat up Bailey.

Bailey …

Her letter is sitting on the table in the main room. I *still* haven't been able to bring myself to open it. Maybe it's time. Maybe I'll get some closure? So, I get out of bed and go and get it.

Reading it is a mistake. I know that almost as soon as I open it. Her message is a goodbye, an ending. It tells me that my instinct was correct and I've destroyed everything that we've built between us over the past ten years.

We're done. We're over. And there's no coming back from it.

By the time Monday morning comes around, I've convinced myself that I'm going to walk into school the most hated student there. All my fears are unfounded, of course, because the second I pull into my parking space, people start calling my name.

"Rush!" I'm almost knocked off-balance as I climb off my bike when I'm body slammed from behind.

Arms snake around my waist and squeeze, and the familiar fragrance of roses hits my nose. I untangle myself, and turn around. Sofia grabs my face and covers me in kisses.

"Enough. Stop!" I grab her shoulders and carefully move her away.

"What the fuck?" That's Seven. "Why didn't you tell me you were coming back today?"

I shrug, evading Sofia's attempt to kiss me again, and walk over to where my friends wait. Riley and Levi do their usual, and pound me on the back. Bellamy and Dom fist bump me. Seven glares at me.

"I got back on Saturday, but I needed some time to clear my head."

"We're your friends."

"I know. I'm sorry."

Seven stares at me for a moment longer, then nods.

"Does Bailey know you're back?" Dom asks as the rest of the

group surround me.

"Oh my god, why are you talking about *her?*" Sofia's voice is shrill.

The boys all turn to stare at her. Her eyes bounce between them, her throat moves as she swallows and she takes a step back, the poisonous smile on her lips faltering.

"I'm just saying that she's to blame for Rush not being on the team anymore."

No one speaks. She looks at me.

"Rush." Her hand stretches out to touch my chest.

I shake my head. Her hand drops, and her eyes narrow.

"Whatever. I'm going to find the girls." She spins and walks away.

I look at Dom. "I don't know if she knows." We make our way toward the entrance. "I've been told I have to stay away from her. We can't avoid each other in class, but I'm not allowed to speak to her."

"You were removed from the investigation, though. It's not your fault someone attacked her."

"No, but it's her parents' request that we're kept separated. I guess they don't approve of all the stuff I *did* do."

I stop, an odd sense of being watched washing over me. Turning my head, my eyes meet blue ones. I look away immediately. I've made a promise, whether she knows it or not, and that includes not looking at her.

"I need to put my stuff in my locker then go and report to the office for some kind of return to school thing." My senses are on high alert as we pass Bailey and her brother, but I resist the urge to turn my head and look at either of them.

Thankfully my locker is a little further down the hallway from hers. I toss all the books I don't need until after lunch inside, slam it closed, and sling my bag over one shoulder.

"I'll catch you all later." I fist bump my friends, and we head in different directions.

When I reach the office, I'm told to take a seat. I feel like I'm being watched, weighed and judged by everyone who walks past me. *How many of them think I'm guilty?*

I'm not sure if I'm imagining the dirty looks or smirks from everyone or if they're really there. Either way, by the time my name is called, I'm half-considering getting up and going home.

When I enter the office, I find Principal Cavendish and Coach sitting there. There's a third person, a woman I don't recognize, also present. The principal waves his hand toward the sole empty chair.

"Take a seat, Rush."

I drop my bag to the floor by my feet and sit down.

"This is Lucinda Bateman, the school counselor. As part of your return to Red Creek High, we're going to need you to see her three times a week."

"Okay." There's no point in arguing. If I want things to get back to normal, I need to play the game by the rules.

"We know the police have marked you down as no longer a person of interest for what happened to Miss Linnett, *but* I cannot stress enough that due to the ..." Cavendish purses his lips. "Due to the unusual relationship the pair of you appeared to have, Mr. and Mrs. Linnett have requested that you keep your distance as much as possible."

"I can do that."

"Your friends on the team have probably already told you that

I've put Jamie Linnett in the center position," Coach takes over the conversation.

I nod.

"I am not ruling out you taking it back, Rush. I need to emphasize that. You're the stronger player, *but* you're going to have to earn it. You'll come to practice as usual, but for at least the next couple of games, you're going to be on the bench. We'll see how you and Jamie work together during practice. *If* you can control yourself, I'll put you in as a forward in an upcoming game. The opportunity to earn back your center position is there, but I'm not going to just hand it to you."

"I understand."

"Ms. Bateman?" Principal Cavendish looks toward the woman.

"I'm going to want to see you Monday morning, Wednesday afternoon and Friday afternoon. Of course, my door is open if you ever want to come and talk to me outside of those appointments."

"Yes, ma'am."

"Our first session will be when we're done here. I've already cleared it with Mr. Taylor." She names the teacher whose class I should be in right now. "But from next week, you'll need to come in earlier so you don't miss any classes."

"The counseling sessions, your behavior during classes and at practice will play a big part in whether your place on the hockey team remains. I don't need to remind you that this is the most important year. We have scouts from all the big colleges turning up at most games between now and graduation. They're looking to hand out scholarships to the best players. If you want to stand *any* chance of one of them seeing you, you need to get back on the ice. I can't do that until I know you can be trusted to play the game and not target your teammates."

"I appreciate the chance you're giving me, Coach." And I do. It's more than I expected. I thought I'd be thrown off the team for good.

"That's all, then. If you'll follow Ms. Bateman, I'll let you get on with your day."

"Thank you, sir." I stand, and follow the counselor out of the office, along the hallway and into her room.

She rounds her desk and sits down. "Close the door, and take a seat, Rush. I don't think you've ever been to see me before, but looking at your record that's a mistake on the school's part. You've been through a lot this year, and I should have seen you at least once after your mom died."

I force myself not to react to her matter-of-fact tone. It's not her fault. She didn't know my mom. She doesn't know me. I'm just another student to her.

I sit opposite her. "What happens now?"

"We get to know each other. I can't help you, if I don't know you."

"What do you want to know?"

"Why don't you tell me why Bailey Linnett became such an issue for you when she first came here?"

20
Bailey

"I DON'T WANT to watch you practice."

Jamie doesn't slow his pace. "Mom won't be back from her shift and Dad got called into the factory early. I'm not supposed to leave you alone at the house. So you have no choice." He sounds as happy about it as I do.

"Just walk me back home, and I'll keep the door locked."

"I don't have time, and with Carter back, it will look good if you come and watch me."

"Look good?"

"Yeah."

"I'm not interested in watching hockey."

"That's funny because you were wearing Carter's jersey often enough, for someone not interested in the game. Or was it just hockey dick you cared about?"

"Don't be disgusting."

"I wasn't the one letting a guy who hated me fuck you. I warned you about him, Bee. You didn't fucking listen. Anyway, the least you can do is support me after everything I've done for you."

"Okay, fine. I'll come."

My brother smirks. "It's not like you had a choice."

I jab him in the ribs with one finger. "Stop being so obnoxious."

Jamie bats my hand away. "Just make sure you cheer for me."

"You said this was a practice, not a game."

"It *is* a practice. We run through some drills and get the blood pumping. Sometimes the Coach has us play short games as well."

Will Rush be there?

The thought distracts me, but Jamie continues to talk, oblivious to the fact I'm not listening.

In every class we've shared since his return, Rush has acted like I wasn't there. Sofia spends each class glaring at me. I overheard her at lunch today bragging to her friends about how she and Rush are working on getting back together.

The thought of her kissing him, *touching him,* turns my stomach.

He called me *his girl* in the letter. I guess that was a lie designed to make his return to school easier.

You're supposed to be letting go of him, a tiny voice in the back of my head reminds me. But thoughts of Rush and the things we did together occupy my mind the rest of the walk to the ice rink.

The rink is closed to the public during hockey practices, and there are large boards surrounding the ice itself. Jamie tells me they're called dasher boards, and are there to stop the puck flying off the ice and hitting the crowd. He goes on to talk about how they can also be used to help execute passes. I mumble a response here and there, not really listening, because my attention is welded to the three boys standing near the penalty box. Rush, Seven, and Dom, are standing together, holding their helmets in one hand, and hockey sticks in the other. Their laughter reaches me, and Rush's smile sets off nervous butterflies in my stomach. It's not directed at me, but that doesn't matter. It's been so long since I saw him smile.

I turn to walk up the steps, and Jamie catches my arm.

"No. Come and sit near the ice."

"Why?"

"You'll be closer to the action. Come on."

Closer to the ice and the players. Closer to Rush.

"I'm happy up there." I gesture up the steps.

"It's too far away."

There aren't many people there to watch the practice. Just me, and a handful of girls on the other side of the rink. I can't shake the uneasiness I feel about being here, so I do what Jamie says and move down to take one of the seats behind the penalty box. Jamie waits until I'm seated, then hurries off to get changed.

Some of the players are already on the ice. Rush and Seven are passing the puck to each other, their lips moving as they talk.

I take the opportunity to look at him properly. If anyone glances my way, they'll assume I am watching all the boys.

He looks pale and tired, but he's smiling.

Is he still drinking? Where is he living? Back at the trailer or is he staying with one of his friends?

Dom looks up at the seats, sees me and frowns. He skates over to Rush and Seven, and says something. None of them look my way. I tear my attention away from them, just as my brother skates onto the ice with a few other players. The team's coach appears and barks some orders, and the boys line up to take turns, gliding backward, one at a time, across the length of the rink.

"Okay, boys. Pair up, and practice square passes," the coach hollers.

My attention latches on to the hockey stick gripped in Dom's hands as he skates past me.

"Keep your eyes up. Work on that balance."

I can feel the solid wood in my hand.

Everything inside me freezes.

"Good job, boys. Let's change the pattern."

The sound of the party emanates from the house to the right of me. I can hear laughter and voices.

Cold sweat breaks out over my body.

Pain explodes across the side of my face, and blood fills my mouth. I hit the concrete of the driveway hard in the dark. Fear chokes me. I can't breathe.

The taste of bile rises in my throat, and I try to swallow it down.

Darkness flows in and out. In my fading vision, I can see a pair of sneakers close to my face. Someone is crouched over me. Fingers brush my cheek ...

I shoot up off the chair and scramble away from the glass. Nausea grows as I sprint away, one hand covering my mouth. Memories of that night sear through my mind and I run blindly for the restroom.

21
Rush

I TAKE MY TURN, sending the puck into the bottom right of the net, then skate back to the end of the line.

"Where's your sister?" Daryl, one of the other defenders, asks Jamie as I pass.

"Probably gone to the restroom or something."

"Is she dating anyone?"

"No."

"She's cute."

"She's dramatic as fuck and a huge pain in my ass. I have to keep her with me all the fucking time because she keeps having stupid panic attacks. The parents make me take her to and from the diner. It's messing up my personal life."

My glance over at where she'd been sitting is involuntary. The seat is still empty, and has been for over ten minutes now. I know that because the second she came in and sat down, half of my attention became attuned to her instead of the practice.

She *still* hasn't returned by the time I take my second go over the ice, and there's a persistent little voice in the back of my head telling me something is wrong. When I reach the rest of the team, I pull off my helmet.

"I need a restroom break," I tell Coach and skate over to the edge of the ice, slide on my skate guards and pull off my helmet and gloves, then set off for the restroom.

There's no one in the men's room, obviously, and I stand outside the women's for a few minutes. There's no reason anyone else will be in there. The only people who come to watch practices are hardcore obsessive parents and whatever girls the team members are dating at that particular moment. The rink is closed off to everyone else. Not even puck bunnies can get inside without an invitation.

I take a deep breath, push open the door and walk inside.

I'll just check and make sure she's okay, then leave. I won't even speak to her.

That promise to myself goes out of the window the second I spot her sitting on the floor, knees drawn up to her chin, with her eyes squeezed closed.

"Bailey?"

At the sound of my voice, her eyes snap open, and she scrambles to her feet. I lift my hands, palms outward.

"I'm not going to hurt you. Are you okay?"

She bites her lip, and shakes her head. I take a step closer, but still keep a decent amount of space between us.

"Do you need me to get someone?"

She gives another headshake.

"Okay … I just wanted to check. You've been gone a while and some of the team were asking about you."

I back away. She moves to the sink, her eyes on me through the mirror. Just as I reach the door, she speaks.

"Why didn't you tell me you were coming back? In your letter, I mean."

"I did. Once I knew for sure, I wrote to you again. It's probably in your box at the post office." I don't wait around for her response, and slip out of the door and head back to the ice.

22
Bailey

THE SECOND THE restroom door swings shut, my shoulders sag. Seeing Rush was enough to ground me at the end of my flashback. *Why*, I'm not sure. Only that the sight of him quietened the images and brought me back into reality.

He's sent another letter? But why send it to my box and not the house?

Maybe he'd been worried about my parents or Jamie finding the first one. I need to check my box.

Jamie … It shouldn't even be a surprise that my brother didn't come to check if I was okay, but it still leaves a faint sense of disappointment, all the same.

Does he really care so little about me, or did he not notice that I was missing?

My sigh is ragged. I stare at myself in the mirror. My face is pale, and my eyes are wide. In my head, I can still see the bruises on the right side of my face. They're no longer there, but *I* can see them. On my forehead, the scar is long and visible. What did Rush think when he saw it?

Why did he check up on me? Was he really worried or did he have another reason? Will he start messing with Jamie again, now he's back on the team?

I wash my hands and dry them. I want to stay hidden in the restroom, but I know I can't. Eventually Jamie will come looking for me. My steps are heavy as I make my way back to my seat.

Jamie spots me as soon as I sit down. He skates over. "Where have you been?"

"I'm not feeling well." None of my inner turmoil bleeds through my words.

"For god's sake, Bee! Get over it already."

"I'm going home."

He scowls. "Jesus Christ, fucking sit down."

I look over his shoulder just in time to see Rush rejoin Dom and Seven. This time he meets my eyes. I'm the first one to look away.

A blonde-haired boy skates over to us.

"Hey Bailey, do you want to meet up for a milkshake later?"

"Shut up, Daryl." Jamie shoves his shoulder.

"Linnett, get your ass back over here," the coach's voice booms across the ice.

"Fuck. Stay here," my brother says and skates away.

Daryl smiles. "I'll stop by the diner later and say hi."

I stand up and move along the glass. Daryl keeps pace on the ice.

"I'm not interested in a boyfriend right now."

Levi and Riley skate closer to us, but he doesn't notice them.

"I'm up for something casual, if you are. We don't have to date."

My stomach lurches. "Casual?"

He nods. "I get it. You don't want anything serious at the moment. You can be my own personal little Puck Bunny."

His words twist the knife Rush left in my heart. They sound so close to what he said that, for a second, the anger that hits me blinds me.

"—at the lake on the weekend," he continues. "I can drive you there and back. I'm already giving Jamie a lift."

"No thanks."

The coach shouts Daryl's name and I use the opportunity to walk away.

Is that how all of them see me now? As a girl ready to spread her legs for anyone in a hockey jersey? Who moves from player to player. A Puck Bunny.

I am *not* like Sofia or her group of friends.

Rush Carter, King of the Ice, might have called me one, but I will never be a Puck Bunny.

L. ANN & CLAIRE MARTA

23

Rush

"It's official. I *hate* being benched." I drop onto the bench seat in the booth and glare around the table.

"Jamie will run his mouth off once too often and you'll be back as center before you know it," Dom says.

"Maybe."

"Snap out of it." Seven bumps my shoulder with his. "He won't be able to hold the position for long. The team is falling apart already."

"That's because they're taking sides. Some are siding with Jamie."

"Only the ones who are benched more than they play. They think sucking up to him will get them on the ice. He's not likely to want anyone who plays better than him out there showing him up."

"What can I get you boys?" The female voice interrupts the shit talking.

"Hey, Sara." Bellamy smiles up at the woman. "Can we get

shakes all round?"

"Usual flavors?" We've spent so many years coming here, she knows all our preferences with food and drink.

"Yes, please."

"There's a party at the lake on Friday night." Levi leans across the table to pick up a paper napkin, scrunches it into a ball and tosses it at Seven. "Are you going?"

Everyone looks at me. I frown.

"It'd be good for everyone to see you," Dom says.

"Why?"

"Because the rumors have been flying since the night Bailey was attacked. You were arrested, then you disappeared out of town. Now you're back and you haven't even looked in her direction."

"So?"

"So, let's not give anyone the chance to say it was you. It's bad enough that you fucked her then invited everyone else to ride the train." Dom's voice is dry.

My fingers clench into fists beneath the table. I can't get angry at the accusation. It's nothing less than the truth. That's exactly what I did. I can, however, get angry with myself for behaving like that in the first place.

"Speaking of Bailey …" Seven's voice is low and full of warning.

Everyone stops speaking as the redheaded girl passes our booth. She doesn't look in our direction, and I keep my head angled downward, although I can still see her out of the corner of my eye.

"I heard Daryl ask her out earlier," Riley says once she's out of hearing. "He invited her to the lake."

I force myself not to react.

"*Daryl?*" Seven does it for me.

"Doesn't that fucker understand the meaning of jerseys?" Bellamy adds.

"She doesn't have it anymore. She gave it back." I lift my head and look in the direction she walked. "I'm sure everyone knows that now."

"Technically, she hasn't given it to you. She gave it to me, and *I* haven't handed it over yet." Dom smirks.

I laugh. "Does that mean *we're* dating now? Are you going to wear my jersey?" I bat my eyelashes at him, feigning amusement I'm not feeling.

"You can take me on a date, and we'll see how it goes."

"Isn't this a date? We're at the diner getting shakes."

"Yeah, but I'm paying."

"Ohhh, so I'm the *girl* in this potential relationship?" I hike an eyebrow.

The guys around us laugh. I let it wash over me. It feels good to be here, with my friends. It's almost like it was before my mom died. Before I decided to punish Bailey.

Before I fucked everything up.

24

Bailey

"It's going to be fun, Bee. You can't avoid being social forever, and this will do you good."

I can hear the smile in Nicky's voice, but I keep my attention on the road ahead of us.

Trent is silent behind the wheel of the truck. I'm next to the passenger door, and she's wedged in the middle between us. I'm still not a hundred percent sure how I got here. Nicky somehow talked my mom into agreeing to let me go to the lake. My friend promised to get me there and back in one piece.

I had every intention of cancelling, yet here I am.

Trent finally breaks the stony silence he's been wrapped in since picking me up. "Have you ever been out to the lake?"

I glance over at him. "A couple of times when I was at Churchill Bradley. We hiked around it."

Nicky smiles. "There's a clearing where we all hang out. Everyone from school knows where it is. We go swimming in the summer, mainly."

I nod, turning to look back out of the window. The autumn light has painted everything in sepia tones.

Fear is a strong whisper at the back of my mind, but I try to ignore it. As long as I stay close to Nicky, everything will be fine.

The pickup takes a sharp left, and we follow a dirt track off the main road through the trees. It's another ten minutes before I see the lake. There's an assortment of cars, bikes, and trucks packed in the clearing at the end of the path. Trent parks in the first gap he finds.

Voices and laughter, mixed with music, reaches my ears the moment I open the passenger door and get out.

Nicky scoots out behind me, a box of beer in her arms. "It's not far."

Trent grabs the other box and hands me the bag of snacks. He makes eye contact with me briefly before looking away. He's not happy with Nicky for allowing me to ride along with them. Not that I care. I still think he's a jerk after the way he treated me on our one and only date.

"You said Jamie was coming, right?"

I nod at Nicky. "He should be already here. Daryl picked him up before you arrived."

He'd tried to convince me to go with him and Daryl, but I'd declined. There was *no way* I was going to give his friend another chance to ask me to be his Puck Bunny.

I follow Nicky and Trent through the trees. The noises grow louder, and after a few minutes we step out into another clearing. Wooden picnic tables are scattered around the edge. In the middle, someone has started a bonfire. There's a large crowd, more than I expected.

Jamie is with Daryl and a couple of his other friends over to one side. Sofia is holding court at one of the tables with her minions, and a few of the hockey players. Dom is sitting at another table with Seven and Riley. There's no sign of Rush.

Maybe he isn't coming? I'm not sure how that makes me feel.

I'd gotten up early this morning and gone into town. I was outside the post office just as it opened. The second letter he'd sent me was in my private box, just like he claimed. Reading it left me messy and confused on the inside.

It reminded me of R.

I miss him. I miss his letters. I miss his words.

They've left a gaping hole in my world. I keep trying to forget about him, but he's a part of me. Embedded deep in my soul.

I shadow Nicky across the open space to one of the tables. I place the bag of snacks down, and a heavy arm drops over my shoulders.

"Hey, Bailey." Daryl pulls me closer. "Maybe we can have a dance later."

I wrinkle my nose. There's a strong smell of beer on his breath. "No thanks."

"Oh, come on. Don't be like that."

"I told you before I'm not interested." I shove him away.

He laughs. "Playing hard to get, huh?"

Nicky pushes between us. "She said she isn't interested."

"You know everyone comes to the lake to hook up."

"Not everyone."

Daryl smirks. "I guess I'll try again later."

She waits for him to walk away before she turns to me. "You tell me if he causes you any trouble, okay?"

"Oh, don't worry. If he tries anything, I'll knee him in the balls."

Her laughter rings out. "Yeah, you do that."

The smile on my lips feels fake.

Was coming here really such a good idea?

The assault has left my confidence shaken. My instinct is to hide away where before I was happy to be a social butterfly. I've turned into a girl who's always looking over her shoulder, jumping at every sound.

I hate it.

I'm not the same Bailey who went to Churchill Bradley Academy.

I'm not the same Bailey who wrote about my hopes and dreams to a nameless penpal.

I'm not the same Bailey who tried to make the best of a bad situation when we moved back to Red Creek.

I'm a weaker version, trapped beneath the weight of my fears, every second of every day.

My world is moving differently than before, and it's hard not to lose myself to the chaos.

I hate the person who stole a part of me … and I hate what they have turned me into.

25
Rush

"I don't think this is a good idea." It's the fourth time I've said it since the guys picked me up.

Seven is the designated driver for the night. He's never been a heavy drinker, claiming he doesn't like the way it feels. I, on the other hand, want a drink so bad it hurts. But this is a test. One Hank thinks is stupid, and was very vocal about it when I told him I was coming to the lake with my friends. He thinks I won't be able to resist temptation. Maybe he's right. But unless I put myself in a situation where alcohol is within easy reach, I won't ever know.

"You'll be fine." Seven unclips his belt and throws open the door.

His words are a reminder that with Seven not drinking, he'll have my back in case I *do* falter.

We all climb out and gather around the front of the car. Laughter and music weaves its way through the trees. I glance in the direction of the lake.

"This is a bad idea." I can't help saying it once more.

Levi throws one arm across my shoulders. "Don't be a killjoy. We haven't been to the lake for ages. It's going to be great. Everyone needs to see you're back, and this is the best way to do it."

"I love your optimism."

Dom slaps my back with one hand. "It would look strange if you didn't come."

"I guess."

Once Seven has taken the cooler out of the trunk, we set off through the trees and down to the lake.

The closer I get, the more uncomfortable I feel. It's as though I've changed in the few short weeks I was away. Or maybe I've been changing since my mom died. Devolving into a lesser version of myself. I'm not sure. All I know is that the noises, the stupid behavior, the music, the smell of beer … all of it makes my stomach churn.

I don't want to be here.

"Rush!" Sofia's squeal is followed by her arms wrapping around my waist and her lips hitting my cheek. "Everyone said you wouldn't be here tonight."

I tense, detach myself from her grip and take a step away. "I wasn't going to come."

"Well, you're here now." She thrusts a red solo cup into my hand. "Here. Take my drink. I'll go and get another one."

The smell of beer hits my nose. My stomach churns more.

"I'll take that." The solo cup is taken from my hand and the contents poured out.

I turn my head to find Seven beside me. "I can't do this."

"You've been here less than five minutes. Come and sit by the lake. Be seen. Remind people that you're back."

"I've been back all week."

"Back at school, sure. But this is different. This is you showing that you're ready to take back your role."

"What role is that?"

Seven rolls his eyes. "Don't be dense." He reaches down to the cooler by his feet. "I brought non-alcoholic drinks for us. Do you want one?"

"Sure."

He hands me a can of lemonade, closes the lid and sits on it.

"I thought you wanted to go down to the lake?" I pop open the can.

"Fuck no. I don't want to watch those idiots making fools of themselves."

An hour into the party and I'm seriously questioning my life choices. The girls laughing, the boys boasting, the drinking and the stupidity is grating on my nerves. I feel like I'm the only adult in a room full of sugar-hyped kids, which is ridiculous when less than three months ago I'd have been out there with them—getting drunk, annoying the girls, using my position as hockey captain to get laid or my dick sucked.

Blowing out a breath, I stand up.

"Where are you going?" Seven peers up at me from where he's sprawled on his back scrolling through his phone.

"For a walk."

There's a clearing about ten minutes walk from the lake and I head there. I just need some space away from the noise to clear my head, before I start snapping at people.

26
Bailey

"I NEED TO pee."

Nicky turns away from the girl she's talking to and reaches into her bag. "Here."

I take the small makeup purse she stuffs into my hand. "What's this for?"

"A packet of tissues, hand gel, and wet wipes are inside."

"But where do I go?"

"Find a tree to squat behind."

I groan. "You can't be serious?"

She nods, laughing. "Don't tell me you've never been camping? Out here you have to rough it, Bee."

I've only been drinking soda. I wish I could hold it in, but the ache in my stomach makes it clear that's not possible. Purse clutched in my hand, I detach myself from the group and head to the tree line.

The light from the campfire stops at the edge, and the darkness lies beyond. I hesitate, torn between my need to relieve myself and fear of the dark.

I don't have to go far.

I glance back to check where Nicky is. She's standing where I left her, talking to Dom.

I can do this.

Taking a deep breath, I step into the dark between the trees. Behind me, the voices and music are loud. The deeper I go into the trees, the faster my heart beats.

Just keep walking.

My feet move me forward. I stop twice to check how far away from the clearing I am.

Still not far enough.

I plunge onward until the noise dims. Another quick check, and all I can see is the flicker of firelight a long way behind me.

Perfect.

I duck behind a tree and do what must be done as quickly as possible, then rise from my crouch and pull up my panties and jeans.

All I want to do is get back to the group. To the safety of the campfire.

A noise comes from my left. A twig snapping.

My heart practically leaps up into my throat. Eyes wide, I turn and stare into the blackness.

Maybe it's an animal? A deer or a raccoon?

A flash of movement catches my eye. It comes running at me, and in my panicked state it takes a second for me to recognize that it's someone in a hoodie.

Rational thought is obliterated by pure undiluted fear. A scream gets lodged in my throat. The makeup bag drops from my fingers, and I turn and take off through the trees. I have no idea where I'm going, whether it's away from the lake or toward it. All I care about is getting away from the monster crashing through the undergrowth after me.

I run and run, my breathing the only sound rasping in my ears.

I can't let them catch me. The words play on a loop through my head.

Branches whip against my cheeks. I stumble out through the trees and right into something solid and hard. Something wraps around me. I lash out, punching whatever has grabbed me.

"Let me go!" I scream and lash out again.

"Fuck." The arms drop away from me. "Bailey, what the fuck?"

The familiar voice penetrates through the fog of panic. "*You!*"

"Why are you out here, all alone?"

I swing my fist at him again. "You son of a bitch." Tears blur my vision, making it hard to see, but I recognize him. I'd know him, blindfolded and deaf, in a dark room.

Rush dodges my wild swing. "What did I do?"

"You chased me."

"What are you talking about?"

The confusion in his voice just fuels my rage. "Back there. It was you."

He turns his head in the direction I'd come from. "Whatever you're running from, it wasn't me."

"Bullshit! You've done it before."

"I know, but this time it wasn't me."

Dizziness hits me and I sink down onto my knees in the dirt. "Oh god. I feel sick."

Rush drops to a crouch beside me. "Have you been drinking?"

"No."

"Then it's the adrenaline rush wearing off."

I close my eyes, my body shaking. I'm not sure if I believe him. He's dressed all in black and he's out here alone. It's strange how he's conveniently out here to meet me right after I get chased. This has to be some dumb set up. The anger inside me builds.

A hand touches my shoulder but I slap it away. "Don't touch me."

"I swear, it wasn't me."

"And you really think I'm going to believe that? Why should I? What have you ever done to make me think otherwise?"

All he's *ever* done is hurt me.

27
Rush

WHAT HAVE YOU ever done to make me think otherwise?

The words hit me like a hockey stick to the head. For ten years, this girl has been everything to me—my friend, my solace, my light in the dark—and in three short months I've destroyed it all.

I shift from a crouch to down on my knees beside her.

"You're right. I fucked everything up. I *know* that. And I know I have no right to expect you to believe me when I tell you I wasn't chasing you. But I swear, Bailey. I *swear* it wasn't me."

She shakes her head. "I don't believe you."

"I know."

I should walk away and leave her, but I can't bring myself to do it. *Someone* chased her through the trees, and it wasn't me. Which means they could still be out there, waiting until she's alone again.

The silence lengthens between us. She doesn't seem to be in any hurry to move away, regardless of her claims to not believe me. And that gives me a tiny bead of hope that somewhere deep inside she *knows* the truth.

"Do you remember me writing to you when I first got accepted onto the Raven's hockey team?"

She doesn't reply.

"I asked you what your favorite number was. You told me it was thirteen because you thought it got a raw deal as a bad luck number and it needed some moral support to make it feel better. When Coach asked what number I wanted to play, I chose thirteen. I thought that if you believed it could be a good number, then it was the one I should have on my back."

I stay still, staring forward, but out of the corner of my eye I see her head turn toward me.

"You told me once that black cats crossing your path are viewed as bad luck here, but in other countries it's good luck." I pull back the sleeve of my hoodie and unwrap the leather wrist wrap I always wear. Beneath it is a small tattoo. "I got this last year. Just after Seven got his driving license, we drove to the next town and used fake ID's to get a tattoo each. I picked the black cat. Trusting you with the number thirteen worked, so I thought having the cat might double that luck. I was made captain of the team a couple of weeks after."

Her arm brushes against mine as she changes position, and stretches her legs out in front of her.

"When your parents told you they were sending you to Churchill Bradley, you told me you felt like an imposter. I sent you a book with something special about you written on each page and instructions to tear one out each time you felt sad or lonely and pin it by your bed."

"I remember." Her words are soft.

I lower myself onto my back and stare up at the sky. "I don't think you ever got to the end of the book."

"I didn't. After a few weeks, I'd made friends and stopped feeling isolated."

I nod. "You should read the last page sometime." I roll my head sideways to look at her. She's lying beside me, hair fanned out around her head, eyes closed. "I messed up when you came to town. My dad died, then we lost the house. When I found out it was your family, at first I thought that maybe the landlord had rented it out to you, but then I found out that your dad *is* the landlord. But, even then, I figured I could get beyond it because I *liked* you. Then my mom died and I ... I just—"

Her mouth covering mine silences me. She braces one hand against my shoulder, leaning over me, while her lips press against mine. Her other hand curves over my jaw, warm and soft. The move surprises me, and I don't react straight away. That doesn't seem to bother her, or she doesn't notice. Her tongue licks across my bottom lip then dips inside, stroking along mine. She tastes of lemonade and peppermint.

Like an idiot, I just lie there and let her explore my mouth, and it's only when the hand on my shoulder moves that I realize I'm not participating. Her mouth lifting from mine snaps me out of my surprise, and I wrap an arm around her waist and roll to pin her beneath me. Anchoring a hand into her hair, I hold her head still and look down at her.

"What are you doing?"

"Proving that you're no more special than any other boy."

My eyes narrow. "What does *that* mean?"

Her tongue sweeps over her lips, and she stares up at me. "Exactly what I said."

"Bullshit."

It's my turn to capture her mouth, and before long it's become a battle, a silent war to see who will break who. The kiss intensifies, tongues tangling, teeth nipping at each other's lips. Her fingers slide into my hair, curl and tug sharply, sending a sting of pain through my scalp. But she's not trying to drag me off her, she's pulling me closer. One of her legs hooks around mine, my thigh pushes between both of hers, and still the kiss continues.

A twig snaps seconds before voices reach me. Bailey's reaction is immediate. Her hand leaves my hair and she slaps both palms against my chest. I roll away, landing on my back beside her.

We both lay there, listening, but the voices don't come any closer. I run my tongue over my bottom lip.

"You should go back to the lake." I lift an arm and point through the trees. "Straight ahead that way. I'll stay here."

She scrambles to her feet without a word, straightens her clothes and turns in the direction I indicated.

"Why did you kiss me?" My words stop her forward progress.

For a second or two I don't think she's going to answer me, then she turns her head slightly. "Actions mean more than words, Rush. If you want me to trust you again, you need to earn it."

And with that, she takes off through the trees.

28

Bailey

I DON'T LOOK back as I head in the direction he sent me.

Why did you kiss me?

There was no easy answer to that. But one reason was that for the first time in months, I felt as though I'd been in control of something. *I* kissed *him*. Not the other way around.

Another reason was the things he told me. About his chosen hockey number. About the cat. It made me feel *seen*.

His words linger in my head, threatening to soften the walls I've built up.

I can't soften.

I'm done with empty words. They mean very little to me now. I don't need a box of empty promises. Like I told him. I need to be shown he's changed, not told.

I emerge from the trees and into the ring of firelight. Nicky is sitting on the bench, giggling at something Dom is whispering. Sofia is with Levi and her minions. My brother is standing with a small group of friends on the other side of the campfire.

Daryl breaks away from them to sway towards me. "How about we go find somewhere to make out?"

"You're drunk."

"I only had a couple of drinks. It won't stop me from kissing you."

"I'm not interested."

When I try to move past him, he grabs my arm. "Come on. You're killing me here. Do you even know how much I want you?"

I pull free. "And I've told you no more than once."

A couple of the other boys join us. I don't know their names, and I'm certain they aren't on the hockey team, but I do recognize them from school. From the year below us. They move to encircle me.

"Is this the sweet little piece you told us about?" The blond one glances at Daryl.

He nods. "Red Creek's newest Puck Bunny."

The dark-haired boy on the other side of him grins. "Well, let's have a party to celebrate."

"I am not a Puck Bunny, and I'm not here to hook up with anyone."

The blond frowns. "Sofia never says no."

"Then go play with her."

I look around, trying to catch Nicky's attention, but she's deeply focused on Dom. My brother has his back to me.

Daryl steps closer. "But I want *you*."

"We can't always have what we want."

My raised voice finally draws attention. Dom looks over at us, and so does Levi.

"I came with my friend, okay? Please, just leave me alone." I try to move around them to get to Nicky.

Daryl blocks my way. "Maybe I can change your mind."

"That's never going to happen."

Sofia and two of her friends walk over. Her smile barely conceals the look of pure hatred on her face.

"Poor little Bailey Linnett," she mocks. "What's the matter? Do you think Rush will take you back? He hates you now. You're nothing to him."

She's nothing but a lying bitch. I *know* that, but it doesn't stop my stomach lurching. "Get out of my way."

"You need to move on. Get down on your knees for Daryl and his friends. Show them what a good little slut you can be."

I stare her down, reaching deep inside for the remnants of the Bailey who would *never* have let her get away with talking to me that way. "You're the biggest whore in the entire school, so why don't you do it? Oh, let me guess, you've already sucked them off and they want something less ...." I fix a sneer to my lips. "Something less used?"

Sofia's laugh is sharp and high. "Look at you being so big and brave. You were running and screaming through the dark thirty minutes ago."

Every inch of my body vibrates with the fury I feel. "That was you?"

Her laughter silences the conversation around us. "Did I make you cry for your mommy because you were scared of the dark?"

Molten rage takes over, and I lunge at her. Sofia attacks back just as fiercely. My fingers tangle in her hair and I yank at it. Her hands snatch up fistfuls of mine, and she wrenches it so hard it brings tears to my eyes. We go down in a pile of limbs and screams. I ram my knee into her stomach. She releases her grip on my hair to wrap one hand around my throat, and claws at my face with the other.

Hands grab her from behind and haul her off me. As I scramble to my feet, Levi steps in between me and Sofia.

"Enough."

My gaze is narrowed on her as she struggles in Daryl's arms to get to me.

"I want to go home."

No one steps forward to offer me a ride home. I turn in a circle looking for Jamie. There's no sign of him anywhere.

"Trent, give Bailey a ride home." Nicky says from somewhere behind me. "I'll get a ride with Dom later."

Trent pushes his way through the group surrounding us. He doesn't look happy, but he nods.

I don't even care at this point. I just want to go home. Where it's safe.

"Did you all see that? She's a complete psycho." Sofia snaps. "She attacked me. I think that blow to the head has made her crazy."

DOM GRABS MY arm the second I return to the lake and drags me away from everyone.

"Sofia and Bailey just got into it."

"Into what?" I look around but can't see Bailey anywhere. Sofia, on the other hand, is wrapped around Daryl while he strokes her hair.

"Apparently Sofia chased Bailey through the trees. Daryl also asked her to suck his dick or something."

"They did *what*?" Anger snaps my spine taut.

"You gave her Puck Bunny status, Rush. Did you think they wouldn't run with that?"

"Fuck." This is all my fault.

Sofia was always going to paint a target on Bailey's back—I haven't exactly hidden my interest in her, whether I was being a bastard to her or not—and Sofia doesn't like *anything* that gives her competition for attention. But Daryl's behavior can't be blamed on anything other than my actions.

"Where is Bailey now?"

Dom shrugs. "Jamie took her home."

I cross the clearing to where Daryl and Sofia are standing.

"Rush!" Sofia untangles herself from Daryl and darts over to me.

I sidestep, avoiding her outstretched arms, my gaze locked firmly on Daryl.

"Stay away from Bailey."

"Why? It's not like you're dating her." An oily smirk stretches his lips. "In fact, aren't you supposed to stay away from her?"

"She's off limits."

"She's a Puck Bunny."

I don't even think about it. My fist just connects with his nose without my brain engaging at all. Shouts erupt from all around us and before long a circle forms with me and Daryl in the center.

We trade punches, aiming for noses and stomachs, anywhere we can inflict damage as fast as possible. Just like on the ice, our fight is quick and brutal and we're dragged apart way too soon.

Seven has his arms wrapped around me, pinning *my* arms to my sides. Dom has Daryl in a similar hold.

"Wait until Coach hears about this," Daryl snaps.

I shrug. "Go for it. And then I'll have to explain why it happened. Do you want him to know that you're trying to force yourself on girls?"

Jamie strolls over, from the direction of the cars. He must have just returned from dropping Bailey home. "Forget about him. He's been benched, so there's nothing he can do, anyway."

"Don't fucking rise." Seven's voice is low. "He wants you to go for him again."

I shake him off and step away. "I'm going home."

"I'll drive you."

Hank is sitting on the steps leading up to his trailer when Seven parks outside mine. He rises to his feet and comes across the grass. I climb out and wait for him to reach us.

"I didn't drink. I got into a fight. I came home." My words are clipped.

Hank's eyebrows rise, and his eyes shift to Seven.

"One of the other players caused shit. It wasn't Rush's fault."

"Is it going to cause trouble for you at school?"

I shake my head. "I doubt it." I move past them both and open the door. "I'm going to bed. You two can sit out here and gossip if you want to."

Truth of it is I'm fucking drained. Going out, interacting with my so-called team and their friends has exhausted me.

But mostly, I want to lie in the dark and replay what happened with Bailey in the clearing.

30

Bailey

The silence between me and Trent is strained as we walk through the trees. The fact he agreed to drive me home isn't lost on me. Maybe he isn't such a jerk after all.

"Hey, wait up."

I turn at the familiar voice. "I'm going home."

Jamie comes to a halt in front of us. "It's okay, man. I'll drive her."

Trent frowns. "I thought you arrived with someone else?"

My brother jingles a set of keys in his hand. "Daryl lent me his car."

I don't say a word. At this point, I don't care who drives me. All I want to do is get home.

Trent's eyes meet mine. When I don't protest, he walks back to the lake. I fall into step with Jamie and head toward the cluster of vehicles. Daryl's car is one of the furthest away from the dirt track, which leads back to the road.

"I need to grab the other case of beer from the back for Daryl before we go." He pops the trunk and opens it.

I turn away and check my phone. The screen lights up, but I don't see any new messages. It's snatched from my grasp.

"What the hell—" My words morph into a scream when I'm lifted off my feet. I don't get a chance to struggle before I'm tossed down into the trunk. I roll onto my back as it slams shut and I'm plunged into darkness.

"Jamie!" I scream. "Let me out! Let me out, god damn it. This isn't funny!" My voice breaks on the final word. I bang against the trunk lid.

"You shouldn't have said no to Daryl."

"Are you fucking kidding me? Let me out!"

"You're always causing drama I don't need."

I slap my palm against the roof of the trunk. "Jamie! Open the trunk. Let me out!"

Silence.

"Jamie?" My voice shakes. "Please, let me out."

Nothing.

"Are you there?"

No answer.

"Jamie!" I shout at the top of my lungs. "Where are you?"

The silence stretches.

He's gone.

Over and over, I bang against the metal and scream his name until my throat hurts. Tears fill my eyes, and fall down my cheeks. My screams for help turn into sobs. No one comes. The sides of the trunk are closing in on me. I can't get out.

Is there even enough air in here?

My nails rake against the roof of the trunk. My sobs soften into fractured whimpers.

All I wanted to do was go home. Why hadn't he just let me leave with Trent?

Time crawls painfully by. Every so often, I slam my hand against the car and cry out. It's so far at the back of the vehicles I know it's a long shot for anyone to hear me.

"Please, someone? " I whisper, and punch the roof again.

The trunk opens, bringing with it a flood of fresh air.

"What the hell? Bailey? How the fuck did you get in there?" Daryl reaches in and lifts me out. "I thought you left hours ago."

"Like you didn't know." I'm shaking so hard, my teeth are chattering.

"I came for a piss and to check on my car."

"Where's my brother?"

"At the party."

I limp back toward the clearing. My eyes feel puffy. Everything hurts.

Jamie is sitting on a bench drinking from a beer bottle, with a girl on his lap.

"Bee? I thought you left?" I hear Nicky's voice to my left but I don't reply.

I stop in front of my brother, grab the solo cup out of the girl's hand and toss the contents of it in Jamie's face. "I can't believe you did that to me!"

He splutters as the girl clambers off of him. "What is your fucking problem?"

"You trapped me in the trunk of Daryl's car!"

Jamie wipes the droplets of beer from his face. "It was just a prank." He laughs.

One of the boys closest to him shakes his head. "No, man. That's not funny."

My brother grins. "Relax. She knew I was going to let her out. Right, Bee?"

The fact he's acting like the whole thing is a huge joke hurts. "Where the fuck is my phone?"

"Oh, I accidentally dropped it in the lake. Oh my god! You should see your face right now." He laughs harder.

"I hate you."

"Where's your sense of humor?"

His face snaps sideways when my hand connects with it.

"What the fuck?" Shock turns quickly to anger, and he rises from the bench, drops the bottle he's holding and grabs my arms.

I raise my chin in silent challenge, daring him to show who he really is to everyone watching.

Nicky's voice shatters the volatile moment. "Bee, we're about to leave. We can drop you home."

Jamie blinks, the fury bleeding out of his eyes, and he releases his grip on my arms. "It was just a joke."

He sits back down and takes his cell from the back pocket of his jeans.

I snatch it out of his hand, and take off in the direction of the lake. The anger driving me dulls any fear I have of the dark. Behind me, Jamie is shouting my name. Without an ounce of regret, I lift my arm, raise it above my head and throw his phone out into the dark expanse of water.

"What the fuck? No!" He skids to a stop beside me.

"Oops, it was an accident."

31
Rush

THE REST OF my weekend is uneventful after the night at the lake. I spend most of Saturday scrubbing the trailer until it shines, then head into work for a few hours in the evening.

I end up leaving work late, because the supervisor wants to talk to me about my hours. That means I don't get to eat because the diner is closed, so I go straight home and fall into bed.

I sleep late Sunday morning. I would have slept longer, only I'm woken up by the sound of my cell phone ringing. I lie in bed and spend half an hour chatting with my grandmother before ending the call and taking a shower.

Hank turns up around lunch time, with sandwiches from the diner, and we sit outside on the steps to eat.

"You didn't call in to the diner last night after work."

"No. I didn't get out of the warehouse until almost two. I came straight home."

"Are you working tonight?"

I shake my head. "School in the morning. I'm only working Saturday nights for now. That's what they wanted to talk to me about. With school and hockey practice, I don't have a lot of free time."

"How's hockey going? Are you back on the team yet?"

"No." I can't keep the bitterness out of my voice.

"It'll all work out."

I laugh. "Before Jamie screws the team up or after?"

"Jamie Linnett? Bailey's brother, right?"

"Yeah. Fucking asshole."

"I don't like him."

"Me either."

Silence falls between us and we eat and sip our drinks. Once we're done, Hank slaps one hand to his thigh and stands.

"Well, I have to get going. Come by the diner later for dinner."

"I'll be fine."

He fixes me with a stern look. "It wasn't a suggestion, Rush. Be at the diner for dinner. I promised your gran."

"I have a freezer stocked full of food."

"Rush."

I blow out a breath. "Okay. Alright. Fine. I'll be there at six."

***

I park my bike outside the diner at five forty-five and walk to the entrance. My steps slow when I spot familiar red hair.

Fuck. I should have considered the fact that Bailey would be working. Pulling a deep breath into my lungs, I continue through the doors and take a seat at the nearest empty table. Sara arrived seconds later.

"Hank said to watch out for you. He said he's paying for dinner. What would you like?"

"He doesn't need to do that."

She flashes a smile at me. "Do *you* want to argue with him?"

"Fair point. I'll take a burger and fries, with a side of onion rings then, please."

"What would you like to drink?"

"Just a Coke. Thanks, Sara."

She reaches out to ruffle my hair. "I prefer this version of you better than the other one. Is he back for good?"

My cheeks heat. "I'm sorry. I know I was being an asshole."

"You had your reasons." She leans down and kisses my cheek. "You're a good boy, Rush. Things will get better. You'll see."

There isn't much I can say to that, so I just smile. Maybe she's right. Maybe she's wrong. Only time will tell.

After a second, she leaves me alone. I stare out of the window and wait for my food. When it arrives, with a clatter of dishes, it makes me jump. I twist on my seat and my hand hits the glass of Coke, sending it across the table and onto the floor.

"Shit." I grab a handful of paper napkins and mop up the spill.

"I'm sorry, let me clean that up for you."

The familiar voice sends a frisson of electricity down my spine. My head jerks up and my eyes meet blue ones.

"It's my fault. Let me do it."

I slide off the bench seat and pick up the glass so I can clean up the rest of the liquid from the table. There's a small pool of Coke on the seat on the opposite side, so I work on that next. And all the while I can feel Bailey watching me.

Is she thinking about the last time I made a mess while she was serving food at my table?

Guilt settles like a stone in my stomach.

I've fucked up so much with this girl, that it's a miracle she even gives me the time of day. Her words from Friday come back to me.

Actions mean more than words, Rush. If you want me to trust you again, you need to earn it.

That wasn't a warning to stay away from her. No matter how I look at it, it comes back to one thing.

She is giving me a chance to earn back her trust. And that starts now.

I pile the Coke-soaked napkins in a neat pile on the table and retake my seat. "Could I get a refill on the Coke?"

"Sure."

"Thanks."

She lingers for a second longer, then shakes her head and walks away. I pull the plate toward me, cover the fries in ketchup and dig in. The entire time I'm eating, I'm thinking about how I can make things right, and by the time I'm done, I have a plan.

32

Bailey

THERE'S NO SIGN of Jamie when I leave the house. I hate walking to school alone, but today I'm happy about his absence. I told Mom about what had happened at the lake and she'd exploded at my brother. Unfortunately, he managed to convince her it wasn't as bad as I made it sound.

Then he'd dropped the bombshell that I'd thrown his phone in the lake. His smug smile as her anger shifted my way hadn't lasted long when I explained how he'd done it to my cellphone first.

I grind my teeth at the memory of the brand-new phone Jamie bought the same day. He borrowed money from Cooper and picked up one of the latest iPhones. It's going to take me forever to save enough money to buy a new phone. No more texting with my friends. I can't even let them know that I'm not ignoring them, until I get to school and use one of the computers to email them. At least all of my photographs are backed up in a cloud drive.

"Bee!"

I turn at the familiar voice. "Morning."

Nicky catches up to me. "I saw Jamie with Daryl earlier. Guess you're not walking with him anymore?"

"He's not talking to me right now."

"I still can't believe what he did."

I fall into step beside her. "He's such a fucking jerk."

"You should have let Trent take you home."

"I don't think he really wanted to give me a ride in the first place."

Lips pursed, she casts a glance in my direction. "I know he was an idiot when he took you out on that date, but he *is* a good guy. He just heard a bunch of stuff about Churchill Bradley girls—"

"That's not really an excuse."

"I know." She pulls a face. "Boys think with their dicks a lot. It makes them stupid."

I laugh at her expression. "You can say that again."

We continue along the sidewalk. Nicky chatters about Dom and how he keeps flirting with her. Her eyes sparkle and her face lights up as she talks. She leans closer.

"He kissed me." Her fingers cover her lips, and she laughs quietly, cheeks red.

"When? At the lake?"

She shakes her head. "No. After we dropped you at your house. He drove to mine, and just as I went to get out of the car, he caught my hand and kissed me."

"Did you like it?"

She grins. "He's taking me to the movies tonight!"

"Hey Linnett, did you pee your pants in the trunk of Daryl's car the other night?"

Laughter erupts behind us.

My spine snaps taut. Sofia and her usual cluster of girls surround us. Her eyes are fixed on me.

"Oh no! Somebody help me." She feigns in a high pitched voice. "Someone is chasing me."

Her friends burst into laughter.

Nicky touches my arm. "Just ignore them."

We do just that, and when the school comes into view, we join the rest of the students walking into the building. Jamie is standing by his locker. Our eyes connect and his lip curls, before he turns away.

Lips pressed together, I go to my locker. I've given up any attempt to understand my brother. We're so different now. Maybe we've always been that way and I just never noticed.

A flash of white catches my eye as I open my locker. A small piece of paper flutters to the ground. I crouch to scoop it up, and unfold it.

Good morning, Bug. I hope your day goes well. ~R~

Rush.

I raise my head to glance up and down the hallway, but there's no sign of him. My day has had a shitty start, yet somehow Rush's note brings a little sunshine to the gray clouds that hang over me.

Don't get your hopes up.

33
Rush

I'm watching the door of the classroom when Bailey walks in. She looks directly at me for half a second, then goes to join Nicky on the far side of the room. The other girl bends her head toward Bailey, and they whisper to each other.

I wonder if she's found my note. *Is that what they're talking about?*

"Alright class, settle down. Open your books to page three hundred and sixty-two. Today we're looking at sonnets."

At the teacher's words, everyone falls silent and heads lower to the text books on the desks. The class passes slowly, but without any interruptions, and when the bell finally rings to indicate the end, everyone rushes out—Bailey included.

I take my time packing my stuff away, letting the room empty of everyone but me and Seven before standing up.

"I'm starving."

I turn my head to look at Seven. He's staring straight ahead.

"Didn't you eat breakfast?"

One side of his mouth quirks up. "Oh, I had breakfast. That's not the kind of starving I mean."

I follow the direction of his gaze and roll my eyes. "Really?"

"You have your obsessions. I have mine." He picks up speed and then stops beside the girl with her nose buried in a book as she walks slowly along the hallway. Reaching out, he tugs on her ponytail. "Hello, Cupcake."

The book drops from her hands and she gasps. I catch the book before it hits the floor, and she snatches it off me.

"What do you want, Brannagh?"

His smile is slow and wicked. "Your frosting all over my tongue."

I snort. Tamara turns red. Seven licks his lips. "I bet you taste sweeter than any cupcake, *Cupcake*. Let me take a bite and find out."

He leans toward her. She shoves him away, and runs down the hallway. Literally *sprints*. Doesn't even pretend she's not running away.

"See you later, Sweetheart."

The door slams on her departing back. Seven laughs.

"Didn't you learn your lesson the last time you fucked with her?" I shake my head.

"Apparently not." He frowns. "Or maybe I did. It just wasn't the lesson they hoped I'd learn."

***

It's raining by lunch time, so we opt to sit in the cafeteria to eat. Our table—the team table—is mostly full by the time we get there, but Dom has kept two seats clear for us and he pushes one out with a foot when we arrive.

"Hey Rush," Daryl leans past Levi and Riley from the other end of the table. "About Friday night ..."

"What about it?" I take a bite out of my sandwich.

"I just wanted to say no hard feelings, right? Jamie said his sister was good for some fun, and you'd marked her as a bunny. I didn't think it'd cause any issues if I made a play for her."

My jaw clenches. "Well, you thought wrong."

"I know that now. And, to be honest, what Jamie did was a little fucked up."

"What Jamie did?"

The table falls silent around us.

Daryl swallows. "You didn't hear?"

"No. Enlighten me."

"Bailey asked Trent to take her home. Jamie said he'd do it and took my car keys. Except he locked her in the trunk for a couple of hours. I found her in there when I went to my car."

Everything inside me turns to ice. "Where is he now?"

"He's off with Sofia, probably under the bleachers while she chokes on his dick."

"I doubt there's much to choke on." Nothing in my voice hints toward the anger slowly building inside me.

My fingers drum against my thigh, a rapid beat that does nothing to calm the fire raging through my veins.

Seven touches my arm. "Now is not the time. Stay calm."

34

Bailey

Raindrops hit my face as I wander around near the football field. But I preferred getting wet than sitting in the cafeteria where Sofia and her friends could laugh at me.

The way Rush watched me in class this morning didn't go unnoticed. Nicky had commented on it. The note he left in my locker is tucked safely in my pocket.

A giggle mingled with a groan breaks through my thoughts. I slow my pace as I reach the back of the school building.

"How can you be hard again?"

"It's the memory of having your lips wrapped around my cock. Do it again."

"But it's raining."

I turn the corner. Sofia is pressed into my brother with her hand down the front of his jeans. Lips locked in a passionate kiss, they're oblivious to my presence.

"*Jamie?*"

He lifts his head and glares at me. "Jesus Christ, Bee. Why the fuck are you watching us?"

Sofia pulls her hand free of his jeans. "That's sick even for *you*."

Anger bleeds through my shock. "I can't believe you're with her."

My brother grunts. "Get over it."

"So, it's okay for you to tell me who I should be with but not the other way around?"

His expression doesn't change. "I have no idea what you're talking about."

"You locked me in the trunk of Daryl's car because I wouldn't go out with him."

"You're imagining things. I never said that."

Sofia giggles. "I think your sister needs some medical help."

Jamie wraps his arm around her shoulders and they both move toward me. "You're just pissed off about the prank at the lake."

"What's the matter, Bailey, didn't you have fun?" she mocks. "I sure did."

She shoves me to the side as they pass me.

I clench my fists. I know what my brother said. It's imprinted in my brain, along with the terror I'd experienced that night.

Please, God, don't let him give her his jersey. The last thing I need is that bitch as my brother's girlfriend.

They'd spend all their time together, and she'd come to the house. The one place I have as a haven would be ripped away from me.

I push through the doors of the school and walk inside, just as

Rush turns the corner and comes down the hallway from the opposite direction. My attention locks on him, ignoring every other student around us. When he goes to pass me, I grab his hand.

He tenses but the second he realizes it's me his fingers close around mine. "Bailey?"

His touch feels solid, and grounding. Without a word, I pull him along the hallway until we reach the space tucked away under the stairwell. It is hidden away from prying eyes. He's the one that taught me that. The Big Bad Wolf who wanted to cut me up to ease his pain. Now it's *his* turn, but it's not a knife I'll be using.

"What are you doing?"

I push him back against the wall and press my mouth against his. Rush doesn't move, seemingly frozen in place, but the second I flick my tongue along the seam of his mouth his restraint crumbles. His lips part and his tongue touches mine. I run my palms over his arms, shoulders and up to loop my arms around his neck.

"Bailey?" He breathes my name.

"Don't talk."

It's not his words I need. It's the heat of his mouth, the feel of his rock hard body against mine, and the fact I can stop this at any time.

I need the control.

35 Rush

WHAT THE FUCK is happening right now?

Bailey's body is pressed so tightly against mine that I can feel every single curve. Her tongue slides along mine, her teeth nip at my lip, and every time I try to lift my head, her fingers curl into my hair and she drags my mouth back down to hers.

The kiss is fierce, almost brutal in the way she's biting and sucking on my lips and tongue. Her nails scrape across my scalp, and the little soft moans escaping from her turns my dick to stone.

This is *not* how I expected Monday to go.

"Carter, put your girlfriend down and get to class." Coach's voice booms out.

Instead of being embarrassed, Bailey drops her hands from my hair and turns to face him. "I'm not his girlfriend. He's my Puck Bunny."

Before I can respond to that, she takes off down the hallway, and

I'm left standing there with a fucking hard-on and my jaw on the floor. I wait for Coach to chew me out for being caught with the one girl I have to stay away from, but he just scowls at me.

"Well don't just stand there. The bell went five minutes ago."

I blink, swallow, shake my head, then blink again.

What the actual fuck just happened. Did she really just call me her Puck Bunny?

Shoving my hands into my pockets and hoping to fucking god that my erection isn't obvious, I step out from under the stairwell. Coach's eyes drop down, and one eyebrow arches up.

Fuck.

"You might want to go and spend a couple of minutes alone in the restroom before heading to class."

I will myself not to react. His lips twitch.

"It's not funny," I mutter.

"That girl has you by the balls, son. You might as well enjoy the ride. I'll see you at practice later. Don't be late for *that*." He walks away.

Doesn't he recognize her? But then, why would he? He's never been introduced to Bailey. He only knows her brother.

By the time I reach the restroom, I've got my dick back under control. I go inside, splash some water on my face and stare at my reflection in the mirror.

I can still feel her mouth on mine. The lingering scent of her perfume is on my shirt, and I catch a hint of it everytime I turn my head. I run my tongue over my lips.

That kiss can't have been because I left her a note. It didn't contain anything to cause *that* kind of response.

I smile at myself.

But that doesn't mean my next one won't.

***

I skip the next class. I'm already late, and I'll get into more trouble for that than simply not showing up. Instead I sit on the floor in the restroom and pull out the notebook from my bag, write out a new note, then take a slow walk to Bailey's locker, where I tuck the folded paper through the gap of the door.

Once that's done, I spend the rest of the hour in the library, ostensibly studying but mostly just reliving the kiss in my head.

Seven texts me once class has ended and I tell him where to find me. He turns up a few minutes later and drops into the seat opposite me.

"Why are you here?"

"I—" I change my mind about what I'm about to say. "Bailey called me her Puck Bunny."

He chokes on the mouthful of water he's just taken. When he's finished spluttering, he frowns at me. "When?"

"Before class. I was at my locker. She came along, grabbed me, made out with me, then told Coach I was her Puck Bunny and ran away."

"Made out with you?"

I nod.

"Are you sure you're not imagining that? Have you been drinking? After everything that's gone down between you, why the fuck would she make out with you?"

I shrug. "I have no idea."

I don't even care what the reasons are. I just want her to do it again.

36
Bailey

"Oh my god," Nicky whispers. "Jamie and Sofia are holding hands."

I turn my head to look over my shoulder and spot them at the end of the hallway. There's a big, bright smile on her face as she clings to his arm. The hope that my brother had just been fooling around with her at lunch time crash and burn.

"Are they dating?" my friend continues.

I shrug, opting for casual indifference. "I have no idea."

I rolled through the afternoon, thinking about the kiss I'd stolen from Rush. Seeing Jamie and Sofia together makes me crave the feel of his lips again. There had been no thought, just sensation. No need to think. No words.

My Puck Bunny.

That's what I had called him.

He didn't show up to the first class after lunch, leaving me to wonder if he'd gotten into trouble with the hockey team's coach, but he reappeared in the next one. I couldn't miss the silent question in his eyes every time he looked my way.

I shouldn't have done it. I *know* that.

Why not? Rush used me. He humiliated me at the house party all those weeks ago.

He apologized.

That doesn't stop the hurt he caused.

Daryl's voice breaks into my thoughts close by. "You guys are together now?"

"Officially dating." Sofia giggles.

Nicky shoots me a horrified look.

I turn away and pretend to search for something in my bag.

"She's coming over to my house for dinner tonight." I can hear the grin in Jamie's voice. "We're going to study."

Daryl laughs. "Study, yeah, right."

"It's not like we can do anything with Bailey in the house. She's been acting like a stuck-up bitch since we started at Red Creek High."

Nicky stiffens beside me but I don't look up.

Is he that desperate for popularity that he's ready to lie about me all the time? What else has he told people? And why, out of all the available girls, did he have to pick Sofia?

It feels as though the universe has decided to punish me again. Pushing obstacles in front of me to see how much I can take until I break.

My anger builds. I close my bag and turn.

"What are you doing?" I ignore Nicky's squeak.

"What did you just say?" I confront my brother.

The crowd around him falls silent.

He gives me an innocent smile. "Oh, hey, Bee. Didn't see you there."

"Did you just call me a stuck-up bitch in front of your friends?"

He shrugs. "I know you can't help the way you feel about everyone here. You were part of Zoey Travers' friend group. No one here has the money her family has."

"You're the one who can't let go of that place."

"I don't know what you're talking about."

"Have you told them how you refuse to find a job because it's beneath you? Or the fact that you're borrowing money from Cooper Dawson?" My gaze moves over the boys around him. "That's his best friend from Churchill Bradley. Jamie thinks this place is trash and the people in this town are nothing."

"Wow, Bee. Why are you saying these things?"

"Because they're true!"

"Look, I apologized about the prank I pulled on you. You don't need to do this."

"How can you spread lies about your own brother?" Sofia demands, her voice shrill.

"I'm not lying."

"Sure you're not." She sneers. "Just like you lied and accused Rush of assaulting you."

My blood turns cold at her words. "I never accused him of anything."

"That's not what I heard. The whole school knows it. All because he dumped you at the party. You need to get over yourself."

I glance around at the faces of the people gathered, mixed emotions in their expressions. Levi is frowning. Nicky's eyes are wide, one hand covering her lips. Trent won't meet my eyes.

Is that really what they all believe?

I turn and walk away. No one calls after me. No one defends me. No one says they don't believe Jamie.

Sofia's laughter echoes down the hallway. The sound grates on my nerves. I force myself to keep moving, until I'm standing outside my locker. When I open the door, there's another piece of paper inside. I pick it up and open it.

I'm not sure why you kissed me but I can't forget the way your lips felt on mine. ~R~

37
Rush

EVERY SINGLE ONE of my friends is wearing the same serious expression on their faces when I walk into the locker room. I stop in the doorway and look at them.

"What's going on?"

"Levi overheard something earlier that you should know." Seven breaks the silence.

"Oh?" I move deeper into the room and dump my bag down onto one of the benches.

"Jamie and Sofia are hooking up," Levi says.

"So?" I unzip my bag and start getting changed.

"So, Sofia accused Bailey of saying you assaulted her."

My brow furrows. "That's not what happened."

"But you *did* get picked up by the police," Seven points out.

"Yeah, but not because of anything Bailey said. She told them it wasn't me." I pull my pads out of the bag. "It's just Sofia trying to stir shit."

"Yeah, well she voiced something a lot of people are thinking, Rush."

"And what's that?" I focus on putting on shin and elbow pads.

"That Bailey might very well be upset because you dumped her."

I snort. "She's not. She's pissed with me because of how I treated her. Which she has every right to be." I turn to face them. "Why the fuck are you all so interested in what Sofia has to say, anyway?"

"Because no one came out and supported Bailey when she said it."

My eyes shift to Levi. "Including you?"

He shrugged. "I didn't see what went down between you at the party, but I've heard the whispers, Rush. Some still believe you're the one who attacked her."

"Some or *you*?"

He jumps to his feet. "I didn't say that."

"You didn't *not* say it."

He glares at me. I glare right back.

"Alright boys, break it up. Keep it for the ice." Coach strides into the room. "Why are you all still in here? Get your asses out there. The rest of the team are already doing drills. If you want to stand any chance of not being benched for the next game, I need to see your commitment."

He doesn't wait for any response. He just turns around and stalks back out again.

"Coach isn't happy."

I roll my eyes at Riley's words. "You think?"

I finish getting ready and we all walk out and make our way onto the ice. Coach is standing in the center surrounded by the rest of the players as he talks about tactics and drills. We join them quietly, and some of the guys shift around to make space for us.

"Okay, so I want you to split into two teams. Rush, you're center and captain for the red team." He tosses a red vest at me. "Jamie, you're team blue." As we separate, he shakes his head. "Oh no. You don't get to choose your teams. Seven, Riley, Daryl, Conrad, and Drake. You're with Jamie."

"What the fuck?"

"No way!"

Seven and Riley speak up at the same time. Coach silences them with a glare.

"Rush, you have Dom, Bellamy, Levi, Jacob and Pasha."

I nod. It's not worth arguing over.

"The team was a mess in the last game. Seven and Riley, you're used to Rush being your center. Jacob and Pasha, you've played more with Jamie. This means you're all going to need to focus and rediscover how to read the game and the players." He blows his whistle. "Fifteen minutes. Two rounds. First team to score six goals wins the position of center for their captain for the next game." He skates off the ice. "And … *Go!*"

***

With the coach's words ringing in my ears, I take my position in the faceoff circle. Jamie is opposite me, and we eye each other. His lips part, but before he can speak the puck drops. Tension zips through me, and I do a quick mental run through of everything I know about him as a player. The Coach blows the whistle and the battle is on.

I win the faceoff with a quick flick of my stick, and send the puck back to Bellamy. As he connects with it, I dart toward the other team's net. Bellamy sends the puck back to me and I sweep it across to Dom. He knocks it across the ice in a clean connection to Pasha who delivers a crisp pass along the boards back to me. I change direction, switching from skating backward to forward, the puck secure on my stick, while I survey the ice, searching for the best play to make.

There's a small opening between Seven and Daryl, and I calculate the trajectory I'm going to need, then launch the puck gently over Daryl's stick in a perfect textbook saucer pass. It lands perfectly on the tape of Dom, who takes full advantage and charges for the net.

I pivot, almost flying across the ice to position myself in front of Drake, who is Jamie's goaltender. Signaling to my closest teammates, I direct them to create a distraction, disrupting Drake's view of Dom as he delivers a blistering shot toward the net.

I brace myself as the puck hurtles toward the goal, ready in case there's a rebound. The shot rings off Drake's pads and I lunge forward to snatch the puck out of mid air, then put on a burst of speed that puts me in a perfect position to spin and fire a snapshot toward the net.

The puck whistles between players and connects with the top corner of the goal. Cheers erupt and I'm engulfed by my team, who slap my back and shout. The back of my neck burns, and I twist around to find Jamie staring at me. I flip him my middle finger. He bares his teeth. I smirk.

As the play develops, we find ourselves coming up against each other time and again, battling for every inch of the ice. With each clash, we go head to head, battling for the puck. Checks and blows beyond the usual intensity of a practice game are dealt every time we face off, until it becomes a battle of wills, a duel that extends beyond the game itself.

When we clash again, in front of my goal, pushes turn to punches and anger finally takes over. I don't know who moves first, but Jamie rips off his helmet and sends it crashing to the ice. My gloves follow it.

Adrenaline burns through my veins. It's just me and him, toe-to-toe, trading blows and insults, shoves and pushes. On the periphery of my awareness, I can hear the echo of our fists smacking against flesh, and our teammates murmuring warnings at each other to not get involved.

"You're such a fucking pussy," Jamie whispers, when I wrap him in a headlock. "What are you really hitting me for? For losing your position? That's all your fault."

"Don't give a fuck. I'm not the one who locks girls in trunks of cars for fucking kicks."

"Better that than what you did."

"What did I do?"

He twists free of my grip and smirks. "Lost your position because you're too fucking pathetic to stay sober."

I launch myself at him and find myself hauled back.

"Enough!" Coach roars. "Penalty box. Both of you!"

I don't even bother to argue, snatching up my gloves and skating off the ice. After a second, Coach blows his whistle and the game resumes without us.

38
Bailey

I LISTEN TO the pitter-patter of the rain on the aluminum roof. The bus shelter is on the edge of town away from the main streets. I tense every time the little light flickers above me to throw the space into darkness for a split second.

My plan had been simple. Walk around for a few hours, grab some food at one of the fast food places, avoid the diner and the house. Basically, stay away from Jamie and Sofia. It had been going fine until the thunderstorm had arrived, unleashing rain from the stormy clouds.

This was a dumb idea. I've let them chase me out of my own house. I could have just stayed in my room. There's no lock on the door, but I could have wedged a chair beneath the handle. I should have just stayed home.

My fingers form fists in the pockets of my hoodie at the thought of Sofia in my room. If that bitch goes through my things I won't be happy, but my biggest worry is her finding Rush's letters. They're well hidden, I think. She'd really have to dig through my closet to find them. But I wouldn't put it past her.

I'm trying my best not to think about the confrontation in the hallway at school. About the things Sofia had said. The way everyone watched. Their true feelings about me written all over their faces.

"Bailey?"

The gruff voice snaps me from my worried thoughts. My gaze lifts to the pickup truck that's pulled up in front of me.

"Hey, Hank."

"Are you going somewhere? I think the buses have stopped for the night."

"No."

"Then why are you at the bus stop?"

"Just waiting for the rain to stop." I keep my tone light. "Are you on your way to work?"

"No. Night off. I can give you a lift home."

"I … No thanks."

He studies me for a moment. "Get in."

"What?"

"Come on, get in." He beckons to me from the window.

"You don't need to take me home."

He sighs. "Fine, I won't but I'm not about to leave you sitting out here in the dark. Now get your ass in the truck."

Thunder rumbles menacingly overhead, and it's enough to get me moving. I jump off the bench and dart out into the rain. I'm drenched before I reach the passenger door. As fast as I can, I jump in, and close it behind me.

"Thanks." I pull the seat belt over me and click it into place. "But I'm sure you've got plans."

"Nothing that can't be changed." He pulls his phone out of his pocket and rattles off a text. "Have you eaten?"

"I'm fine."

"Bailey." The growl of disapproval is soft.

"No." I reply quietly. "Look, I don't want to be any trouble."

Hank slides his phone back in his pocket, then reaches to switch on the heater. "We'll go get something to eat."

"Not the diner … please."

He nods. "Okay, sure."

He drives us out of town to a drive-thru burger place. I can't remember the last time I'd been to a place like this. The line moves slowly, and he fiddles with the radio until he finds a local station. I don't recognize the song but it sounds like something old.

"Are you cold?"

I nod.

Without another word, he turns up the heat.

It doesn't take long for us to place our order. When I offer him the money, he refuses to take it. He pays for our meals, thanks the woman at the service window, and hands me the large paper bags. I settle them on my lap while he smoothly drives the truck away. We don't go far before he pulls over on the side of the road.

He flicks on the interior light and turns in his seat to face me. "You going to tell me why you don't want to go home?"

I hand him one of the bags. "You'll think it's stupid."

"Try me."

"My brother brought his new girlfriend over for dinner, and I don't like her."

His lips purse. "When I saw you at the bus shelter. I thought you'd decided to take off. Your parents must be wondering where you are."

"I told them I had an extra shift at the diner tonight." Opening my paper bag, I take out the burger box.

"After what happened to you, you know how foolish that was, right?" His voice is soft. "If I hadn't been driving by, no one would have known where you were."

My stomach twists. "I didn't think of that."

He sighs. "Eat your food."

I take a bite out of my burger, and my stomach gurgles into life. Hank chuckles, then tucks into his own food. We eat and listen to the radio. One song flows into another, and I relax, enveloped in the cozy warmth of Hank's truck.

Once we're done eating, I gather up the garbage and put it all into the bags.

Hank makes no move to start the engine. "You ready to go back now?"

"What time is it?"

"Ten."

"I don't want to get back home before eleven. If you need to go somewhere, just drop me back off at the bus stop." I don't want to keep him from whatever it is he had planned for this evening.

"You're determined to keep up the pretense you went to work?"

"Just this one time. *Please.*"

"Okay, kid."

"Okay?"

He smiles. "We can sit here a while longer, and if you want to talk, I'm a good listener."

"I think I just want to listen to the radio."

He nods, and turns to look out of the window. The fact he doesn't push me to talk eases some of the tension I've been carrying around.

There's no criticism.

No disapproval.

No judgment.

And for those handful of hours I feel like I have a real friend.

39
Rush

THE HEADLIGHTS OF a vehicle reflect through the window as it drives along the narrow road through the trailer park. The rumble of the engine is clear above the TV show playing on the television, and I glance outside, curious who would be out this late.

Hank's truck pulls into the parking space beside his home, and I can just about make out the shape of someone in the passenger seat beside him. I smile to myself. He'd told me earlier that he was going out on a date—his first since getting out of prison. I'd teased him about being a born-again virgin and asked how many centuries had it been since he last got laid. Finding out the man is only thirty had been a shock to the system. I'd been pretty sure he was older, but looking at him more closely I realized it was the look in his eyes that gave off an older vibe.

I briefly consider sticking my head out of the door to acknowledge his return, but doubt he'd appreciate me gatecrashing his date, especially if it's been successful enough to bring her back with him. Instead, I get up and switch off the television. It's not late, only eleven-thirty, but I have school in the morning and my body is still aching from the clash with Jamie on the ice.

Outside, the engine cuts off and is followed by the slamming of car doors. The murmur of voices, one male and deep, the other softer and more feminine can be heard through the thin walls of my trailer, but I can't make out the words. I *don't* want to know what they're saying anyway. The last thing I want to do is think about what Hank's seduction techniques are like.

Laughing to myself, I start walking toward my bedroom, only to stop at a soft knock at the door. I change direction.

"Really, Hank? You need advice on how to—"

It's not Hank standing on the top step.

"*Bailey?*"

Her hands lift, curve over my cheeks, and then her mouth is on mine. I get a distinct sense of deja vu at her action, and just like earlier she doesn't give me a chance to speak. Her mouth is firm against mine, her tongue insistent as it licks across my lips, and even though my mind tells me to back away, my body does its own thing.

I wrap one arm around her waist, and pull her against me while I take a step back and shove the door closed. Pulling my mouth free from hers, I stare down at her.

"What are you doing here?"

She reaches for me again, her palm sliding down my chest, over the front of my sweats and down to my dick. She curls her fingers around it and squeezes me through the material.

"Isn't it obvious?" Her other arm loops around my neck and she raises up onto her toes to find my mouth again, but she doesn't kiss me. She rests her lips against mine, her eyes wide and focused.

"Make me scream," she whispers, then sinks her teeth into my bottom lip. Her tongue licks over the sting. "Make me bleed."

And with those words, all logical thought leaves my mind.

I wrap my arms around her waist and lift her off her feet so I can back across the floor and into my bedroom. My legs hit the mattress and I freefall back onto it. She gives a small shriek, but I don't release my grip on her and she lands on top of me. I roll, pinning her beneath me and capture her mouth with mine in a quick kiss, then reach back to grasp the back of my shirt and pull it over my head. Her hands slide over my chest, down my ribs and beneath the waistband of my sweats.

The second her fingers make contact with my dick, I groan and bury my face against her throat, sucking at the soft, fragrant skin pressing against my lips. Reaching down, I grope around the floor at the side of the bed until I make contact with the cold metal of my knife. Securing my grip on it, I grasp the hem of her shirt, lift my head and bring the knife up to slice through the middle of the material. It parts easily beneath the blade and I pull both sides apart, revealing a pale pink bra. My tongue runs over my bottom lip.

"Pretty." My voice comes out husky.

Her breasts rise and fall with each breath she takes. The outline of her nipples are clear against the lacy bra and I lower my head to capture one between my teeth.

It's her turn to release a soft moan. Carefully, I slide the blade beneath her bra and cut it in two. One side falls away, and I run the tip of my knife over the nipple it's revealed. The nipple in my mouth hardens further and I bite gently before letting it go and pushing the bra away so I can pinch it with my thumb and finger.

Her back arches, her hand falling away from my dick to clutch the sheets. I pinch her again, and add a small twist. Her teeth sink into her bottom lip and her hips shift restlessly beneath me.

"Use your knife." Her voice is breathless.

I circle her nipple with the blade, press the tip against it, then stroke it down over the curve of her breast. I'm careful not to cut her.

"Harder," she demands. "I want to *feel* it."

Fuck. Her words make me harder. I drag the knife over her flushed skin, down her ribs, around her navel. Her hips lift when I reach the waistband of her jeans.

"Take them off."

I unbutton them and drag the denim over her hips, taking her panties with them, then crawl between her legs, pushing her thighs apart. Her breath hitches when I press the flat edge of my blade against her pussy.

"Why are you here, Bailey?"

"For this. For what you make me feel."

"What do I make you feel?"

Her fingers slide into my hair and she pushes my head down until my mouth is against her pussy. I drag my tongue over her. She shudders.

"What do I make you feel?"

"Control."

RUSH FROWNS, AND the knife stills between my legs. "Why control?"

This is the only thing that's remained untouched out of everything going on around me, because no one has any idea I've been near Rush when I'm not supposed to.

But this is just physical, nothing more. I can't let him in. It's power over me I am not willing to give him again. I'm not ready to trust him with my reasons, maybe I never will be. Right now, we're a million miles from where we used to be.

I lick my lips. "I'm not here to talk. Cut me or fuck me."

His gaze narrows. "Bailey—"

"If you're not up to it, then I'll find someone else who is."

My words have the desired effect. Rush's eyes darken, and a growl vibrates up his throat. The cold hard blade of the knife caresses my pussy lips. I arch my neck back, the sense of danger it invokes spreading heat through me.

Maybe there's something wrong with me. It shouldn't be right to find pleasure in what Rush is doing to me. Would I enjoy it if it was someone else wielding the knife? I push aside the question, not ready to acknowledge the answer.

The skin of my inner thigh stings, and I moan. I don't have to look to know he's nicked me.

Rush groans. "You're so fucking wet."

He dips his head down to lick my clit. I open my legs a little more and raise my pussy to his mouth. His eyes are pinned on my face as he pushes his tongue inside me. Teeth sinking into my lower lip, I resist the urge to close my legs around his head. The knife skims over my stomach while he fucks me with his tongue. I lift my hands to cup my breasts to pinch and twist my nipples. Each tug sends a dart of desire straight between my legs.

"Fuck me, Rush." I whimper.

He rises from between my legs and drops the knife on the mattress. I watch with greedy eyes as he strips out of his sweats and underwear. He's all muscle and sharp edges. He grabs a condom from the floor.

"I want to do it."

He doesn't argue, tossing me the foil packet and sprawling onto his back. "It's all yours."

I rip it open, pull out the condom and roll it carefully over his length. If he notices how my hands shake, he doesn't comment. I straddle his lap, keeping my attention on his face, and guide his dick to my pussy, and sink slowly down on him.

Rush's lips part. The feeling of being filled with him again is perfect, so right ... *so wrong.*

"Ride me, Bug." His voice is husky and strained.

I don't want to hear that nickname. Not tonight. I'm not his Bug. I flex my hips experimentally. "You're not the one in charge here." He groans.

I start to move up and down. One hand braced on his chest, I tip my head back and focus on the pleasurable pressure as I fuck him.

"You look so fucking beautiful on top of me." His hands move to my hips.

Instead of replying, I quicken my rhythm and close my eyes. I want to come. *Need* it to take away the tension that has me wound up tight. It's not the same using my fingers. It's never enough to make me see the bright burning stars that I do when Rush makes me come.

One second, I'm on top of him, the next, I'm flat on my back with his hand around my throat. My eyes snap open to meet his hard stare.

"Why did you close your eyes?" His thrusts slow.

"I don't want to talk," I snarl.

"No, you want my dick and this." The knife gleams in the light as he brings it to my throat.

Excitement courses through me.

Yes, yes cut me. Make me feel something other than the darkness that's been smothering me for weeks.

"You want control or are you using me as a substitute fuck?" The metal ghosts along my skin. "Why won't you look me in the eyes while you fuck me?"

Because I don't want to see the concern in his eyes. Softer emotions that might stop me from using him.

I arch my hips up to meet his. "Shut up and make me come." I drag my nails down his back. "Harder!"

Something dark flashes in his eyes.

My lips curl up. "Maybe the Big Bad Wolf should be wary of Little Red Riding Hood. I *said* harder!"

Rush snarls, teeth flashing in the darkened bedroom. His free hand tangles in my hair as he drives into me violently, making the bed shake. His pace is ruthless, fast, punishing … almost as if he wants to fuck the life out of me.

It's *exactly* what I want.

Not the boy from my letters.

Not my friend.

But the wolf who chased me through the woods in the dark.

41
Rush

"Is THIS WHAT you want, Bailey? A quick, dirty fuck with no feelings or attachment?" I punctuate each word with a thrust of my hips, driving us both up the bed. "You just want to scratch an itch, is that it?"

She doesn't deny what I've said. "Make me bleed!"

I lower my head and sink my teeth into her bottom lip in a sharp bite, then rise up slightly to meet her eyes.

"*You* make *me* bleed."

In answer, her nails rake down my back, and she wraps her legs around my hips. "Make me scream, Rush."

My hand tightens around her throat, and I force her head back with my thumb against her chin. "Beg for it."

Something flares in her eyes, and her lips curve up. "Fuck me, Rush. Fuck me like a Puck Bunny. Make me come."

"You're not a fucking Puck Bunny."

Her smile stretches wider. "No, but *you're* my Puck Bunny."

My hand on her throat tightens a little more. "I *play* hockey, I don't chase hockey players. I can't be a Puck Bunny."

"Then you're my Puck Fuck." She laughs, and I squeeze her throat, cutting her off, but not before I hear the desperation in the sound. "My Puck Fuck with a dirty mouth." Her fingers tangle into my hair and she drags my mouth back down to hers. "Let me hear those dirty words, my filthy Puck Fuck."

"What do you want me to say?" My lips brush against her, while I drive into her body again and again. "Do you want me to tell you how your pussy feels around my dick? The way I can feel every single time it tightens its grip on me?

"Do you want me to tell you how I've imagined being inside you, coming inside you without a condom, filling you with my cum? Or do you want to hear about how I want to take you to the woods again? How I want to stalk you, find you, strip you and fuck you? How hard it makes me when you beg me to hurt you, to cut you, to make you *bleed*?"

My hand gropes for the knife on the bed and I drag it along her jaw. "Your pussy is gripping me so fucking hard right now."

Releasing her throat, I use that hand to brace myself and lift my body up slightly so I can run the knife down her throat and over her breast. Her nipples are hard, tight, pointing upward, begging for the kiss of my blade. And I give it to them, using the point to run a circle around each peak.

"Do you like that?"

"Yes!" She arches her back, pressing her nipple against the knife.

"Do it again."

Her pussy contracts around my dick when I press a little harder, and she throws her head back, clutching at the sheets. She looks fucking amazing. Her skin is flushed, her nipples hard. I look down the length of her body to where my dick is sliding in and out of her pussy, and the visual is almost enough to send me over the edge.

But she hasn't come yet.

And there's no *fucking* way I'm going to come first.

I drop the knife and dip my hand down over her stomach to find her clit. Her entire body locks up tight when I stroke a finger over it, and a strangled moan leaves her lips. I repeat the action, adding a little flick and then pinch it. Her hips jackknife upward and she grabs my wrist.

"Oh god, please stop!" She begs, her voice breathless.

I arch an eyebrow. "You don't get to dictate what the wolf does to his prey, Little Rose." I pinch her clit again, and she moans. "You're going to come all over my dick, but first you're going to ask for it." I stroke a small circle around her clit. "Say please."

"Rush."

I tap her clit with two fingers and she hisses.

"Say please let me come."

Her nails dig into my wrist.

"Rush, please."

"Not quite. Try again." I give a slow roll of my hips, driving my dick as deep inside her as I can get, and tease her clit again. "You're so wet, you're soaking my sheets. I should make you lick me clean when you're done so you can taste for yourself just what I'm doing to you. Do you want to do that, Little Rose? Do you want to get on your hands and knees and use your tongue to clean up the mess you're leaving?"

"Rush." My name is a low moan.

"I could fuck you from behind and press your head into the wet patch you've made. You could lick it all up like a good girl should."

Her breath hitches, her legs locking tight around me while she meets me thrust for thrust.

"But you're not a good girl, are you, Bailey?" I bring my mouth close to her ear and lower my voice to a whisper. "You're a *dirty* girl. My own personal little Puck Bunny who wants to get off on the edge of my knife."

I nip her ear.

"No, you're definitely *not* a good girl. You're a *bad* girl. And bad girls have to scream before they get to come."

RUSH'S DIRTY WORDS penetrate my brain and a surge of wetness floods between my legs. I've never been this aroused before, and it's both frightening and addictive.

How different would it feel if he came inside me without the condom? Would he do it if I asked? The thought is as reckless as the emotions that drove me to demand he fuck me in the first place.

"Make me come." I dig my nails into his back and rake them over his spine until he hisses.

"You know what I want." His fingers fist my hair, hard enough to blur my eyes with tears of pain.

Ankles locked behind his back, I writhe against him, desperate to find release. The determination to make him do what I want isn't as strong as the need to come.

"Please, Rush." I whine. "Make me come all over your dick. I want to feel you come inside me again."

"Scream for me." His growl is low and deep.

The sound vibrates straight through me right down to my pussy. I suck in a breath and part my lips. As the scream rises from my throat, his palm covers my mouth and muffles the sound.

His teeth bite down on the curve of my shoulder, and a million fireworks explode before my eyes. My spine arches up as the orgasm rips through me. It's so powerful, my vision dims, and all I can hear is the rapid beat of my heart in my ears. When awareness returns, it's to Rush still fucking me. His movements have changed, become edged with the same desperation I felt moments ago.

He thrusts into me over and over until his rhythm shatters into uncoordinated jerks, and he shudders with his release. Panting heavily, his weight drops down on top of me, knocking the air from my lungs. His lips kiss and lick their way up and down the side of my neck. I skim my hands down to his ass, and squeeze. The intenseness of the moment slowly eases and reality creeps back in.

He pulls out of me, rolls off the bed, and walks toward the door. I wince but keep my attention on the ceiling. I don't want to look at him. I got what I came for. I roll onto my side. I'm right on the wet patch but I don't care. Eyes closed, my body finally relaxes.

"Bailey?" Rush's voice is soft. "We need to talk."

I pretend to be asleep.

"Bug?" The side of the mattress dips.

When I don't reply, a finger gently ghosts down the length of my spine. My teeth sink into the inside of my cheek at the gentleness of the caress.

This is just physical, I remind myself. It's just sex. No emotions. No cuddles. If I thought he'd let me go, I'd walk out right now. But he won't, and I don't want to walk back to the house in the dark. So, I'll pretend to be asleep and wait until dawn, then slip out.

Rush moves behind me. A blanket brushes my legs and rolls up to cover the length of my body. He shifts closer. Frozen to the spot, I don't make a sound as he spoons me with his body, his front to my back. I can handle Rush at his nastiest. I can't deal with him when he's kind. His face presses against my shoulder, his breath warm against my neck. And then an arm curls over my waist, his fingers flattening against my stomach.

"Good night, Bailey," he whispers.

Tears prick the back of my eyes, but I keep up my pretence of sleep.

He's my Puck Fuck, nothing more.

I'm not sure how much time passes when I wake from my doze. It's still dark outside. Sleepily, I roll to face Rush, and brush my lips over his while my hand snakes down to wrap around his dick. He groans into my mouth as I stroke him from base to tip.

His hand rises to cup my breasts, his fingers plucking at my nipple. The only sounds in the room are our moans, groans and harsh breaths. His other hand moves down between my legs and I part them willingly as he finds my pussy and pushes a finger inside, then he breaks away and rolls me onto my front.

His hands clasp my hips, and I raise my ass in invitation. The sound of foil being torn fills the room. I'm so wet, his dick slides into me easily, and he moves in and out of me with leisurely strokes.

Neither of us speak. This feels different from the last time, but

I'm too tired to examine that thought. Face buried against the pillow, all my focus is locked on where we're joined and the sparks of pleasure he's building.

The world outside is gone.

The only thing that matters is this moment and the ecstasy I know will follow.

***

My eyes crack open and my gaze settles on the fingers of weak light that filter in through the window. Panic jolts me out of my sleepy daze. I must have fallen asleep.

Shit, what time is it?

Rush doesn't move, his breathing slow and even. As carefully as I can, I untangle the arm still wrapped possessively over my waist and slither down the bed. My body aches, reminding me of the things we did in the dark.

I tiptoe around the narrow space to gather my clothes. The bra and T-shirt is ruined from where he cut them off with his knife. Heat flashes through me as I remember the bite of the blade.

Dressing quickly in my hoodie and jeans, I stuff the ruined garments in a grocery bag I find on the countertop.

I toss one last look at Rush. He's sprawled on his front now, one arm thrown out across the sheet where I'd been asleep.

I had taunted the wolf in its lair until he devoured me.

I walk through the trailer and pull the door open. It squeaks and I cringe, waiting for Rush to wake up. There's no call behind me, no sounds at all. As carefully as I can, I close the door and step outside, breathing a sigh of relief when Rush doesn't appear behind me.

"Oh!"

Hank is sitting on the steps of his trailer, one hand clasped around a white mug. "Morning."

My cheeks burn with embarrassment at being caught. "Oh, hi."

"You said you were going home last night."

"I changed my mind."

"Where's Rush?" His eyes shift over my shoulder to the door behind me.

"Asleep." Head down, I walk away. "I'll see you at the diner."

43

Rush

I DON'T MOVE until I'm sure she's gone, and even then I wait another five minutes just in case she comes back. When I'm certain that isn't going to happen, I roll onto my back and stare up at the ceiling, my mind playing back scenes of the night before like a movie reel in my head.

Something about it is bugging me. The sex was amazing, *more* than amazing, but her behavior was not what I associate with Bailey. Don't get me wrong, I *loved* the way she demanded what she wanted, but there was something … something that wasn't quite right.

I laugh. *Nothing* about the night was right. She's supposed to hate me and not want anything to do with me, so why was she in my bed, demanding my dick and marking my body like it was her property?

My dick stirs at the memory of her nails on my back, and my hand wraps around it and gives a long, slow stroke. The sensation isn't as good as Bailey's pussy, but it'll do … and if I close my eyes

I can imagine it's her hand getting me off.

It's pathetic how quickly that happens. All it seems to take is the image of her face, the memory of her moans, and a few swift pumps of my dick before I come all over my fingers.

I'm losing my fucking mind.

Rolling off the bed, I take a quick shower, then strip off the bed sheets and take them to the on-site laundromat before heading to school.

I'm early by at least forty minutes, which means the hallway where our lockers are is empty and silent. I stash my stuff in mine, then walk down to where Bailey's is situated. Glancing up and down to make sure I *am* alone, I take out a notepad and pen from my bag.

Hey Bug,

I had the weirdest dream about you last night. You turned up at my place and fucked me until I couldn't see straight, then you slipped away while I was sleeping without saying goodbye.

Or maybe it wasn't a dream and it really happened. In which case, I'm a little annoyed with you this morning. Even puck bunnies get treated better than that. I think you need to make it up to me. I look forward to seeing what you come up with as an apology for my mistreatment.

~R~

I fold it up and slip it through the gap between the door and the edge of her locker, then take a slow walk to the cafeteria to grab some breakfast, thoughts of Bailey's reaction to my note keeping me occupied until my friends show up.

**

Bailey isn't in class when I get there, but Jamie is with Sofia straddling his thighs while they make out at his desk. I ignore both of them and go to the back corner of the room, where Dom and Seven are already seated. Dom jerks his chin toward Jamie and rolls his eyes.

"Definitely making a meal of things over there."

"Not sure which one is the most desperate." Seven doesn't bother lowering his voice. "Sofia trying to make you jealous or Jamie for trying to prove someone wants his dick."

"Not really a win when the girl sucking on your dick is known to open her mouth for anyone who plays hockey." Dom leans forward. "I hope you're using protection, Jamie. Sofia isn't known for her high standards."

"Don't talk about my girlfriend like that!" Jamie lifts Sofia off his lap and stands up.

"Girlfriend." I laugh. "Sofia is the ultimate Puck Bunny. Once someone else shows interest, you'll be yesterday's news."

"Fuck you, Rush!" Sofia snaps.

I smirk and lean back on my chair. "No thanks, I have my sights set on someone way more special than you'll ever be."

"You mean Bailey?" Her fingers curl into fists. "She'll never do the things you like to do. She's too much of a prude!"

A smile stretches my lips. "Be careful, Sofia. Your claws are showing."

"You better not be fucking Bailey." Jamie crosses the room and glares at me from the other side of my desk.

"Or what?"

"Is that where she was last night?"

"If she didn't tell you where she was, then it's not my place to do it for her. You're not her keeper, and she's older than you, anyway. So what fucking business of yours is it?"

The inevitable fight is stopped by the teacher arriving, followed closely by Bailey who takes her seat without looking in my direction.

I spend the entire class staring at her, boring a hole in the side of her head, *willing* her to look at me. But she doesn't, and the second the bell rings, she's out of her seat and gone before I can even move.

I consider going after her, but Seven's hand on my arm and the reminder that we have extra hockey practice turns my attention back to the day in front of me instead of the girl who'd spent the night in my bed.

44

Bailey

WITH THE CLOUDS a dark silver gray and threatening to rain for the second day in a row, the bleachers are practically empty of students. The majority have chosen to have lunch in the cafeteria. I sit with my chin tipped up to the sky and watch the storm above slowly take form. Nicky tried to talk to me earlier, but I'd just walked away. I haven't been in the mood to hear what she has to say.

"You lied to me."

I sigh at the accusation in Jamie's tone, and turn my head to find him on his way toward me. There's no sign of Sofia with him, which surprises me. They've been joined at the hip all day. I should have known he'd seek me out, eventually.

His eyes are narrowed. "You were with Carter last night."

My stomach clenches in knots but I hold my ground. "No, I went for an early morning jog."

The lie slips from my lips as easily as it had the first time. Mom caught me sneaking into the house and her raised angry voice had woken my brother. A run had been the first thing that had popped into my mind as a flimsy excuse.

"That's not what he fucking said," he snaps.

A few students gathering at the other end of the bleachers look our way.

"I don't know what he's talking about." I rise from my seat and walk past him.

It's been hard to ignore Rush's intense stares in every class. The silent challenge for me to look at him. I'd resisted the urge, even after I'd read the note he'd left in my locker.

There's no way I want anyone to know what we've done. When people are around, I'll just pretend he doesn't exist. When we're alone, then I'll lose myself in what he can offer. If he doesn't like that … well, it's not like he gave me any choice when he used me.

A hand clamps down on my wrist. "I'm talking to you."

"Jamie!"

He drags me through the gap in the bleachers. The second we're hidden from view, he spins me around and shoves me back against one of the supports.

"I told you not to mess around with him. Are you fucking deaf?"

Teeth gritted, I push him just as hard. "You're allowed to fuck around with that bitch."

Jamie stands his ground. "Don't call her that."

"Or what?" I raise my chin in challenge. "She's only with you because she wants to get back at me."

"That's a lie."

"Are you really that stupid?"

Fury flashes in his eyes, and he leans so close I can smell the peppermint on his breath.

"You're just jealous of what I have and insecure because no one wants you. No one likes you. Everyone is laughing behind your back."

Voices reach us from the seats above us. I freeze. We haven't been talking that loud so probably no one has heard us. Jamie glances upward, then back to my face, and a slow smirk spreads across his face.

"Jesus, Bee. I didn't think you'd be this upset about me dating Sofia," he shouts. "I can't believe the stuff you just said about her!"

Eyes wide, I open my mouth to reply. Only he grabs me around the waist, pins me to his chest and smoothers my response with his palm.

"That shit you're saying about Rush makes you sound like a psycho," he continues. "Trash his locker? No fucking way. I don't want anything to do with your crazy vendetta."

I try to escape, but he subdues my struggles. His mouth brushes my ear as he whispers.

"I'm all you have here, Bee. You should remember that. Pissing me off will not work out well for you."

I stumble back when he releases me, push past him and run through the gap. Angry tears blur the faces of the people nearby. Head down, I stride back toward the school and I don't stop moving until I'm back in the hallway and standing in front of my locker.

I slam my fist into the metal door. Pain shoots down my knuckles.

Jamie's words hurt. The little show he's just put on back there feeds the negative feelings that try to choke me. Hate slithers through my veins. Eyes closed, I rest my forehead against my locker and try to breathe.

45
Rush

"DID YOU HEAR what Jamie's sister is saying about you?"

I roll my eyes at Levi's question, but don't answer him. I'm sitting at our regular table in the cafeteria. Dom and Seven are either side of me, Bellamy and Riley are opposite, and the rest of the team are scattered around at various points. They all fall silent at Levi's words.

I don't look up, and continue to eat my pasta salad.

"Rush, did you hear me?"

Sighing quietly, I let my fork drop and lift my head. "I heard you."

"She was trying to talk Jamie into trashing your locker."

I shrug.

"The bitch is really out to get—"

I'm across the table, one hand wrapped into the front of his shirt before he finishes speaking. "Why the fuck are you listening to anything Jamie Linnett has to say?"

"I'm not!"

"This is the second time you've been there when he's claiming shit about Bailey. Are you friends with him now?"

"No."

"Then why are you just taking his word as the truth?"

He tries to pull my hand away from his shirt. I tighten my grip.

"Jesus, Rush. All I asked is if you'd heard about it."

"Did you hear Bailey say the bullshit you want me to know about?"

"Well, no but—"

"Then it's a rumor."

"Jamie was talking *to* her about what she said. She didn't deny it."

"Did you ask her to?"

"Of course not!"

I shove him away from me. "Then why the fuck do you think it's the truth? What has she done to make you think—"

It's his turn to interrupt me. "She accused you of beating her up. Don't fucking deny it, Rush. The police arrested you because of what she said."

"And later she said I didn't."

"Only after witnesses came forward that proved she was lying."

I shake my head. "If you would rather believe Linnett and his bullshit, then go and hang with him. I won't listen to the crap you're spouting about Bailey." I sweep my gaze over all my friends. "You hear me? You either treat Bailey like she's wearing my jersey, or you fuck off and run with Linnett."

Silence falls around us. Nobody moves. Then Seven touches my arm.

"You've made your point. Bailey is still your girl, even if she's pretending otherwise. Levi thinks he's being a good friend by telling you what he's heard, that's all. Don't throw away years of friendship over this." His attention shifts to Levi. "*Either* of you."

We glare at each other for a second longer, then Levi nods.

"I just don't like the way she treated you, Rush." His voice is quiet.

"I didn't exactly welcome her with open arms. It goes both ways. But all this bullshit coming from Jamie is to cause problems, that's all."

Levi blows out a breath and nods. "He's claiming she tried to get him to trash your locker."

I laugh. "What would be the point in that?"

"To get your attention, maybe?"

"She doesn't need to do that to get my attention. She already knows she has it."

***

The rest of the day is uneventful. The classes blend into one another. Bailey continues to ignore me and I barely listen to anything any of the teachers are saying.

When the bell finally rings to signify the end of the day, I can't stuff my things into my bag fast enough. We have practice straight after school, which leaves me barely enough time to get out of school and make my way across to the rink. So when I reach my locker and find the door hanging off the hinges and the contents scattered across the floor, my first reaction isn't anger but annoyance that I'm going to be late for practice.

There's a small circle of students watching Dom as he gathers up the papers and books that have been strewn around. I stop in front of him.

"What happened?"

"It was wrecked when I got here. I think whoever it was got disturbed as not everything has been destroyed." He rises to his feet, holding something in one hand.

When I reach out for it, he hesitates.

"Rush, I need you not to lose your shit."

"What is it?"

He holds my gaze for a moment longer then holds out his hand, revealing a photograph ripped into four pieces. I stare at it, then slowly lift my eyes to look at him.

"Where's Bailey?" I don't recognize the sound of my own voice. There's an alien tone to it, a bite that has the students surrounding us shifting back a step.

"You tell me. You shared the last class."

I swing around. "Has anyone seen Bailey Linnett?"

"I saw her leaving a few minutes ago with her brother."

I nod, stuff the torn up image into my back pocket and walk toward the exit. Whispers erupt behind me. I know what they're saying without listening. They think I'm going after Bailey.

Let them think that.

I'm not, though. I'm going to hockey practice, and then I'm going home.

I meant what I said to Levi. Bailey wouldn't do this. I don't care what anyone claims.

I know deep in my soul that she wouldn't tear a photograph of my mom to shreds and leave it for me to find.

46

Bailey

TENSION RADIATES OFF me as I walk beside my brother in the direction of the house. I'm not talking to him after what he said at lunchtime, but he doesn't seem to care. He'd greeted me with that easy charm he wields as if nothing had happened when we met outside of school to walk home.

I try to ignore his husky laughter as he chats with Sofia on his phone. I'm not sure if he told her what happened, but she'd aimed a vicious little smile in my direction every time I caught her gaze.

"No, I miss you more." He coos into his cell.

I roll my eyes. They're so sugary sweet, it makes me want to vomit.

"Let me grab my stuff, and I'll meet you at the rink," he continues. "Of course you're invited. It's only puck bunnies who can't come to practice, you know that. Okay, later babe."

There must be hockey practice this evening. Sofia is probably only going so she can keep an eye on Rush. Her attempts to make him jealous are just as pathetic as the girl herself.

He ends the call and shoves the phone into his pocket. "Are you going to stop acting like a child and talk to me?"

I don't even bother to look in his direction.

"Why are you making such a big deal over what happened?"

My lip stings as I bite down into it.

"Oh, I forgot you like playing the victim, don't you?" he continues. "You're overreacting, you know that right?"

That comment takes me over the edge. I spin to face him. "Can you hear yourself?"

"I'm just telling you the truth, Bee. You're way too sensitive."

"I am *not* overreacting." I yell. "And I'm tired of you trying to control my life."

"You always take my help the wrong way. I'm only looking out for you."

"No, you're only looking out for yourself."

He frowns. "Do you know how irrational you sound?"

It's like hitting my head against a brick wall. The need to lash out is strong. Instead, I grit my teeth and walk away.

"Bee, don't be like this," he calls after me. "Why are you being such a bitch?"

I flash him my middle finger.

Fuck them. Fuck Jamie. Fuck Sofia. Fuck the asshole who attacked me. Fuck Red Creek High and all its students. And Fuck Red Creek. I wish we'd never moved here because maybe, just maybe I would never have realized what a jerk my brother can be.

Was everything really so perfect when we had money or were all the cracks in my family I now see hidden beneath a golden veneer?

Mom calls out a greeting from the kitchen when I finally get home, but I ignore her, rushing up the stairs to my room. I kick the door closed behind me. I'd planned to call into the hardware store and buy a new lock, but I flop down onto my bed instead. Grabbing one of the pillows, I punch my fist into it over and over, pretending it's my brother's face.

When I hear Jamie's footfalls on the stairs, I lunge up off the bed and cross to the bathroom. Darting across the tiled floor, I turn the lock in the door that leads to his room, just as the handle rattles.

"Bailey are you in there? I need to take a shower before practice."

I ignore his shout and cross back to the door on my side so I can close and lock that one, too. Sealed inside, I strip out of my clothes and switch on the shower. The cascading flow of hot water over my head drowns out the sound of my brother's angry shouts. Face raised to the spray, I close my eyes.

After a while, his shouts and the bangs on the door stop. I stir from the semi-trance I'm in and scrub my body clean, wash my hair and then linger until the water becomes cold. When I finally wrap myself in a towel and return to my room, it's safe in the knowledge that Jamie will have left for practice.

I cross the room and pull out clothes from my dresser. A clean hoodie, a soft pair of yoga pants and a plain white T-shirt. With what I have planned tonight, I don't bother with underwear. Once I'm dressed, I put on my sneakers and walk out.

"Bailey?" Mom sticks her head around the kitchen door when I come down the stairs. "Where are you going?"

"I'm going to hang out with Nicky tonight. Have a pizza and watch a movie."

"Okay, but make sure you're back by eleven."

"I thought I could sleep over at hers, if it gets too late. Is that okay with you? Her mom said she didn't mind as long as I got permission from you."

I'm pretty sure she's about to say no, but then her expression softens. "Enjoy the sleepover sweetheart."

"Thanks, Mom." I don't wait around for her to change her mind.

I take a quick detour into town to withdraw money from my bank account and stop at the hardware store to buy the new lock for my bedroom door. Done, I head for my true destination.

It's already getting dark when Rush rolls home from hockey practice. The second he sees me sitting on the step of his trailer in the shadowy dusk, our eyes lock. A frisson of anticipation has me clenching my thighs together.

He doesn't slow his pace as he moves toward me. "Back again?"

I smile. "I'm here to make up for sneaking out on you this morning. That's what you wanted right?"

"You going to do it a second time?"

"It's just sex Rush."

The chaotic mess of my emotions churn and shake. Every muscle in my body throbs with the effort to contain them, but I keep the smile pinned on my face. I can't afford to shatter and break.

Rush is attracted to me enough not to say no to what I'm offering, and like an addict I'm not about to stop this if it gives me a way out of my life for a few hours.

47

Rush

I SKIRT AROUND where she's sitting, walk up the steps, and open the door to the trailer.

"Come in, then."

I don't check to see if she's following me, and walk inside, dumping my bag with my hockey gear inside on the floor. My plan when I got back was to shower and find food. It had been a tough practice, with Coach working us hard, and all I wanted to do was clean up, eat and sleep.

The soft click of the door closing tells me Bailey has moved from her perch on the steps and come inside. I don't look around and move to the kitchen so I can open the refrigerator and take out a bottle of water.

Hands slide over my back and around my waist as I drain half the bottle. I drop one hand to cover hers as it slides down to my dick, and stop its downward progress.

I toss the empty bottle into the trash and turn to face her. "I need to shower first."

"No, you don't." She steps closer.

I shake my head. "I'm sweaty, tired and hungry. Take a seat, watch television, read a book." I hike an eyebrow. "Unless waiting an hour will change your mind about fucking me?"

"I've been sitting outside for an hour already. I guess waiting for another sixty minutes won't matter."

There's a tone to her voice, an edge that I don't like. It raises the hairs on the back of my neck. She turns away. I stay where I am, watching as she crosses the room, drops her bag onto the small wooden coffee table, lowers herself to the couch, and curls her feet beneath her. Her head swings in my direction.

"What?"

I give myself a mental shake. "Nothing. I'll be back soon."

Heading into my bedroom, I make sure the door is closed securely then strip down to my underwear—the tiny bathroom isn't big enough for me to change in there. I lay fresh clothes out on my bed, grab a towel and slide open the door. Bailey is where I left her, and she doesn't look up as I take the few required steps to enter the bathroom.

I want to stay under the heated water, but don't linger, staying in the shower long enough to wash and get clean. Once I'm out, I wrap the towel around my hips, then eye the door.

There's a risk Bailey will jump on me the second I step outside, and if I'm honest with myself, wearing only a towel there's very little hope of me turning her down. But there's a niggling whisper in the back of my head telling me that giving in to the temptation of losing myself in her body right now would be a mistake.

I ease open the door as quietly as I can, search her out, then dart back into my bedroom. Relief washes over me when she doesn't stir from where she's sitting on the couch, head bowed over whatever she's reading. I throw on a pair of gray sweats and a hockey jersey, then make my way back out into the main room.

My stomach chooses that moment to make an unholy grumble, and I change direction from the couch to the kitchen. The creak of the floor warns me she's on the move seconds before her arms wrap around my waist and her body presses against mine. I swallow a sigh and continue searching through the small freezer for something to eat.

"You smell good." Her tongue licks over my throat.

"Better than I did when I came home." There's not a lot in the freezer. My gran is due to send me grocery money tomorrow.

I purse my lips. *Do I have enough cash to order food?*

"Do you want to split a pizza?"

"No." Her hands are on a downward path to my dick again.

I grab her wrists and pull her hands off me. "Stop it, Bailey."

"I thought you wanted me to make up for sneaking away?"

"Not like this."

"Not like *what*? It's just sex, Rush." She repeats the words she'd said when I first arrived home. They hit like poisoned darts.

"It's never just sex, Bug."

Her lips compress at the nickname. "Don't call me that."

"Why not?"

"Because it's not who I am anymore."

"Then who are you? People don't change that fast, Bailey."

"*You* did." The words are sharp.

"I didn't. Not really. I was grieving. I still am. But I chose to embrace my anger and drinking amplified the things I was dealing with. I blamed your family for what happened, and you became the physical target that I could use to make it hurt a little less. And now you're doing the same thing to me. I don't know what's going on with you, but this isn't the way to deal with it."

Her bottom lip wobbles, then firms. "So you're not going to fuck me?"

"No, I'm not going to fuck you. But we can order pizza and talk."

She spins away. "Then there's no point in me being here." She stalks across the floor and stoops to snatch up her bag. Her hand delves inside and comes out clutching a white envelope. "Here." She tosses it at me.

I frown, and catch it. "What's this?"

"I was going to give it to you later, but since sex is off the table you might as well have it now." She walks to the door. "Maybe there's someone else around here who'll give me what I want."

I drop the envelope, unopened, onto the countertop and intercept her before she reaches the door.

"Where are you going?"

"I came out to have sex, Rush. If you're not going to give me that ..."

"Like fuck are you going out to hook up with someone."

Her head tilts back and she rakes a hard-eyed glare over me. "You're not giving me any choice."

"Bailey—"

"No! I don't want to hear it. Either fuck me or cut me, Rush." She shoves at my chest. "That's all I want."

"What about what I want?"

"I don't care what you want!" She screams the words at me. "You got what you wanted for months. Don't I deserve to get what I want?"

"This isn't what you want." I keep my voice level. I don't know what's going on with her, but this isn't the Bailey I know. Not even at my worst moments had she been wrapped in this layer of desperation.

"Don't pretend like you know me."

"I *do* know you. Let's order food." I wrap a hand around her arm and draw her across the room.

She wrenches free. "Fuck you, Rush. You don't get to act concerned. Not now. Not *ever*."

She makes a break for the door, and I'm not fast enough to stop her from throwing it open and running down the steps.

"Bailey, wait!" I take off after her and pull her back around to face me. "What the fuck is going on? This isn't you."

Pain radiates out across my cheek. I frown at her as her hand drops back down to her side.

"How *dare* you tell me who I am. How fucking dare you! This is what you turned me into. *You* did this to me!"

She twists away and I don't stop her from leaving.

Because she's not wrong.

I *did* turn her into this … this broken version of the girl I fell in love with through the letters we wrote.

48
Bailey

I RUN OUT of the trailer park as fast as I can. The tears I've been holding back spill free to stream down my cheeks.

Rush Carter knows nothing. Nothing!

Is it so wrong to want to empty myself of everything and fill myself with this dark-haired boy instead? Not the words in the letters and notes he's sent me, but with his breath and hardness and heat.

He took what he wanted from me when he was bullying me, so why can't I just do the same to him?

It's not fair.

What gives him the right to tell me what I can and can't do? He sounds just like my brother.

I scrub a hand over my face to wipe away the tears, angry at myself, at Rush and the whole fucking world.

He wanted to talk.

What was I going to say? That everything is out of control, and even if I told him, what would he say? That I'm overreacting about everything just like Jamie claims. I'm not about to have my heart ripped out of my chest again. It's already been carved into pieces by the people I love.

Why couldn't he just kiss me? Why couldn't he have just fucked me like he did last night?

That's all I wanted. The rejection stings and a sob is wrenched from my chest.

The darkness seems to close in around me and I bolt across the road not caring about the car that screeches and swerves to miss me.

Maybe I should just find someone else to fuck? Be the Puck Bunny they all want me to be.

It wouldn't be the same. You wouldn't fit together the way you do with Rush.

I shake my head and laugh through another sob.

The lust, the magnetic pull between us, a spark that's been there since the first day I set eyes on him. I'm so messed up I can no longer tell the difference between red flags and the butterflies in my stomach.

A shadow detaches from the darkness at the side of the house as I draw closer. My heart leaps up into my throat with fear. It takes me a split second to recognize who it is.

"Jesus, Jamie. You scared the crap out of me."

He moves closer, his face painted with shadows, his lips twisted. "Where have you been?"

"I went to see a friend." I walk past him, and let myself into the house. The light in the hallway is on, but the silence is unsettling.

"Where's Mom?"

Jamie kicks the front door closed behind us. "She went out to drop something off to Dad at the factory. Who were you with?"

"Why are you so obsessed with interrogating me?" I wipe the sleeve of my hoodie over my eyes, and hope that he hasn't seen my tears. "Nicky, if you must know."

"Nicky was out with Dom tonight. I saw them at the diner." His voice is icy.

"It's none of your business who I was with. I'm eighteen. I can do what I want."

"It was fucking Carter, wasn't it?" His voice follows me. "You're just fucking him now to piss me off, aren't you? Because of what happened at lunch."

I huff out a breath. I'm tired, hungry, and empty. "I'm not doing this again."

"Tell me."

"I'm going to bed." A hand closes over my wrist in a steel-like grip, when my foot touches the first step.

"Don't you fucking walk away from me." He yanks me backward.

I turn and shove him away. "Just leave me the hell alone. Go play with your girlfriend before she dumps you for someone else."

Pain explodes across the right side of my face.

Jamie lowers his hand. "You're making me do this, Bee. This is your fault, not mine! All you do is push, push. Fucking push."

"You ... you just hit me."

"I'm not going to apologize." His voice is fierce. "You hurt me. You have no idea how you're making *me* feel. You shouldn't have said those things about Sofia."

"I hurt you?"

"I didn't want it to be like this. I'm not to blame. You are."

I push myself away from the wall and scramble up the stairs. "I'm going to tell Mom and Dad what you did."

"They won't believe you."

I turn at the top to glare down at him, tears spilling free. "Yes, they will."

"You've already caused them enough stress." He rakes a hand through his hair, and stares up at me. "They'll just see it as another cry for attention. Besides, I'm staying at Daryl's place tonight. I'm not even here as far as Mom knows."

I run across the landing and into my bedroom. Once I'm inside, I push a chair under the handle to keep him out. Pain throbs over my face. I rub at it and sink to the floor.

Jamie hit me.

There's a sick feeling in the pit of my stomach.

He's grabbed me before but I never thought he'd ever actually do something like this.

They'll just see it as another cry for attention. His words echo in my head.

Is that really what Mom and dad will think?

49
Rush

I GIVE UP trying to sleep when three a.m. passes and I'm still staring at the ceiling.

I should have gone after her. I should have made sure she got home safely. I should have made sure she didn't meet some other guy and go home with him.

My jaw clenches and roll out of bed, pull on my clothes, shove my feet into boots, and walk out of the trailer. I stop beside my bike.

"What the fuck are you doing?"

I walk back inside. I can't just ride to Bailey's house and wake everyone up to check she's there and demand to know if she spent the night alone. Rubbing the back of my neck with one hand, I pace the floor.

Would she really hook up with someone random?

A day or two ago, I'd have said no. But now? With the way she's behaving, I'm not so sure.

I drag a hand through my hair and drop heavily onto the couch. Tipping my head back, I close my eyes.

I'll corner her at school and make her talk to me.

I must fall asleep because I jolt awake sometime later, with a crick in my neck and someone banging on the door.

"Fuck's sake. I'm coming!" I shove myself off the couch and aim my tired body at the door.

When I throw it open, it's to find Dom, Seven, and Bellamy outside. I frown.

"What are you doing here?"

"Thought we'd pick you up for school," Dom replies.

My frown deepens. "Why?"

"Can't friends pick up friends?" He comes up the steps and I move back to allow him inside. "You're already dressed, so grab your stuff and let's go."

I throw him another scowl, but grab my stuff.

"Do we have practice today?"

"No. Leave your gear here." Dom follows me around the trailer.

"Why are you so eager to get to school?"

"We have things to do." It's Seven who replies to that question.

I swing around to face him. "We do? What kind of things?"

"We know who trashed your locker."

"Who?"

My friend taps the side of his nose. "Patience, grasshopper."

"Seven ..."

"What's this?" He picks up the envelope Bailey tossed at me last night.

"Haven't opened it."

He doesn't wait for permission, and tears it open, then frowns. "Why is there an envelope full of money on your coffee table, Rush?"

"What?" My eyes jerk down to the envelope in his grip. "Give me that!" I snatch it off him and thumb through the bills inside. "What the actual fuck?" I stuff it into my bag and stalk out of the trailer. "Let's go."

We pile into Dom's car, Bellamy calling shotgun and taking the front passenger seat. Seven sits beside me in the back.

"Where did the money come from?"

"It's mine."

"Did you rob a bank?"

"Don't be stupid."

"There was a couple of thousand in that envelope ..."

"Three thousand." My fingers drum over my thigh.

"Where did you get three thousand dollars from?"

I roll my eyes. "It's nothing nefarious, Seven. It's my savings."

"You withdrew it all?"

"A while ago. And gave it to Bailey because her mom was demanding back rent."

He straightens in the seat beside me. "She fucking *what*?"

"It doesn't matter. Don't worry about it. Who trashed my locker?"

"Riley's sister was out of class and saw Murphy Peterson do it."

"Who the fuck is Murphy Peterson?"

"A junior. He's also Daryl's cousin."

"You think Daryl got him to do it?"

Seven shakes his head. "No, I think *Jamie* got Daryl to make him do it."

"So, what's the plan? Are we dealing with Murphy, Daryl, or Jamie?"

As it turns out, we don't deal with *any* of them because the second I walk into school and see Bailey, everything else becomes unimportant. There's a bruise on her cheek, and she's hurrying along the hallway with her head down. She's so focused on the floor she isn't aware of me stepping into her path. I hook a hand around her arm and force her to a stop ... then duck when her fist comes swinging toward my face.

"Fuck. It's me."

She pulls the punch just before it connects with my jaw and yanks her arm free. "Leave me alone."

I ignore her, catch her arm again and drag her into the nearest empty classroom. Kicking the door shut, I lean back against it so she can't escape.

"What happened to your face?"

50

Bailey

"Nothing," I take a few steps back. The classroom is empty and I can see Dom and Seven through the window as they guard the door.

Rush mirrors my moves. "Did someone hurt you on the way home last night?"

My stomach tightens with nerves. "No."

"I can see the bruise on your cheek even with the makeup you've plastered on."

Hand lifting, I touch the sore, discolored skin. "I told you it's nothing."

He steps closer. "Bailey—"

"I don't want to talk about it. Get out of my way." My ass hits the edge of a table.

"No." He puts his hands down on either side and traps me between him and the wood. I flinch at his closeness. "Did you hook up with someone after you left me?"

Is he jealous? I don't know if I want to laugh or cry at the revelation.

"And what if I did? You have no right to be jealous. I'm not your girlfriend."

Rush stills and tilts his head to the side. "Talk to me."

"You're not my therapist."

He lets out a breath and lifts a hand. I flinch. His eyes narrow and he continues the move to shove his hair away from his face.

"I'm not going to hurt you."

Why can't he leave me alone? I can't tell him what happened. He won't believe me. Why would he? Not even mom believed me when I told her this morning. She called Jamie, who denied everything.

I never did that, you're crazy. Why can't you stop making things up, Bee? I'm worried about you. I'm going to have to tell Mom and Dad that you lied about staying at Nicky's. You know that doesn't make you look good right? All the lies, are you doing drugs?

Every word he spews, mom takes as gospel.

My gaze darts toward the door, then back to a spot just below his chin. I don't want to look him in the eyes because he might see right through the mask I'm trying to wear.

"Bailey, who hit you?" His voice is soft.

"Why the fuck do you care?"

"Because we're friends."

"Yeah, right." I snort and shake my head.

He lowers his head and tries to capture my gaze. "I mean it."

I turn away, avoiding his eyes. "If you were my friend, you would have given me what I wanted last night. You'd give it to me now."

The tip of his nose brushes my unhurt cheek. "I recognize the desperation I see in your eyes because I saw it staring back at me from the mirror after my mom died. I drowned it with alcohol. You're doing the same thing with sex."

Eyes closed, I don't reply.

His nose nuzzles gently against my ear. "Why did you give me the money back?"

"Because it's yours." I whisper.

"You thought I stole it from you."

"My savings weren't that much. It was Jamie who took it" I blurt out before I can stop myself.

"Your brother stole your money?" Anger laces his words.

I bring a hand up between us and push him away. "He does a lot of things."

Almost reluctantly, he lets me force him backward. "Like what? Stop being cryptic. What's going on? You can trust me."

Noise comes from behind the closed classroom door. Dom's voice is loud, talking to a teacher. The door opens, and I circle around Rush and hurry through it before he can stop me.

51
Rush

He does a lot of things.

The words echo around my head as I walk slowly out of the classroom, and along the hallway. Dom and Seven fall into step either side of me.

"What's going on?"

"Have you seen Jamie?"

"Not yet. The plan is to confront him at lunch."

I throw open the door of my locker and grab my math book. "Fuck that."

My hand hits the door and it slams shut. I stalk down to where Bailey is staring into her locker.

"We're not done talking."

"Yes, we *are*." She pushes past me and walks away.

"Bailey, wait!" I go after her. "What did you mean by he does a lot of things?"

She doesn't reply, picking up speed until she's almost jogging through the hallways.

"If you don't tell me, I'll ask him."

That gets her attention. She stops and spins to face me. "Stay out of it, Rush."

"I can't do that."

"Yes, you can. It's none of your business."

"You *are* my business."

She rolls her eyes. "The *only* business we have between us is you giving me sex and orgasms. If you can't supply me with that, then leave me alone." She surges back into movement.

I keep pace beside her, unwilling to end this conversation until I've got answers. "Stop behaving like there's nothing but sex between us."

Students side-eye us at my words. I glare at them and every single one of them looks away.

"That *is* all that's between us."

"Bullshit. I have thousands of letters that prove otherwise."

Her laugh is brittle. "Really, Rush? *Really*? The boy you shared with me in those letters is a *lie*. You showed me how little I mattered to you when you decided to blame me for everything. You're just another in a long list of people who don't give a single fuck about me. Stop pretending you do!" She takes a sharp left turn and disappears through a door.

I don't even look at where she's gone, I just follow her ... and am greeted by female shrieks.

"Oh my god, *get out*!"

"This is the girls bathroom, asshole."

"*Rush?*" Nicky enters my view, blocking Bailey from sight. "What are you doing in here?"

"I need to talk to Bailey."

She glances over her shoulder, then looks back at me. "You should maybe wait until later? Someone is going to report you for being in here." She hooks her hand around my arm and draws me back outside. "You should go to class. I'll make sure Bailey is okay."

My focus zeroes in on her face. "What do you know?"

She frowns. "What do you mean?"

"Don't bullshit me, Nicky."

She gives a small headshake. "I don't know anything. She's blocking everyone out. She barely talks to me these days."

"I think Jamie hit her."

Her eyes round. "No way! He wouldn't do that, surely? He's her *brother*. Did she tell you that?"

"No."

"Are you sure it's not just your own dislike of him making you say that?"

"I know what I know." Now I've voiced it, that's exactly what I think happened.

Her expression troubled, she worries at her bottom lip with her teeth for a second before speaking. "I'll see if I can get her to talk to me. But Rush? If he *did* hit her, throwing your weight around, yelling and demanding answers, isn't going to make her feel like she can talk to you."

I know she's right, but I don't like it.

"Just find out what you can and let me know."

"I'll try my best."

52

Bailey

"Hey, Bee. Wait up."

I debate whether to slow down. It's lunchtime and I don't want to be out in the open where Rush can find me. He stared non-stop at me through the last few classes and it's amped up my anxiety. I shouldn't have let anything slip about Jamie.

"Bee!" Nicky calls again.

I dive into the closest empty classroom and hide behind the door.

Footsteps stop on the threshold. "Where are you?"

Lips pressed together I remain silent.

"Unless you climbed out of the window, you're hiding in there. Stop avoiding me."

"Why? I know you believe all that stuff Sofia said about me."

"That's not true." Nicky's voice is firm.

"You just stood there with everyone else when she said it."

"She caught me off guard. I tried to tell you that, but you didn't want to talk to me. I even came around to your house the other night. Jamie answered the door. He told me you were working at the diner, but when I got there, Sara told me it was your night off."

The night Hank found me. The night I made Rush cut me and fuck me.

"I'm worried about you, Bee."

"I'm fine."

"No, you're not. I'm your friend. I'm sorry I wasn't fast enough to back you up before, but I'm here for you now. Even if I have to follow you around for the next month I won't stop until you let me help you. Please talk to me."

A tiny part of the wall I've built inside me cracks. "I'm sorry."

"There's nothing for you to be sorry about. Please open the door. Let's talk."

I've been such a fucking mess since last night. Since the attack, I've been looking at everyone as my attacker. After Jamie hit me, it's amped up the fear of people to new levels. But I know I can't carry on this way. Something has to give.

I wipe my eyes and sniff, then pull open the door. Nicky steps through it.

"Have you eaten lunch?"

I shake my head. "I'm not very hungry."

"Then you can share my sandwich."

"No, it's okay."

She smiles. "No arguments."

We push two tables together and sit down. Nicky pulls a

Tupperware box out of her bag and peels off the lid. A sandwich wrapped in Saran wrap is inside.

"It's just cheese and ham." She removes one half and hands me the other.

"Thanks." I take it, but leave it on the table in front of me.

"You want to tell me what's going on?"

"It's …I don't know."

"Who hit you?"

My hand rises to my cheek, but I don't reply.

Nicky gently reaches over to touch my shoulder. "Did someone attack you again? Is that why you've been acting so weird lately?"

The shock, shame, anger and guilt that's been my constant companion merges with the helpless loss of control.

Would she even believe me if I told her Jamie hit me? He's my *brother*. Why do I feel responsible when he's the one who did it?

Because he's made everyone think I'm crazy.

Because brothers aren't supposed to hit their sisters. Families love each other.

"You can tell me."

I close my eyes and bow my head.

You made me do this, Bee. This is your fault, not mine. All you do is push, push. Fucking push. Jamie's words ring in my head.

Did I? Is it because I kept telling him to get a job? To stop borrowing money from Cooper?

"Is it someone you know?"

I nod.

"Someone at the school?"

I nod again.

I didn't want it to be like this. I'm not to blame. You are.

Am I?

"Someone close to you?"

The knot in my stomach tightens. There's no way in a million years she'll say his name.

"Bee, did ..." She licks her lips. "Did Jamie hurt you?"

For a second I'm sure I haven't heard her correctly. Guilt, fear, embarrassment, and *shame* wind themselves around me. *Should I tell her?*

I push back my chair and stand. "I need to go."

"Bailey?" She tries to grab my hand. "Oh my god, it *was* him. Wasn't it?"

"No!"

She calls after me as I run out of the room. I don't stop, don't look back. I feel sick to my stomach with the fact that she knows.

53
Rush

I'M SITTING ON the bleachers, eating lunch with my friends, when Nicky finds me. She hovers at the bottom of the steps, and waves to me.

"I'll be back in a minute." I head down to meet her.

"I think you're right." She doesn't wait for me to ask.

"Did you ask her?"

Nicky nods. "She denied it, but …" She gives a helpless shrug. "She looked terrified when I said his name. Rush … Rush? … *Rush*, where are you going?"

I ignore her, and pull out my cell, firing off a text to my group chat.

Me: Cafeteria. Now!

I don't wait to see who reads it and push through the doors of the school's main building. I take the stairs two at a time to the top floor and stop just inside the entrance of the cafeteria. My eyes sweep over the interior, searching ... searching ... *there!*

I walk over to the table where half the hockey team are sitting and take a seat.

"Hey, Rush." Daryl slaps my back. "Where are the others?"

"On their way up." I don't take my eyes off Jamie.

"Are you ready for the game on Saturday? Coach hasn't shared the final list of who's playing yet. Do you think it'll be you or Jamie?"

At the sound of his name, the boy in question looks up. "It'll be me."

"You think?" My voice is casual, almost bored.

"Well, yeah. Coach benched you. He's not going to swap back to you this close to the game. The team is used to playing with me as center now."

"Used to losing, you mean?"

He surges to his feet, fingers curling into fists.

I stay seated and smile up at him. "Gonna hit me, Linnett?" I lift my chin. "Give it your best shot."

A muscle pops in his jaw, but he doesn't move.

"No?" Slowly I rise to my feet. "Why not? Not brave enough to face me with no padding between us now that I'm sober?"

"Fuck off, Carter." He turns away.

"Or is it because I'm not a girl?"

He swings back to face me. "What the fuck does that mean?"

"You going to deny hitting Bailey?" I hike an eyebrow.

"Of course I am. What the fuck are you talking about?"

"You know what I'm talking about and ..." I take an exaggerated look around the room. "It makes me wonder ... Where exactly were you when she was attacked at your party?"

The team seated around us falls silent, and the tension building between us slowly spreads to other tables, until all eyes are on us.

"See, I've been thinking about it a lot lately. Other than me, the only person with any reason to be angry with her is you."

"How'd you work that out?"

"It was your car she was smashing when she got beat up, wasn't it?"

Someone gasps. I don't look away from Jamie to see who.

"No one else had any reason at all to target your sister."

He shrugs one shoulder. "She turned down Cooper for a date earlier that night."

"Wow. You're really going to throw one of your friends under the bus?" I laugh. "Take note, everyone. Being friends with Jamie Linnett means you're going to be used to get him out of trouble."

"Everyone knows it was you. I don't know what the fuck you're talking about."

"It wasn't me. I already proved I wasn't there."

"Well, Bailey says otherwise."

I shake my head. "That's just it, Linnett. *She* doesn't. You keep claiming she's saying it. But no one has actually heard *her* say it. Why don't we ask her?"

His eyes dart around the room, and the relief on his face is clear when he doesn't see his sister. "She's not here to ask."

"I can rectify that." I pull out my cell, and tap Seven's number. He answers on the first ring. "Can you find Bailey and bring her up to the cafeteria with you?"

"Sure. We're on our way. Be there in five."

I CLOSE MY locker door, and turn to find Seven, Dom, Levi and Nicky right behind me. My stomach drops at the sight of them.

Oh my god, did she tell them what I said?

"I need to go study for the math test." I blurt out before she can say anything.

Dom smiles. "Then why don't you come do it in the cafeteria with the rest of us?"

"No, thanks"

"It wasn't an invitation. Come on," Seven says.

"No."

"You either walk or I carry you."

Nicky puts herself between us. "Guys, relax. Bee, it's okay. We just need you to come with us."

"Why?"

"You're needed in the cafeteria." Dom answers me this time.

"By who?"

"You'll find out when we get there."

"Nicky? What did you do?"

The compassion in her eyes makes me want to run and hide. When I turn in the opposite direction to do just that, Seven blocks my way.

He gestures down the hallways. "Let's go."

"Leave me alone!" Panic is clear in my voice.

"Please, Bee." Nicky's voice is soft. "It's going to be okay."

They're not going to give me a choice. It's clear on their faces. Whatever they've planned for me in the cafeteria, they're going to force me to face it. The boys surround me to prevent my escape, Nicky takes up a position beside me, and they escort me through the school and up to the cafeteria.

All eyes turn in our direction when we enter. The tension in the air is palpable. My mouth dries up when I see Rush and Jamie facing off across the table.

No, no, no.

I go to turn, and a hand clamps around my bicep.

"Oh no, you don't." Seven forces me back around, and drags me across the room.

For a room full of people, the silence is deafening. Dom, Levi and Seven move to join Rush.

Somehow, I find my voice through the panic threatening to drag me under. "What's going on?"

Rush's head turns my way. "Do you think I'm the one who

attacked you at the party?"

"What?" The word comes out as a croak.

"Tell them, Bailey." Jamie's voice is hard.

"Shut the fuck up, Linnett, and let her talk."

"You just want to scare her into saying what you want."

"No, I want her to tell the truth."

"Of course, it was him." Jamie's eyes burn into mine. "Right, Bee?"

My mouth opens to agree with him, but then I look at Rush. At the way he's looking at *me*. There's nothing but patience on his face.

"I ..."

"Everyone knows the truth. You're just a fucking piece of trash, Carter." My brother sneers. "A violent drunk. A *bully*. Everyone saw what you did to her at the party. No one believes she agreed to you fucking her like that." His gaze moves back to me. "Unless she's a slut. *Are* you a slut, Bee?"

His taunting words twists through me, and the hate he can't hide breaks through my apprehension, and forces me to respond.

"No."

The entire room gasps.

"See. You did it." Jamie sounds exultant.

"No, I mean ..." I swallow. "I mean, it wasn't Rush."

Jamie's triumphant smile falls away. "What did you fucking say?"

"I said no. It...it wasn't Rush."

"You're confused."

"No, I'm not."

"Who put the bruise on your cheek?" Rush isn't looking at me anymore. His focus is on Jamie.

Something in my chest tightens painfully.

Why is he doing this to me? Everyone is watching. Is this because I refused to talk to him?

Shame and embarrassment snuff out my temporary confidence, and I take a step back. The need to fight or flee surges through me. My back hits something solid, and an arm wraps around my waist, securing me in place.

"Don't run." Dom's voice is soft in my ear. "Trust him."

Rush turns his head, eyes finding mine. "It's okay, Bug. Don't be scared to tell the truth."

Bug.

I lick my lips. "I …"

Jamie pushes violently away from the table. "What are you trying to prove?"

"I'm not trying to prove anything. I just want confirmation of what I already know. What are you scared of, Linnett?"

"I don't have to fucking stand here and listen to this." He steps away from the table, and turns toward the door.

"Coward."

That one word, uttered in such a mocking tone, stops him in his tracks. His fingers curl into fists and he slowly turns back to face Rush.

"I'm not a fucking coward."

Rush snorts. "Then let's hear what Bailey has to say."

"She's a fucking lying little psychopath."

"Pretty sure that's you, not her."

I must make some kind of noise, because both boys swing around to face me. Rush holds out a hand. "Come on, Bailey."

I shake my head.

"What the fuck are you trying to do here?"

Rush smiles. "I'm giving Bailey her power back."

"What power?" Derision drips from Jamie's tone.

Nicky must have told him. Does he believe me?

A tiny trickle of hope tumbles through the negative emotions, loosening their grip on me.

"Jamie," I whisper.

Rush cocks his head. "What was that?"

"Jamie," I repeat louder. "It was Jamie. Jamie hit me last night."

Whispers erupt around us.

My brother shrugs it off, laughing. "Don't be fucking stupid. She's lying."

"You hit me, and you told me it was my fault." My voice grows stronger. "You said that I *made* you do it."

"This act of yours is getting a little desperate, Bee."

"She's your sister, man." One of the boys at the table gives him a disgusted look.

"She's crazy. I didn't touch her," Jamie insists. "Bee, tell them you're fucking lying."

Gathering up the threads of courage, I straighten, and step away from Dom. His arm falls away, letting me go. I lift my head and stare my brother straight in the eyes. "I can't do that."

"Tell them!"

I shake my head.

"Fucking. Tell. Them," he snarls. "Don't fuck up my reputation."

"Yeah, you wouldn't want Coach to hear about this, would you?"

Rush's voice is dry. "Guess you won't be center after all, huh?"

"This is all your fault, you stupid fucking bitch. A real sister would have had my back. This just proves how fake you are."

"A real sister?" I jump on the words.

"You're not my sister." He spits. "I found the adoption papers in a box in the attic we bought from the old house."

Adoption papers? What? No, he has to be lying.

"Mom and Dad should have left you to rot in whatever shit home you were in, instead of letting you ruin my life." Jamie's cool veneer snaps, and he lunges at me, his weight propelling me backward into a table. My hip connects with a corner, sending a sharp stab of pain through me. His hands wrap around my throat. "I should have fucking finished what I started with that hockey stick."

And just like that, the torn and tattered corners of my world implode.

I gasp for breath, nails clawing at his wrists. Rage contorts Jamie's face. It's twisted with so much hatred, I don't recognize him.

"You fucking bastard." The snarl comes seconds before Jamie is dragged off me.

55
Rush

"Are you *sure* he admitted to it?"

I tip my head back against the seat and blow out a breath. "Everyone heard him. He said '*I should have fucking finished what I started with that hockey stick.*' What else would he be talking about?"

I'm sitting in the principal's office, Seven and Dom on either side of me. School security have taken Jamie into another room, where they're watching over him. Bailey was taken to the school nurse. Nicky went with her.

"It's a serious accusation, Rush."

"I'm not making an accusation. I *told* you, everyone heard him say it. Can I go now? I want to make sure Bailey is okay."

"Her parents arrived earlier and took her home."

I sit up straight. "What about Jamie?"

The principal sighs. "That's up to Bailey. The police were

called. They're going to want to take statements from everyone who witnessed the situation."

My lips twist. "The *situation*? Is that what we're calling it?" I stand. "Can I go?"

"You have to stay away from Jamie Linnett. We just had to drag you off him. They might want to press charges."

"I have no intention of going anywhere near him."

"This is serious. I *mean* it, Rush."

"So do I. I know it's fucking serious. He beat the shit out of his sister ... *twice*."

He sighs, then nods. "Alright, boys. I'm giving you the rest of the day off. Go home. The police will be in contact to speak to you."

"That's it?"

"It's with the authorities now. Beyond that, my hands are tied for the moment. Go home. *Stay* away from the Linnett's house."

We leave the school, make our way to where Seven's car is parked, and stop beside it. Dom rubs the back of his neck. Seven leans against the door and folds his arms.

"Are we really staying away from him?" He nails me with a hard look.

"It'd be obvious if we make any kind of move right now, so we need to wait and see what happens next."

"Do you think Bailey will press charges?"

I roll my bottom lip between my teeth, thinking about it. "I don't know. Just because he's said she's adopted, doesn't mean it's true. And even if he's *not* lying, they were raised as siblings. I'm not sure she'd want to press charges against her brother."

"What's your plan for this afternoon?"

"I'm going home. Since school has brought the police into it, they will have contacted the parents of everyone involved. Which means my gran has probably been informed, so I'll speak to her and let her know what happened."

"We're supposed to have practice tonight."

"I'll be there. I doubt Coach has been left out of the loop."

***

The police turn up shortly after I get back to the trailer, and I give them my statement. I keep my answers to their questions brief. They refuse to tell me whether Jamie has been arrested, or if they've spoken to Bailey, and eventually leave with a repeated warning to stay away from the Linnett household.

Once they've left, I call my gran, who spends five minutes ranting about how I can't be left alone before calming down enough for me to explain. Once I do, she tells me she's coming home, and no matter what I say, she can't be swayed from the decision. Part of me is relieved, another part is annoyed that *this* is the thing that brings her back instead of my descent into madness a few short weeks earlier.

When I finally get off the call, I spend an hour cleaning the trailer … and then it's time to head to the barn for hockey practice.

Everyone is sitting in the locker room when I arrive, talking in subdued tones. I dump my bag on the closest bench.

"Where's Coach?"

"Running late. He said to start warm ups and he'll be here in half an hour." It's Daryl who answers me.

I change out of my street clothes and into my hockey gear, then follow the rest of the team out onto the ice. We're taking turns sending the puck into the net when Coach finally shows up. He blows his whistle, then bellows my name and waves me across to the players bench.

"I've just come out of a meeting with the principal. It's been decided that in light of what happened today, Linnett is off the team and I'm officially reinstating you as captain and center."

"Thanks, Coach." I'd have preferred to get my position back by proving I am the better player, so the news is a little bittersweet.

"Obviously, with everything that's come to light, you being seen with the girl is no longer an issue. I'm glad it was proved without any doubt that you didn't do it, Rush. I always knew you were better than that." He pats my shoulder. "Get back out there. We have a game to get ready for."

He works us hard for the next two hours, and by the time he lets us off the ice, we're hot, sweaty, and tired. I opt to shower at the barn, and when I finally get back to the trailer park, the sun has set and it's getting dark.

Deja vu wraps around me when a figure detaches itself from the shadows cast by the trailer and comes toward me. The street lights reflect off red hair and pale features a second before the wind is knocked out of my lungs by a body throwing itself at me.

"*Bailey?*"

"I had to get out of there. I didn't know where else to go."

56
Bailey

THE DOOR TO the nurse's room swings open and Dad strides in. "What the hell is going on?"

My attention jerks away from Nicky, who's been comforting me through my turmoil and tears for the last thirty minutes. The police have already questioned me and taken photographs of the bruises around my neck.

For one brief second, I'm terrified Jamie is with him, but only Mom follows him into the room.

"Well? The school called to say you and your brother were fighting."

"Jamie attacked her!" Nicky answers before I can. "There were dozens of witnesses. He even admitted to being the one who assaulted her outside the house with the hockey stick."

"Lies!" Mom snaps.

"Shawna." Dad's tone is a low warning.

"Jamie is a good boy. You know that."

"He hates me. He's done nothing but make my life a misery since we started here." I stifle a sob. "He said—"

"Mr. and Mrs. Linnett. You were supposed to go straight to the office. The principal wanted to speak to you before you came here." The nurse interrupts me.

Dad casts a dark look in the woman's direction before turning back to me. "Wait here. We'll sort this mess out."

I don't reply as they both follow the nurse. I'm numb inside. Have been that way since school security dragged my screaming brother out of sight. I can still feel his hands wrapped around my neck.

Nicky pats my arm. "It will be okay."

"I don't think it will ever be okay again."

"I just…I just wanted to make you feel better."

I bow my head and don't reply. Nothing can fix what happened today. This is just the beginning.

Will Mom and Dad believe me, or will they take Jamie's side?

Twenty minutes later, my parents return. This time they both look pale. Whatever has been said to them appears to have left them both shaken.

"Come on, Bee. We're taking you home." My dad's voice is quiet.

Mom doesn't say a word.

I glance at Nicky.

She smiles. "I'll come and see you tonight."

I follow my parents out into the hallway. It's deserted, and we don't see anyone at all as we walk to the entrance and head outside. There's a rental car parked outside. As soon as we climb into it, Mom turns in the passenger seat.

"You are not pressing charges."

"Shawna," Dad snaps.

"Kelvin, he can't have a criminal record."

"For Christ's sake, he *attacked* his sister. Do you think that's normal behaviour?"

"Maybe not, but he wouldn't have assaulted her! That's the other boy trying to put the blame elsewhere."

Her denial of the truth makes me feel sick. Even after all this, she *still* believes Jamie. I rest my cheek against the cool window, close my eyes, and let my parents argue. By the time we reach the house, my head is pounding.

We're barely through the front door when I blurt out the question that's been spinning around my head. "Am I adopted?"

Both my parents freeze. The color in my mom's face drains away.

"What did you just say?"

"Is it true?"

I wait for the string of denials but they don't come.

Dad rubs a hand over his face. "We never wanted you to find out like this."

"Oh my god." My body sways. "I am!"

"You ... you went digging through the boxes in the attic!" Mom's voice is shrill.

"No, Jamie told me."

"Let's go into the kitchen and sit down." Dad gestures at the doorway.

I follow them into the room. Everything I thought I knew about myself has been turned upside down.

I'm not their daughter.

Jamie isn't my brother.

I'm not a Linnett.

Who am I?

Where did I come from?

I sink down into one of the chairs. "Why didn't you say anything?"

"Because there was no point." Dad replies. "We … we had problems conceiving. The doctors told your mother she couldn't have children."

"But Jamie—is he adopted, too?"

"No! He was a miracle baby." Mom's voice is soft. "I wanted more, but there were complications and that dream ended. You can't send him to prison, Bailey. Not my only baby."

"What about me?" My stomach twists." You raised me, too!"

Her eyes meet mine. "You need to do what's best for the family. Don't be selfish."

"*Selfish?*"

Dad slams his fist down on the table. "Shawna, stop it! Leave her alone."

"She owes us for giving her a life, Kelvin. Jamie shouldn't be made to pay for a stupid mistake."

"I am not responsible for what happened. All I did was stand up for myself, and he attacked me! I'm not the cause of whatever trauma he is dealing with, and I *won't* be used as a punching bag to make him feel better. Jamie needs to take fucking responsibility for his emotions and actions. He can't blame someone else for things that happen to him through the choices he made." I'm shrieking by the time I finish speaking.

"You ungrateful little bitch." Mom spits.

Dad blocks her way when she tries to rise from her chair. "Can you hear yourself, woman? What's wrong with you?"

"We can't let his future be destroyed because of one stupid mistake."

I've heard enough. I leap up from my chair and run from the room. Dad shouts after me, but I don't stop, until I'm through the front door and halfway down the street.

I hate the way she spoke to me. How she defended Jamie because she loves him more.

The truth is obvious to me now. The ways she always doted on him, supported him, *loved* him more, because I'm not really hers.

It hurts so fucking much.

I roam aimlessly around town, ducking behind walls anytime I see a face I recognize, until shadows start to stretch through the dusk. There's *no* way I can go back to the house. Not tonight. My feet move in the direction of the one place where I feel safe.

I knock on Rush's door, but there's no answer. I peer through the window. It's dark and empty inside. Restlessly, I circle around the outside of the trailer a couple of times. On my third circuit, I find the boy I'm waiting for walking toward me. I break into a run at the sight of him and throw myself into his arms.

"*Bailey?*"

"I had to get out of there." I hang onto him. "I didn't know where else to go."

His arms wind around my waist. "It's okay. Come inside."

"Are you sure?" The tension inside me eases a little.

"You're always welcome here."

His gentle voice reaches something inside me. A jagged sob explodes from my lips, and everything I've been bottling up for the past few hours spills out.

"I don't know who I am, Rush. Nothing in my life is real. Is my name Bailey? Did they change it? Who am I?"

57
Rush

"COME INSIDE." I reach behind me to unwrap her arms, and take her hand, so I can lead her up the steps.

Her fingers are tight around mine, and she follows me inside, dashing at her eyes with her free hand. I guide her across to the couch, and pull her down beside me. She immediately crawls across my legs and wraps her arms around my neck, burying her face against my shoulder. I loop one arm around her and brush the hair away from her cheek with my other hand.

"Do you want something to drink?"

She shakes her head.

"Have you eaten?"

Another headshake.

"Do you want to talk about it?"

"I don't know what to say." Her voice is muffled against my shirt.

"Anything you want. Was Jamie telling the truth?"

She nods.

"That explains a lot."

Her head lifts. "What do you mean?" There's a slight tremor to her voice, and her eyes are shiny with tears.

"You don't have the asshole gene." I use one thumb to wipe away the tear making its way down her cheek. "I'd be celebrating that."

"I don't know who I am anymore." The words are a broken whisper.

"You're the same person you were yesterday ... and the day before that. You're Bailey Linnett, hot as fuck girlfriend of the Red Creek Raven's hockey team captain." I press a finger to her lips to stop her speaking. "You're the girl who didn't give up on a boy who lost his way. You're the Big Bad Wolf's Little Rose." I press my palms to her cheeks and tilt her head up. "You're my Bug." I kiss the tip of her nose.

She sniffs. "I'm your girlfriend?"

"You've always been my girlfriend."

"But I'm not Bailey Linnett. I don't even know if *Bailey* is my name. Did they change it?"

"Does it matter if they did? Your name doesn't define you. Who you are in here ..." I drop one hand and place it over her heart. "This is what defines you, Bailey. Not your name, not who your parents are. None of that matters."

"I feel like my whole life is a lie. My parents aren't my parents. My brother isn't my brother. He hates me. Why does he hate me? Why does my mom hate me?"

I slide my arm around her waist and pull her closer. "I don't think your mom hates you." I don't deny her claim about Jamie. It's clear to me that he does hate her, otherwise he wouldn't have hurt her the way he did. I shove aside the stab of guilt and the whisper reminding me that I'd treated her just as badly. Now isn't the time to bring that up or deal with it.

"She told me it would be selfish to press charges against Jamie. All she cares about is Jamie not having a police record."

I sigh. "That's fucked up."

"Is that what I should do? Should I—"

"The fuck you should. Did you talk to the police?"

She gives a small nod. "They asked me what happened."

"Did you tell them?"

"I think so. I ... My head is so mixed up. I don't know what I told them. What do you think I should do?"

I have opinions on that, but in the state she's in I don't want to tell her.

"You need to sleep." I tighten my hold on her and stand, scooping her up into my arms. "Get some rest, let your head clear, and then think about what you want to do tomorrow."

I carry her through to my bedroom and lower her to the bed. "Clothes off and get under the sheets."

"I don't think I can sleep." Her teeth worry at her bottom lip. "I have too many questions going around my head."

I lean over her, sliding one hand around her neck to tangle in her hair. I tug her head back until I can meet her eyes. The despair is clear in her gaze. She's adrift and desperately trying to find something to cling to.

I can give her that. The same way she did for me. By being

what she needs. And what she needs right now is someone to make decisions for her.

"I'm going to get you some pills for the headache you're pretending you don't have, and a glass of water."

I release my hold on her hair and straighten. "Clock's ticking, Bug. I'm prepared to cut you out of those clothes if they're not off your body by the time I get back."

I head back out, fill a glass with water, find the pills and tip two into my palm. I detour into the bathroom on the way back, and take the tub of Vaseline out of the cabinet. When I return to the bedroom, Bailey is under the covers. I hold out the glass and pills. She takes them from me, pops the pills into her mouth and washes them down with the water.

"Good girl. Now roll onto your stomach and close your eyes." I reach back and pull my shirt over my head, then crawl onto the mattress beside her.

She frowns, but does as I say. She tucks her hands beneath the pillow and turns her head toward me. I smile, then rise up and straddle her hips, pulling the sheet down to reveal her bare back.

"What are you doing?"

"Hush." I open the Vaseline, scoop some out and rub it between my palms, then smooth them down her back. Pressing my thumbs down against her skin, I rub small circles on either side of her spine, moving back up to her shoulders. "Unfortunately, I don't have any massage oil, so I'm going to have to improvise."

It doesn't take long for the tension to loosen its grip from her muscles, and before long her breathing turns deep and steady. I stay where I am for a little longer, stroking light patterns over her skin, until I'm sure she's asleep, then carefully inch my way down the bed and out of the room. I close the door behind me, wash my hands and walk out to the kitchen to find some food. I'm pretty sure Bailey will sleep the night through, but I want to have something ready, just in case she does wake up and is hungry.

Plus, I'm fucking starving. I haven't eaten since lunch time. I opt for ease and make a pile of ham and cheese sandwiches, cover some in saran wrap and put them in the refrigerator, then take the rest to the couch, where I demolish them and two bottles of Coke.

I'm washing up my plate and silverware when there's a tap on the door. Drying my hands, I walk across the floor, make sure the safety chain is on, then open the door.

Bailey's parents are standing beyond it.

"Can I help you?"

"Is Bailey here?" It's her dad who speaks.

"She is."

"Bailey. Come out here!" At his raised voice, I step outside and pull the door closed.

"She's asleep."

"We need to talk to her."

I look from him to her mom, who says nothing.

"She was pretty upset when she got here. She's taken some headache pills and gone to bed."

"I need to know what she's planning to do!" Her mom's voice is sharp.

"Shawna!" her dad snaps.

Dismissing the woman from my attention, I focus on Bailey's dad. "Look, finding out she was adopted was a shock. And after the way Jamie's been treating her ..." I shrug. "You can't blame her for needing some space."

Her dad nods. "I don't blame her at all. The police brought Jamie home earlier. I know why she doesn't want to come home, and I completely understand, but I really want to talk to her ... to explain more."

"I'm not sure that's wise—"

"I know. I know she won't want to come home with Jamie there. Will you ask her to meet me ... at the diner, maybe?" He hands me a piece of paper with a cell number scribbled on it. "This is my number. If you could let me know what she decides, I'd really appreciate it."

I take the paper and stuff it in my back pocket. "I'll talk to her when she wakes up, but I'm not making any promises." I nail her mother with a glare. "Jamie needs to pay for what he did."

"He did—"

"I was there. I heard him admit to everything, so I don't recommend standing there and claiming he's innocent." I nod to her dad. "Nice to meet you, Mr. Linnett. I'll pass on your message. Now, if you don't mind, it's late and I have school in the morning." I close the door without waiting for a response.

Turning back to face the room, I rub one hand down my face.

How did I go from blaming Bailey for everything that happened to me, to having her in my bed while I defended her from her mom and brother?

Life is so fucking weird sometimes.

58
Bailey

MY FEET POUND across the street, darkness closing in around me. I can sense him. Malice surrounds him like an aura. Sucking in a ragged breath, fear tries to smother me as I sob. The second I stop, he'll catch up to me. I have to keep moving. As fast as I can, I race across the road toward the trailer park.

A hand shoves at my back. The weight of it sends me stumbling forward, a scream tearing out of me. I hit the ground, hard.

"No, no, no. Please." I roll sideways.

The shadowy figure lunges at me, the hockey stick swinging toward me with such violence I raise my hand to protect my head.

I wake with a start, skin slick with sweat. A pair of arms are wrapped about me, holding me tight, and I fight against them. "No!"

"Bailey, it's me."

It takes a few seconds for the fog to fade and the realization of who is holding me to filter in.

"Rush?"

"You were having a nightmare."

"It … it was d-dark and something was ch-chasing me."

"You're safe." He pulls me closer to him.

My body sags into his. I bury my face against his neck and close my eyes. His fingers stroke along the length of my spine.

"Are you hungry?"

"No."

"You need to eat."

My stomach chooses that moment to rumble.

He presses a kiss to my forehead, directly over my scar, before he untangles my arms from around his waist. "I'll be right back."

He climbs out of the bed and leaves the room. I roll onto my side. It's still dark outside, and I have no idea what time it is. My head feels thick, my eyes gritty, and I'm yawning when Rush reappears with a plate of sandwiches in one hand and a bottle of water in the other.

He places it down on the mattress beside me, then sits on the edge of the bed. When I'm done demolishing the sandwiches, he takes the plate back to the kitchen. I open the bottle of water and take a sip.

"Your parents came over after you fell asleep," he says when he comes back into the room.

"My parents?"

"Yeah." He rejoins me on the bed. "Jamie is back at the house."

"He's *home*?"

He reaches for the bottle of water and removes it from my hand.

"Your dad wants to talk to you. He left a number for you to call."

"I …I can't go back there."

"Just breathe, Bailey."

"Can I stay with you?"

"My gran is due back in a couple of days. I'll have to clear it with her first, but I doubt she'll say no."

"What if she does?" My tongue darts out to wet my lips. "Rush, I can't go back there. Not with Jamie in the house. Not when my parents don't want me."

His fingers curl around the back of my neck and he tugs me down against his side. "Your dad loves you."

I swallow hard. "I-I don't know if that's true."

Lips press to my forehead. "Everything is still raw right now. It's going to hurt, but eventually you'll be able to see through the pain."

"Why can't this all just be a nightmare?"

"I wished for the same things for months after my mom died."

"I'm sorry."

"It's not your fault." His fingers trace over my arm. "Try and get some more sleep. We'll deal with this tomorrow … together."

Together.

He called me his girlfriend. Did he really mean it?

59
Rush

I WAKE UP before Bailey, and creep out of the bedroom as quietly as I can, grabbing clothes as I go. I'm sitting on the couch with coffee and toast when she finally wakes up. My eyes move over her as she walks toward me, starting at the tousled red hair falling around her face, over the hockey jersey falling off one shoulder and down to her bare legs and feet.

"Why are you smiling?" She comes to a stop in front of me.

I tip my head back against the couch. "You're wearing my jersey."

Her cheeks turn pink, and she plucks at the hem. "I just grabbed the first thing I saw."

"It looks good on you." I hold out my hand and pull her down beside me when she takes it. "How are you feeling this morning?"

She curls up beside me, tucking her feet beneath her legs. "Numb."

I nod. "Understandable. Do you want to go to school?"

"No. Everyone will stare or ask questions."

"Okay. I'm going to need to go in. We have practice this afternoon, but you can stay here. No one other than your parents know you're here, so you won't be disturbed. Hank lives next door. You can go to him if you need anything." I stand and walk over to the kitchen. "Coffee? Toast?"

"Yes, please."

I make her breakfast and coffee, and take it over to her. "I need to shower and get ready for school." I reach out and tip her face up with one finger beneath her chin, then lean down and press a kiss to her lips. "It might not seem like it right now, but everything is going to work out. Eat your breakfast."

I take a quick shower, brush my teeth, and get dressed. She's sitting where I left her when I return to the main room.

"I'm going to check in with Hank before I go. If you need me, text me."

"I don't have your number."

I frown. "You don't?"

"No. Not that it matters, Jamie broke my phone."

"You don't have a phone?"

She shakes her head. I pull my cell out of my pocket and toss it onto her lap. "The lock pin is five seven nine two. If you need anything, call Seven and he'll tell me."

"You don't need to leave your phone here."

"I don't want you to have no way of contacting anyone." I walk toward the door, then stop and turn. "I guess you didn't tell your dad about your phone?"

"No."

"Maybe you should call him and tell him everything."

"I don't want to talk to him."

I retrace my steps and crouch in front of her. "Bailey, listen to me. *Nothing* in life is guaranteed. The day my day died ... I had an argument with him before he left. I never got the chance to clear the air. When my mom died—" My voice breaks and I clear my throat. "I never got the chance to say goodbye."

"He's not my dad."

"You don't mean that. He might not be your biological dad, but in all the ways that matter, he is. Moving here has been a huge upheaval for your entire family, and I think it's brought to light certain characteristics that might have remained hidden, but your dad seems like a decent enough guy ... all things considered." I doubt I'll ever forgive him for his part in what happened to my mom, but that's just a small part of a bigger situation for Bailey. "Just promise to think about it, okay?"

She lowers her gaze. "Okay."

Rising to my feet, I reach out to squeeze her hand. "I promise, it'll all work out. Help yourself to food and drink. Gran won't be back until Saturday. If she calls, just ignore it and I'll speak to her later."

It takes every ounce of willpower to walk out of the trailer and leave her there, but I eventually manage it and head over to Hank's place. He opens at my first tap on the door.

"Bailey is staying with me for a couple of days. She's not going to school today. Could you check in on her for me?"

His brow furrows. "Is everything okay?"

"Her asshole brother attacked her yesterday, *and* admitted it was him who beat her up."

Something dark passes over Hank's face. "You witnessed that?"

"I did. He also dropped the bombshell that she's adopted. She turned up at my place late last night. I have to go to school. I can't miss practice, but I don't want to leave her alone."

"Go to school. I'll look after her."

"She has my cell, if she needs to contact anyone."

"Alright. Go on, get going, I'll walk over in an hour and make sure she's okay."

I hesitate for a second longer.

"Rush, go to school."

60
Bailey

I DON'T MOVE after Rush leaves the trailer, and just enjoy the silence. It's nice to sit there, without anyone asking me questions, demanding answers, *judging* me. Like he said, no one knows I'm here.

I hope mom and dad didn't tell Jamie where I am. Maybe he'll leave me alone now.

At that unsettling thought my gaze moves to the door. I stand up and double-check it's locked, then return to the couch. Rush's cell is on the cushion beside me. If anyone turns up, I'll call Seven.

How long has he known I'm not his sister?

He mentioned something about papers in the attic. I recall the day he asked me to go find his stuff up there.

Was it then?

I still can't believe Mom and Dad never told me.

"Stop thinking." I tell myself. "Take a shower."

The cramped bathroom holds a tiny cubicle with enough space for one person to stand in. I find a towel, fold it across the sink and strip out of Rush's jersey. I wish he'd stayed with me, but he needs to maintain an appearance at school. His life has been in enough upheaval.

I turn on the water and step into the shower. The water is cold enough to break out goosebumps over my skin. It takes a few moments before it heats up, I scrub my body, wash my hair and get out before it turns cold again.

I'm not sure what I should do with myself today. Rush told me to call my dad. I don't think I'm ready for that.

What if he tries to talk me into going back to the house?

No way do I want to go back there.

My internal debate is interrupted by a knock at the trailer door. I'm tempted to ignore it. But it could be Rush. Maybe he changed his mind and came home.

I redress in Rush's jersey, and walk across to answer the door. Hank is on the other side of it.

His gaze moves over me, frowning at the Raven's logo on the front of the jersey. "Rush said you were here."

I nod. "He went to school."

"I know. I came over to check on you."

"You don't have to do that."

He shrugs. "I'm free, and you look like you could use the company."

The thought of not being alone is appealing. "Okay."

"Give me five minutes. I'll just go and lock up." He turns and heads back off toward his trailer.

I close the door and dart back toward the bedroom. I find a pair of oversized sweats and pull them on. They're baggy on me, and I have to pull the drawstring tight to make sure they stay up.

I need someone to collect some clothes for me. Maybe Nicky? But will Mom and Dad let her bring them? They might make me go over myself.

Hank bangs on the door a few minutes later with two mugs of coffee. I open the door and step back to allow him inside.

He moves to the couch and places the mugs on the table. "You got anything for lunch later?"

"Rush said there was stuff in the freezer."

"Don't worry about that. I'll fix you something when I make mine."

I arch an eyebrow. "Did he tell you to keep any eye on me?"

"He cares about you."

I pluck at the hem of the jersey. "You don't have to hang around here and babysit me. I know you must have things to do."

Lifting his mug up, he settles back on the couch. "I'm good."

"You sure?"

He nods. "Rush said your brother attacked you."

"At school." My voice is low. "He … he said he was the one who hit me with the hockey stick at the party."

Hank's expression is like stone, but there's a nerve ticking in his jaw. "The little shit should pay for what he did to you."

"The police asked if I wanted to press charges."

"What did you say?"

"I don't remember. Everything from yesterday is mostly a blur, but my mom … I mean, *Shawna* doesn't want me to press charges."

Hank is silent.

I reach for my coffee to give myself something to do. "I found out yesterday that I'm adopted."

"I know." His voice is soft.

"Rush told you."

"No," He cradles his mug against his chest. "I've known since the day you walked into Darla's diner looking for a job."

61

Rush

FINGERS SNAP IN front of my face and I blink, focusing on the frowning features of Seven.

"Sorry, what did you say?"

He shakes his head. "What is wrong with you today?"

"Nothing." I move toward the main doors of the school.

"Don't lie to me, Rush."

I shrug. "I'm just wondering what's going to happen today. Has Linnett been thrown out of school, or will he be allowed back? Coach said he's off the team … but that doesn't mean it'll stay that way."

"He tried to strangle his sister in front of half the school yesterday. I don't think he'll be back any time soon." Seven's voice is dry.

"Doesn't mean he can't spin it to make it look like something else."

"Too many witnesses. I doubt anyone is taking his side." He bumps my shoulder with his. "Why are you so concerned? Something you want to share?"

There's so much I want to share, but I won't betray Bailey's confidence. She came to me, trusting I would be there. I'm not going to share her fears without her permission. But I need to talk to someone …

"Bailey was waiting at my place when I got back from practice last night."

One eyebrow hikes. "Oh?"

I stop in front of my locker. "Her parents turned up, looking for her, and told me Linnett had been allowed home. She stayed with me. I couldn't send her back to the house, knowing he was there."

"Where is she now?"

"Still there. She didn't want to come to school. I guess she doesn't want to face whatever questions people would have."

Seven gives a slow nod. "Understandable."

I take out the books I need for the morning, slam my locker shut then follow Seven down to his.

"Are you and Bailey together now?"

Are we? "I don't know. We haven't really talked about it, but I called her my girlfriend last night and she didn't argue so …" I shrug. "Maybe?"

Seven snickers. "You should probably figure that out then."

"What about you and …" I jerk my chin to where Tamara Rees is standing at the end of the hallway.

"Rees?" A slow smile spreads across his face. "That little cupcake is in denial of the truth."

"Which would be?"

His smile drops away. "That she belongs to me."

62

Bailey

It takes a split second for his words to register. When they do, all I can do is stare at the man seated beside me. "You did?"

He nods.

"How? Is that why you kept staring at me so much? Do … Do you know my real parents?"

"You look like your mom."

My heart slams against my ribs. "I do?"

"She lived here in Red Creek." He drains the rest of his coffee and places it on the table.

"Where is she now?"

"She died when you were little."

The knowledge brings a twist of pain. I'll never know the woman who gave birth to me. "That's why I was put up for adoption?"

"Yeah."

"What about her family? Didn't she have any parents or siblings?"

"She was an only child." Hank's expression is somber. "Her parents were older. They passed away before you were born."

"You knew her?"

Slowly he rises from his spot on the couch. "I have something to show you. I'll be right back." He strides out of the trailer.

My thoughts are all over the place.

Does he really know where I came from? If my mom lived here in Red Creek, was I born here? Where did we live? Why hasn't he said anything until now?

He reappears a few minutes later in the doorway with a book in his hands. It's not until he places it down on the table that it becomes clear that it's a photo album. The cover is worn and scratched.

I place my mug down, and lean forward. Nervous apprehension sets off butterflies in my stomach.

He flips the first page over to reveal four photographs. The pale, redheaded woman in the images looks a lot like me. Her hair is the same fiery color, only she wears it shorter. Freckles decorate her nose, but her eyes are brown, not blue like mine. There's a baby tucked under her arm and a little boy standing next to her in each one.

"Her name was Emily. No one was sure who fathered her kids. She had a string of boyfriends. They might have the same dad, they might not."

I touch the picture, my fingertip tracing over the woman. "I have a brother?"

"The two of you got separated at the group home. He was sick, and the Linnett's were only interested in a little girl."

My gaze moves over the boy, looking for anything that could tell me who he is. "How can I find out what group home he was in? Do you know where he is?"

Hank's big calloused hand gently settles over mine above the photograph. "I'm right here, kiddo."

My chest constricts. "You? You're my brother?"

His gaze softens as it meets mine. "When you stepped into the diner looking for a job, it was like staring at a ghost. Darla recognized you too, although it took her a while to figure out why. She advised me not to say anything, in case you didn't know you were adopted."

"They weren't going to tell me."

"I figured as much."

"Jamie found some papers in the attic, and that's how I found out." I blurt out, bitterness making my voice sharp. "I think that's what set him off."

He sighs. "I tried to look for you a few times, but it always stopped at dead-ends. I had no intention of interfering with your life. I just planned to watch from the sidelines, until I was certain whether you knew or not."

"You mean like a guardian angel?"

"Like a big brother."

There's a lump in my throat so thick, I can barely swallow. "What happened to Mom? How did she die?"

He releases my hand and sits back. "Drug overdose. I wish I could tell you a better story, but the truth of it is that she was a junkie, who turned tricks to get money to pay for her next fix."

My gaze returns to the unsmiling image of the young woman. It sounds like she had a tragic life that had been cut short too early. I may not have known her but it doesn't stop my heart aching for the parent I never got to know.

"Did you get adopted, too?"

A million questions tumble through my brain.

Is this all real, or am I dreaming? If we hadn't come back to Red Creek, would I have ever learned the truth?

"No, I went from home to home, and eventually fell in with the wrong crowd. Ended up going to prison before I came back to Red Creek. Darla knew our mom when she was alive. Even babysat us a few times. She offered me a job at the diner and the rest is history."

"Is my name really Bailey?"

A smile curves his mouth. "Mom named you Rosie because of the birthmark on the back of your neck. That was how I knew for sure it was you."

"Rosie." I test the name out.

"Rosie and Hank Hicks." He hands me the photo album. "If Rush's gran won't let you stay here, you're more than welcome at mine."

"I don't know what to say. It's so much to take in."

Hank nods. "I know. If you need more proof—because, let's face it, Bailey, I could just be spinning you some bullshit story—Darla can back me up. And I have this album, and some of Mom's old jewelry. With everything that's happened it must be overwhelming. I wasn't going to say anything, but I wanted to let you know that you're not alone."

63

Rush

"HEY, GRAN." I'M sitting astride my bike outside school, using Seven's cell.

"I'll be home at eleven-thirty on Saturday morning. How are you? Is everything okay?"

"I'm good. Listen, I need to ask you something."

"What's wrong?"

"Nothing, but … did school tell you about Bailey?"

"That's the girl you write to. The one who moved back into the house and you were mean to for a while? Her brother attacked her and you got involved, and it's the reason I'm coming home. *That* girl?"

"Well, yeah. Look, she's going through some shi—stuff. Her brother dropped the bomb that she's adopted, he attacked her, and was then released back home. She came over to the trailer. She doesn't want to go home—"

"And you wanted to know if she could stay with us?"

"Yeah."

"Rush, are you sure? You hated her not that long ago."

"She was just a convenient target. It was never really her I was angry with."

She sighs down the line. "Honey, you're eighteen. I assume she is as well?" She pauses while I confirm it, then continues. "We don't have a lot of space, but if that's what you want she's more than welcome to stay."

"I'll sleep on the couch."

"Because that's where you're sleeping while I'm not there?" Her voice is dry. "Rush, I'm not stupid. I know what you kids get up to."

I laugh quietly. "Sorry."

"I'm looking forward to meeting this girl of yours. She's inspired a lot of different moods in you."

"Thanks, Gran."

She ends the call, and I hand Seven his cell back.

"Thanks."

"No problem. So, you and Bailey are officially living together, huh?" There's a slight curl to his lip.

I ignore it, and turn the ignition on my bike. "I need to get home. I'll see you tomorrow."

I give him a wave and ride off the school grounds and back to the trailer park.

Coming to a stop in my usual parking space, I climb off and chain my bike up, then walk toward the trailer. The door opens before I reach it. I smile at the redhead framed in the doorway.

"Hey."

She smiles back at me. "Hey, yourself."

I walk up the steps and stop in front of her, eyes moving over her face. She doesn't look as pale as she did this morning.

"How are you feeling?"

She moves back inside the trailer and I follow her. "You told Hank to check on me."

I nod. "Was that a problem?"

"No. He ..." She sucks in a breath. "Rush, he's my brother. My *real* brother."

I frown. "What?"

"His mom ... *our* mom died when I was a baby. We were taken into care. The Linnetts wanted to adopt, but only wanted a girl. They took me and left him."

I glance toward the window which faces Hank's trailer. "Are you sure? It seems a little coincidental, don't you think?"

She shakes her head. "He showed me a photo album. Rush, I look just like her." There's a note of awe in her voice. "He let me keep it here to show you." She grabs my hand and pulls me over to the couch, pushes me down and hands me a large book. "Look."

She curls up beside me, and we look through the photographs together. I can see why she believes Hank. The images of the woman in the album are eerily similar to Bailey. We stop on the photograph of a baby. She's asleep, lying on her side, the birthmark in the shape of a rose clearly visible on the back of her neck. There's a boy beside her, smiling at the camera.

"Is that Hank?"

She nods.

I look closely. I can see hints of the man in the photograph of the boy, and the baby's birthmark is hard to deny. I close the book and turn to her.

"Are you sure?"

She nods again, then bites her lip. "I've arranged to meet my dad ... I mean Kelvin."

"He's still your dad, Bug." My voice is soft.

She shrugs. "Anyway, he's agreed to meet me at the diner tonight. Just him. Hank is working, so he'll be there. Darla also knows who I am. Hank says she's known from almost the first time she met me."

"Do you want me to come?"

She hesitates, then shakes her head. "I think I need to do this alone."

"I'll give you a ride there, at least."

Her head drops to rest against my shoulder. "I'd like that."

"And I'll pick you up afterward." I slide my arm around her waist. "I spoke to my grandmother. She's fine with you staying here."

"Really?"

"Yeah. She said she's looking forward to finally meeting you."

64
Bailey

Rush presses a kiss to my lips. "Remember to get Darla to call me when you're done. Don't leave the diner before I get here. Okay?"

I nod. "I will. I promise."

"Good." He takes my hand and walks with me toward the doors. "Are you sure you don't want me to stay with you?"

"I'll be okay. I have to do this by myself."

My dad is sitting at one of the booths. He's alone. There's an untouched strawberry milkshake in front of him and he's toying with the edge of a menu. I'm not sure what I'm going to say to him.

"You have Darla, Sara, Dennis and Hank in there with you," he reminds me softly. "I can be here in five minutes—"

I tug my hand free and wrap my arms around his neck. "Thank you."

He smiles down at me. "For what?"

"Being here with me now." I press a kiss to his lips to prevent him from answering, and then break away from him and enter the diner. Every step I take closer to where my dad sits, I swear I can feel Rush's stare burning into the back of my neck.

My dad's face lights up at the sight of me. "Hey, Bumblebee. I'm so glad you agreed to meet me."

"Hi." I take the seat opposite him. "What's the food like here?"

"Good."

He nods. "What would you like? My treat."

"I'll just have a strawberry milkshake. I'm not really hungry."

Dad's brows knit together. "Sweetheart you need to eat. Please?"

"I'll have a plate of fries, then."

Sara appears beside the table, her note book and pencil already in her hands. "What can I get you?"

Dad places our order, and she doesn't stop to chat. He waits until Sara leaves to talk again.

He clears his throat. "How are you doing?"

"Still reeling from everything that happened," I tell him honestly. "Everything I thought I knew is gone."

"You're still my little girl, Bailey. I might not be your biological father, but I love you."

"Mom … Shawna doesn't."

His sigh is heavy. "She loves you in her own way."

I remain silent. I don't believe it, not looking back with the knowledge I now have. It's obvious to me that she *never* loved me, she merely tolerated me. I consider telling him about Hank, but decide against it. I'm not ready to talk about him, or the fact I know who my real mom is. I can't help but worry it might get snatched away from me. The only thing that seems stable in my life right now is Rush.

But what if I lose him too? It's already happened once. What if something happens to make him hate me again?

"Is Jamie—"

"At home with your mother."

"Let me guess, he's pleading innocence."

"He is. I don't believe him, though. I had no idea what Jamie was doing. You should have come to me, Sweetheart. I'd have stopped it. We've all been under a lot of pressure since the move"— He falls silent when Sara arrives with our food and drinks.

I smile and thank her. She gives my hand a squeeze, then turns away.

Dad huffs out a breath. "I'm not going to make any excuses for him. Your mom has always spoiled him. But I'm not empty of blame. If I hadn't pushed to adopt you—"

That catches my attention. "Wait, *you* wanted to adopt me?"

"We fostered you to begin with. I fell in love with you from day one. A sister for our son. Shawna had her doubts, but I talked her into keeping you. I thought it would help her get over the pain of not being able to have anymore kids. I'm sorry Bee, I should have been around more."

The pain in his voice twists in my heart. "You've been working hard to support us."

His laugh is humorless. "Things would be so different if I hadn't messed everything up. I've tried so hard to fix things."

I reach across the table to touch his hand. "You can't control everything. I've come to learn that the hard way."

His smile is sad. "Don't press charges against Jamie."

I snatch my hand away from his, the warmth I'd felt toward him cooling. "Is that why you're here? To soften me up so I agree to forget what he did?"

"We're getting a divorce."

"D-divorce?"

"This has been coming for a long time. I promise, it's nothing to do with you or what's happened recently. Your mom and I have been pretending we're happy for a very long time. It's just reached the stage where we can't pretend anymore."

Would things have been the same if they hadn't adopted me at all?

No. I can't think like that. This *isn't* my fault. No matter what Jamie has claimed in the past, I'm not responsible for the actions of those around me. Everyone has a choice in what they do. I refuse to take the blame for everything that happens. It's not fair.

I take a sip of my milkshake to distract myself from the burn in my eyes. I'm not going to cry. Everything fell apart weeks ago. This is just another part of the fallout as my family crashes and burns.

"Your mom has agreed to take Jamie to California to stay with your Aunt Carol."

My gaze rises to his. "California?"

He nods. "She's already started packing."

"I thought Aunt Carol didn't have any room?"

"They'll be roughing it until they find a place to live."

"What about you?"

"I'm going to stay here. With you. Red Creek is my home now.

Has always been my home. We're selling the house, and splitting the money."

I lick my lips. "Selling the house?"

"It's for the best. I thought moving back here would be like old times. I've never been so wrong in my life."

I pause and collect my thoughts. "I forget about the charges and he leaves?"

"You won't have to see him again. I'll visit Jamie in California, whenever I can. You don't have to have any contact with him, unless you want to. I'll make sure Shawna gets him into therapy. He may have fucked up but he's still my son … and your brother."

His words stir memories of the little brother who'd played with me in the garden when we'd been small. A bright-eyed boy with the biggest smile. When had he changed? Why hadn't I seen it?

"We're still family, Bee. Maybe he can change. We won't know unless you agree to let him go. Please, give him this one chance."

I hate Jamie for what he did to me, but I love my dad, and I can see on his face how much this is hurting him.

If I say no, will he hate me? Would Jamie be sent to prison if I went ahead and pressed charges?

California is far away from here. Maybe that would be enough?

"As long as he goes to California and never comes back here."

I gave Rush a second chance. He's no longer the cruel boy who blames me for the loss in his life. He's grown. Maybe the same thing will happen with Jamie.

BAILEY IS STILL sitting with her dad when I enter the diner. I scan her features as I move toward them. She looks a little pale, but there's no evidence that the man has made her cry. When I reach their table, I stop.

"Hey, Bug."

Her head turns toward me, and she smiles. "You got here fast. I only asked Hank to call you ten minutes ago."

I shrug. I'm not about to tell her I was lurking down the road, just in case everything went sideways and she needed to leave in a hurry.

"Rush Carter, right?" Her dad speaks up.

I nod. "Mr. Linnett."

"You were the one who lived in our house."

"That's right."

He waves a hand to the space beside Bailey. "Would you sit

down for a minute?"

"Why?"

"Please? I'd like to talk to you."

I slide onto the bench seat.

"If I'd thought for a second that taking the house back would have resulted in your mom's death, I would *never* have done it. The lease she'd signed was up for renewal, and she hadn't paid rent for months. We … No, *I* thought it would be easier for her to start afresh somewhere else, somewhere more affordable. I'd spoken to her a couple of times beforehand. She never gave any indication that moving out was going to be a problem for her, Rush. I *swear* had I known—"

"*No one* knew."

"Maybe so, but I want you to know how sorry I am."

A month ago, his words would have made me angry. Now, it brings up nothing more than sadness and regret.

"Thank you. I appreciate that."

Beneath the table, Bailey's fingers interlock with mine and she squeezes gently.

"I appreciate how you've been there for Bailey during this mess."

She tenses, and it's my turn to squeeze her fingers.

"She deserves to know she's loved and supported."

He nods. "That she does." His attention goes back to Bailey. "Sweetheart, if you *need* anything—"

"I need my clothes. I don't want to come back to the house for them." She's squeezing my fingers so hard, the tips are turning numb.

"I understand." He doesn't even try to convince her otherwise. "I'll go home and pack you a case and drop it off later."

"Okay, good. Thanks." She looks at me. "Can we go?"

"Sure." I slide out of the booth and wait for her to join me.

"Bailey?"

She pauses at her name.

"No matter what, I *do* love you. You're my daughter. *Nothing* will ever change that."

She nods, but doesn't reply. Fingers still tangled with mine, she sets off across the floor to the entrance. I let her pull me along, glancing back when we reach the doors to find her dad's gaze on her, expression sad, as he watches her leave. She doesn't stop until we're beside my motorcycle.

I hand her the helmet, climb on, then hold out a hand to help her take the seat behind me. Her arms slide around my waist and she rests her head against my back. I cover her hands with one of mine.

"Okay?"

"Yeah." Her voice is muffled by the helmet and my shirt. "No ... I don't know."

"Is there anything I can do?" I fiddle with my key while I wait for her reply.

"Could we go for a drive? I don't think I can stand sitting in a room and staring at the walls right now."

"Sure. Make sure you're holding on tight." I jam the key in the ignition and start the engine.

She tightens her grip on my waist, and I reach back to pull her closer until her legs are pressed close to mine, and then send the bike forward.

We ride aimlessly for a while, from one end of town to the other. Her body is warm against my back, and her fingers toy with my shirt.

The first time they brush over the front of my jeans, I think it's an accident. The *third* time she does it, I know I'm wrong.

Letting go of the handlebar with one hand, I reach down and press her palm against my dick. She doesn't pull away. That's the only signal I need to take the next left turn instead of the right, which would take us back to the trailer park.

I park under the trees, then climb off. Bailey is slower to move, unbuckling the helmet and looking around, a small frown creasing her brow.

"Do you remember the last time I brought you here?" I pitch my voice low. Sound travels at this time of night in the woods.

Her head swings back toward me, and her tongue swipes over her bottom lip.

Reaching out, I help her get off the back of my bike. I keep my fingers curled around her wrist and tug her around to face me.

"Do you remember, Bailey?"

Her throat moves as she swallows. "It was the night you climbed through my bedroom window."

I tilt my head. "That was later. What happened in the woods?"

Her eyes are wide as they stare up into mine. "You chased me."

My lips curve up into a smile, and I dip my head until my mouth is close to her ear.

"Run, Little Rose."

66
Bailey

I DON'T EVEN think. The second the words leave his lips, I spin away from him and take off through the trees in the darkness. But once the trees surround me, I stop.

What if someone is out here? Waiting for me.

I shake my head.

Rush won't let anything bad happen to me.

That one thought stops me from calling an end to the game before it's begun. Every snap of a twig or rustle of a leaf makes my heart beat faster.

I *want* him to catch me, but I don't want to make it easy for him. All the worry and fear of the past few weeks dissolves, replaced with the need to be hunted by Rush.

My breath comes out in sharp, short pants, adrenaline buzzing through my veins. After a few minutes, I stop beside a tree to catch my breath.

How far is he behind me? Was he counting or did he just wait until I ran? Can he really find me out here? What if I get lost?

A twig snaps.

My heart jolts.

I push away from the tree trunk and lunge away from the sound. An arm snakes around my waist and I'm jerked back into a hard chest.

"Got you." The voice is low and husky.

Instinct takes over and I struggle against his hold. "No."

I dig my fingernails into his skin and twist in his grip, but he's too strong for me to break free.

"Bailey, it's me."

Rush.

The concern in his voice cuts through my panic. Shaking, panting, the fight drains out of me. He turns me in his arms. One hand remains around my waist while the fingers of the other sink into the hair at the back of my head as he hugs me to his chest.

"I didn't mean to scare you."

I wrap my arms around him. "You made me jump. That's all."

"Maybe this wasn't such a great idea." His voice is uncertain.

I press a kiss to his mouth. "I want this. I want *you*. I don't want to be frightened of the dark anymore."

I'm safe with him. Here. Now. That's all that matters.

He kisses me more forcefully, parting my lips with his tongue. I clutch the material at the back of his T-shirt. In two steps he has me back against a tree. He rolls his hips and a groan tears from my throat, as I arch into him. I can feel the hardness of his erection through his jeans.

His mouth moves to my jaw. "I caught you, Little Rose, and that makes you mine."

We're not even naked but the way he moves against me sends waves of lust through me.

"Rush."

His teeth scrape and nip across my skin, followed by his tongue. "This Big Bad Wolf is going to devour you."

"Yes." The word leaves me on a hiss.

"You want me to mark you, don't you?" He buries his face in my neck, biting at my throat in a way that makes everything inside me melt.

I tilt my head. "Do it!"

"I'll cover you with bites so everyone will see that you belong to me."

"I need you inside me."

I'm not even sure he knows how much I need this tonight. God, the way he touches me ...

His hands move to my ass and he lifts me. "I want to hear you scream my name."

My legs wind around his hips, and I cling to his shoulders."Fuck me. Please fuck me."

His mouth finds mine again and I lose myself in the heat and passion.

L. ANN & CLAIRE MARTA

67

Rush

HER HANDS ARE everywhere. Running over my shoulders, into my hair, over my arms. Her legs are wrapped around my hips, her back braced against the tree trunk, and she writhes against me, rubbing her pussy over my dick through my jeans. Soft whimpers leave her lips every time our mouths part to snatch in a quick breath.

Wrapping one arm around her waist, I use my other hand to pull her top up.

"Lift your arms."

She doesn't argue, raising her arms above her head so I can drag her T-shirt the rest of the way off, and toss it to the ground.

"Lower your legs."

I hold her steady so she can unhook her legs from around my hips and set her feet on the ground. The second she does, I pull down the zipper on her pants.

"Wait." Her hand covers mine. "There's something I want to do first."

She drops to her knees in front of me and works on the buttons of my jeans.

"Bailey?" I groan when her hand slips beneath my boxer-briefs and wraps around my dick.

"You've had your mouth on me so many times. I want to do the same for you." She takes my dick out of my pants while she talks.

My thoughts go to the last time she sucked my dick. I'd humiliated her, and then her brother had attacked her. "You don't have—"

"No." Tipping her head back, she gazes up at me. "I *want* to."

Before I can say a word, she runs her tongue over the head of my dick, and then sucks me into her mouth.

The chill in the air is negated by the heat of her mouth, of the way her tongue laps at me, swirling around the head, licking away the precum I know is collecting there. She makes a sound in her throat, and it vibrates along my entire length.

"Fuck." The curse is harsh in the dead of the night, and she stops her movements.

I don't even think. My hand wraps in her hair and I urge her forward, so my dick slides deeper. Her hand moves over my thigh, nails digging into the denim but she doesn't stop, rocking back and forth, lips moving up and down my dick in a perfect rhythm.

"That's good, baby. Can you take me a little deeper?" I cup the back of her head and push forward, groaning when my dick hits the back of her throat. "So fucking good. That's it. Good girl. Take all of me."

My fingers curl, nails scraping against her scalp, as I tug her head back slightly so I can see her face as I fuck her mouth. Tears are streaming down her cheeks, but she continues to suck and lick my dick.

"You look so fucking good on your knees for me, taking my dick like a good girl." I reach back and pull my cell out of my pocket. One-handed I navigate to the camera, angle the screen down and focus on the way my dick is sliding in and out of her mouth, then hit record.

"I want to watch this back with you later. I want you to see how fucking sexy you look, okay?"

She blinks up at me, and I wait to see if she wants me to stop. Instead, she eases back until my dick is resting on her lips, and smiles up at me. Her eyes close, lashes resting on her cheeks, and then she *really* gets to work.

Her tongue laps around the slit in the head, probes gently, sending a sharp stab of lust through my entire body, then she kisses down my entire length until her nose brushes against my skin. She changes direction, licking her way back to the head, then opens her mouth and takes me inside again.

Her body shifts, lowering until her head is tipped back, throat straight and then she slowly inches her way up my erection, until I feel the head hit the back of her throat. She retreats, then tries again, each time taking me a little deeper, sending me a little closer to heaven.

My fingers are loosely clasped in her hair. I'm not even pretending to have control over this situation, I'm just along for the ride ... and what a fucking ride it is. Every nerve ending is sparking, each slight touch of her mouth, her tongue, is sending my body haywire with the need to come.

And, fuck, I want to come so bad.

But where?

In her mouth? On her face? On her tits? Each one has its appeal.

But there's really only one place I want it to be.

Tightening my grip on her hair, I pull her off my dick, and shove my phone back in my pocket.

"Enough. Now it's my turn." I shove her back and she sprawls in the dirt. "Take off your bra and play with your nipples."

Her hands immediately go to the scrap of lace concealing her breasts and she pulls it off. I smile.

"That's better." Crouching, I drag her pants down her legs, then kneel between them.

Her pussy is wet, gleaming in the moonlight. I reach out and run one fingertip over it, flicking her clit. She gives a quiet whimper.

"Lie back, twist your nipples until they're hard and spread your legs wide."

I grab her T-shirt and tuck it under her head, then put my hands on her thighs and force her legs further apart.

"This Big Bad Wolf has a pussy he wants to eat."

But I don't. Instead, I push one finger inside her. Her hips lift.

"More."

"I don't see your nipples being teased." I stretch out one hand and do what I told her myself, plucking at one nipple with thumb and finger, twisting it and stretching it upwards until it pulls free.

"Rush."

"Nipples."

I push a second finger inside her. She moans, her fingers finding her nipples so she can pinch and twist them.

"Good girl."

"Do you have your knife?"

"If I said yes, how much wetter will you get?" A third finger slides in easily, and I laugh. "I guess that's my answer." I pump them in and out of her pussy, watching as she writhes and moans. "Do you want me to fuck you with my knife, Little Rose? Stroke around your clit with the blade? Do you want me to make you bleed, then lick you clean?"

"Oh god. Rush, please."

I take the knife out of my hoodie and flick it open, lifting it for her to see, then flip it around so I'm holding the blade. Pulling my fingers free from her pussy, I replace them with the knife's handle and slowly push it in.

She gasps. The metal is cold, my fingers were warm.

"Look at you. So fucking beautiful. You're taking it so well. Such a good girl for me, Little Rose. Fuck my knife, baby. Show me how much you want it."

She's so fucking wet, the handle slides in and out of her body with ease. Her hips rise to meet every thrust until she's fucking it eagerly, begging for me to make her come. My fingers tease her clit, stroking, flicking, pinching, and I move carefully until I can reach her breasts with my mouth while continuing to push the knife's handle in and out of her pussy. My lips find one nipple, taut and sensitive from the way she's been twisting it, and I bite down gently before sucking it into my mouth. I torment it with my tongue and teeth, nipping and licking, until she's an incoherent babbling mess. The hand holding the knife is soaked with her arousal, and my dick feels like it's going to explode at any second.

"I want to fuck you, but I don't have a condom."

"Do it."

"Are you on birth control?"

"No. I don't care. Fuck me. I need it, Rush."

I toss the knife to one side and fist my dick, line it up with her pussy and slowly push inside. "I'll pull out."

We groan in tandem at the sensation of me inside her with nothing between us and I still for a second while my entire body processes the way it feels. I've never fucked a girl bare before, and I want to hold onto this feeling forever.

Her legs lift to wrap around my waist, her feet digging into my back, bringing me back to the moment and I start to move, slowly at first, rocking into her body, savoring each thrust. But all too soon, slow is not enough, and I move faster, harder, slamming into her body, driving my dick as deep as I can get while my fingers move over her skin.

I pinch her nipples, play with her clit, cup her ass, and fuck her under the moon until I lose track of where she ends and I begin.

"Harder." I beg. "Faster."

Rush obliges and drives his dick deeper. The discomfort of the leaf-strewn ground barely registers as he thrusts into me in the dark. I cling to him, my hand sliding beneath his T-shirt so I can dig my nails into his flesh. Our frenzied movements are in sync with the wild rhythm that has us both swept up. A familiar intoxicating feeling builds deep inside me as my climax draws closer. There's a loud buzzing in my head. A single-minded need to find release.

One hand in Rush's hair, I drag his mouth to mine. His groan mingles with mine as my tongue mimics the thrust of his dick.

"Let go, baby. Let go."

"Rush." I break apart around him.

He claims my mouth again, hard and desperate, still thrusting in and out of me.

My eyes roll into the back of my head and I arch up into him, mindlessly. He rises, gripping my thighs, our bodies still joined, and kneels between my legs.

"Fuck, yes." He drives into me in long hard thrusts as I twitch around him.

The night is filled with my pants and his grunts and growls ... and then something inside my chest cracks open. All the emotions from this evening erupt and tears fill my eyes. I cover my face with my hands as they slip soundlessly down my cheeks, my body still vibrating from my orgasm.

Rush pulls out of me, and I feel the emptiness inside me so profoundly a whimper escapes my lips. He gives a long drawn-out growl, and then shudders. A moment later something warm and wet covers my stomach.

Breathing harshly, he drops down beside me. A hand strokes over my breasts then up to my hair. The gentle gesture rips a sob from my throat.

The hand stills. "Bug?"

I drop my hands and turn on my side, the cum he's left over my stomach forgotten. Tears stream from my eyes as I bury my face against his chest.

"Fuck. Did I hurt you?"

I shake my head. "No"

Lips brush my forehead. "Why are you crying?"

"I-I don't know."

His fingers find my chin and he tips my head up. He leans in and presses his lips to mine. The kiss is gentle, unhurried, the complete opposite of the others we've just shared. It eases the mess of emotions inside me. The connection I feel to him right now is so fierce, it hurts.

"Let's go home."

I get out a shaky breath, and nod.

He stands, and pulls up his jeans, then uses the edge of my T-shirt to clean off the cum on my skin. I slip it back on over my head when he's done, gasping when the wet part hits my still-heated skin.

He laughs softly, and helps me up off the ground. "I'm sorry. Fucking you out here wasn't part of my plan. I didn't come prepared."

I shake my head. "No, it was perfect. Everything I needed. I'll just take a shower when we get back to the trailer." I fix my clothes, then smile at him.

He laces his fingers with mine and pulls me closer. Our mouths meet in another quick kiss before he leads me through the trees. By the time we reach the bike, my emotional outburst has caught up with me.

When we stop beside the bike, I tug on his hand. "It wasn't you."

He turns. "What wasn't?"

"Well, I guess it was."

"Bailey, I don't know what you're talking about."

"When I cried." I explain. "There was just so much bottled up inside me, and when you made me come it all just exploded—"

He snickers. I frown.

"What?"

"It just exploded." He breaks down halfway through the final word, laughing, and covers his mouth. But his shoulders are shaking and his eyes dancing.

I try to hold onto my frown. "I'm being serious."

I aim a punch at his shoulder. He laughs harder, and something lightens inside of me. A giggle escapes. Then another, and before long we're both standing there staring at each other, laughing until tears roll down our cheeks. Then Rush pulls in a steadying breath and reaches for me. Arms looped around my waist, he smiles down at me.

"I get it. You don't need to explain anything."

"I didn't want you to think that I didn't enjoy what we did."

"Oh, I *know* you enjoyed it. You were so fucking wet, there was no way you were going to hide it."

"*Anyway!*" I mock-scowl at him. "What I'm saying is that if you wanted to do it again. I wouldn't say no."

He pulls me closer. "This Big Bad Wolf isn't done chasing you. I'm still hungry for you, Little Rose."

Butterflies take off in my stomach. "I love you."

Rush stills.

Oh god, did I just blurt that out loud?

I'm drained, mixed up and saying things I shouldn't be confessing. I don't want him to think I'm saying it because of all the mess my life has descended into.

What if all he feels is lust toward me?

I untangle myself from his arms and grab the helmet, cringing internally.

"I mean love that you're taking care of me. I appreciate it a lot. Thank you."

69

Rush

I PAUSE NEXT to my bike, arguing with myself, while she shoves the helmet onto her head. She clearly didn't mean to declare her love for me, and I'm not one hundred percent certain it isn't just a typical post-coital bliss statement. When she continues to babble, trying to explain her true meaning, I let her talk.

She won't meet my gaze, fiddling with the chin strap of the helmet. I say nothing. I don't think anything I can come out with right now would be right. If I told her I felt the same, she'd think I was just trying to make her feel better. If I agree with her reasoning, she'd think I didn't love her. If I say nothing, she'll think …

Fuck it.

I pull the helmet off her head and drop it to the ground, then palm her cheeks and tilt her head up.

"Look at me."

Her eyes dart to one side, looking somewhere over my shoulder.

"Not at the trees, Bailey. At *me*. Stop fucking talking, and look at me."

I slide one hand over her jaw and down to wrap around her throat. My thumb forces her head up. The words she is babbling stall, and she swallows.

"Are you done?"

"Done?" She licks over her bottom lip. "Done with what?"

"Done with the bullshit you're spewing."

"I don't—"

"Enough." I flex my fingers, squeezing her throat. "Do you think you can lie to me, Little Rose?"

Her sharp intake of breath tells me she's recognized the tone in my voice. The one I use when I'm stalking her, *fucking* her.

"No, but—"

"I *said* enough." I press my other palm against her mouth. "Don't you think there's been enough lies spread around over the last few months? Aren't you tired of them?" I dip my head and rest my lips close to her ear. "Wasn't it written in the bible that the truth will set you free? So tell me the truth. Do you love me? Just a one word answer, Bug. Yes or no."

I uncover her mouth. She stares at me.

"Rush, I—"

I shake my head. "Yes or no. That's it. That's all I want to hear from you."

"Can't you just forget I said anything and take me back to the trailer?"

"I could. But I'm not going to." I stroke a finger over her lips.

"But I'll take you home and fuck you again, *if* you tell me the truth."

"That's not fair," she whispers.

"No, what's not fair is you telling me that you love me, and then taking it back in the very next breath. Other than my grandmother, I've lost *everyone* who loved me, Bailey. *Everyone*. So don't fucking mess with me on this." I didn't realize how true the words were until I sent them out into the world.

When she told me she loved me, something inside me had unlocked for the three seconds it took her to backtrack. Something I hadn't realized I'd cut off in the first place.

"Would it help if I told you I loved you? That I have done since the day I found that first letter you left, hidden beneath the floorboards in our bedroom. I was new to Red Creek. We moved here from New York, and I was lonely and scared about leaving everything behind. That letter helped me, made me feel less alone, and my mom encouraged me to write back. You have no idea how much I bugged Mom and Dad the entire two weeks it took for you to reply. Every single day I'd ask if there was a letter for me, and the day it arrived, I was too scared to open it straight away. I tucked it under my pillow and took it out day after day. I was worried it would be a letter to tell me not to write to you again. But it wasn't ... and from that moment on I. Loved. You.

"I loved you the way an eight year old loves ice cream. I loved you the way a pre-teen crushes on an actor or model or singer. I loved you the way a teenager falls in love for the first time, and now I love you the way a soul finds its missing half. You've always been my Bug, you became my Little Rose, and I loved you as both." I crouch and scoop up the helmet and push it back onto her head. "Get on the bike."

"Rush—"

"I love you, Bailey. Now if you don't tell me you love me, and then get on the fucking bike, I'm going to leave you here in the dark to make your own way home."

She throws herself at me, arms wrapping around my waist, and narrowly misses headbutting me with the helmet when she kisses me.

"I love you." She kisses me again. "I love you!"

***

My plan to whisk her back to my trailer and fuck her again is delayed by Hank sitting on the steps when we park outside. He watches as we both climb off and I chain up my bike, then rises to his feet when we walk toward him.

"Everything okay?" I ask once we're close.

He nods. "I just wanted to check in. I spotted your bike wasn't here, so thought I'd wait. You picked her up over an hour ago."

"We went for a drive. She wanted to clear her head."

"I can understand that." He turns to Bailey. "Are you okay?"

She slips her fingers between mine and leans against my side. "I'm okay. Da—Kelvin said he was going to drop some of my stuff off."

Hank waves a hand toward an overnight bag beside the door. "He did … about twenty minutes ago. He also asked me to give this to you." He hands Bailey a small cardboard box.

"What's this?" She takes it from him.

"He said it's a cell phone to replace the one Jamie lost."

"I don't want—"

"You need a phone," I cut in. "Jamie should really be replacing it, but don't turn it down out of some misguided sense of pride, Bailey."

"It's not—"

"I agree with Rush. I know you don't feel like it at the moment, but he *is* your dad, Bailey. In all the ways that matter." Hank's voice is gentle.

Bailey glares at him. He holds his hands up.

"I'm just saying, that's all."

I take the box from her and shove it into the pocket of my hoodie. "How about you sleep on it? See how you feel in the morning? If you still don't want it, I'll drop it by the house on the way to school."

She thinks about that for a second, then nods. "Okay, that's fair."

"Speaking of school," Hank says. "It's late. You two should get some sleep, you have to be up early."

"I'm not going back."

"Bug, you can't stop going to school." I squeeze her fingers. "You'll go in, with your head held high. You have no reason to hide. *You* aren't the problem. I'll be with you, and the classes I don't share with you, I'm sure Nicky or Dom and Seven do. You won't be alone at any time, I promise."

"But what if Jamie comes back?"

"There's no way they'll allow him on site. He's been thrown out."

"You don't know that."

"I *do* know that. Security won't let him through the doors. School is probably going to be the safest place you can be. And I don't like leaving you here while I'm there. If he was going to do anything, it'd be easier for him to get to you here than it will at school."

"He's right," Hank says. "I don't want him anywhere near you, and with Rush at school and me working at the diner, there won't be anyone here to stop him. Plus, you can't afford to miss any more classes. It's your final year. You need to graduate."

"Look, just because you're my brother, it doesn't mean you get to tell me what to do," she snaps.

"I know. I'm sorry." He gives her a small smile. "I just don't want to lose you now I've found you again."

70
Bailey

R‍USH AND H‍ANK's words do nothing to soothe my worries. After everything he's done to me, all the gaslighting and lies, the thought of seeing Jamie again makes me sick.

We say goodnight to Hank, and I collect the bag while Rush unlocks the trailer. He takes the bag from me and carries it inside. Arms wrapped around myself, I follow him inside.

"Hey." He pulls me into his embrace. "I promise, I won't let Jamie touch you again."

"What if he comes here?"

"Then we'll call the cops."

"I keep waiting for him to show up."

His lips brush my forehead. "He'll be gone soon."

I fist the front of his T-shirt in my hands. "I hope so."

He hugs me tighter.

"It's constantly in the back of my mind. He hates me so much."

"I'll protect you."

My eyes close and I rest my head against his chest. What is this boy doing to me? He hunted me down and fucked me, then gave me his heart back in the woods.

"I promised to fuck you again." He kisses over my cheek. "I don't break my promises."

Desire awakens at his words. "I should shower."

"After. I want my smell on your skin." His hand slides down between our bodies, and I moan as he unzips my jeans.

I pull my T-shirt over my head, and throw it to the floor, then press my lace covered breasts against his chest.

His fingers slip under my panties to stroke through my wetness. "You're so fucking wet for me already."

The need he's ignited inside me roars to life. "I want you so much, it hurts."

He lifts me up and I wrap my legs around his hips. His mouth captures mine as he carries me through the trailer. When we reach his bed, we eagerly strip off our clothes in silence. The second we're both naked, he crawls over me to kiss, nip, and lick a path up from my stomach to my breasts.

"Did you think of me when you touch yourself in bed at night?"

"You're the only boy I've ever fantasized about."

"Are you telling me that every orgasm you've had belongs to me?" He slides a hand down my stomach to stroke across my clit.

Eyes closed, my head arches back into the pillow. "Yes."

His lips find the side of my neck biting and sucking. "I'm hungry for you again."

Without a word I widen my thighs in invitation, the emptiness inside me desperate to be filled. Rush reaches for a condom, tears open the foiled packet and rolls the condom down his dick. Lifting my legs, he settles them over his shoulders, wraps a hand around his dick, then thrusts inside me and buries himself to the hilt. At the angle he's positioned me, I feel him deeper and it makes everything within me tingle and buzz.

He moves slowly in and out of me, his eyes on my face.

"You're going to wear my jersey to bed tonight."

I arch up to meet his thrusts.

"And you'll wear it at school tomorrow," he continues, his rhythm slow and languid, arms braced on the mattress either side of my head. "I want everyone to know that you're mine. From the marks I leave on your skin to my number you wear. You are *mine,* Bailey. Every fucking inch of you … just as I'm yours."

His words fill my heart.

His pace changes, becomes hard and fast. I suck my bottom lip between my teeth, but he pulls it free and bites down. The sharp sting of pain makes my pussy throb and pulse around his dick. I wrap my arms around his neck and pull him closer.

His mouth on mine, his dick possessing me, the warmth of his body wrapped around mine, is everything I need. Everything I *want.*

He drives me deeper into the mattress until my orgasm bursts and spreads in a wave through my body. His thrusts become jerkier, less coordinated until he shudders above me. A few more shallow pumps and he collapses on top of me, burying his face into the curve of my throat. I brush through the slick strands of his hair with my fingers.

It's just the two of us and for now nothing else matters in Red Creek.

71
Rush

BAILEY'S FINGERS ARE tight around mine as we stand beside my bike outside the school. None of my friends have arrived yet, and it's almost like a moment of peace before the chaos will begin.

"This is a bad idea."

"It's not. The sooner you get back to school and into a routine, the easier it'll be for you to move forward." I stop her from untangling her fingers from mine. "Bailey, you can do this."

"But—"

I pull her around until she's in front of me. "We talked about this. Someone will be with you in every class. Me, Nicky, Seven, Dom, and the others."

"Seven doesn't even like me."

I laugh. "Seven behaves like that with *everyone*. He doesn't hate you at all."

"You'd know if I hated you, Bailey. Ask Cupcake over there. She can tell you all about it." Seven's voice preceded him stepping around me and bumping my shoulder.

"Cupcake?" Bailey frowns.

Seven jerked his chin toward Tamara Rees, who was walking up the steps toward the main doors.

"Why do you hate Tamara?"

All three of us watch the girl, her nose buried in a book, as she moves forward.

"We don't have enough time to list all the reasons. Let's just go with she fucked me over and it's almost time for her to pay."

Bailey gives a little laugh. "Isn't that a little dramatic?"

Seven doesn't smile. I shake my head. I know the reasons why Seven hates Tamara the way he does, but it's not my story to tell.

I release her fingers, so I can pick up both our bags. "Let's go."

Before we can move, a female voice shouts Bailey's name, and then Nicky is hurrying toward us. She throws her arms around Bailey when she reaches us, and hugs her tight.

"Oh my god. Bailey! I stopped by your house and your dad said you weren't there. I've been so worried about you. Are you okay?"

Bailey holds still for a second, then relaxes against the other girl. "I'm okay. I'm sorry, I didn't think to let you know. I've been staying with Rush." She untangles herself from Nicky's embrace.

"And you're back in his jersey." Nicky takes a step back, smiling at me.

"And is going to stay in it." My voice is firm. "Where's Dom?"

Nicky blushes. "What makes you think I know where he is?"

I hike an eyebrow. She giggles.

"He's parking his car, and dealing with the idiot who stole his usual space. He said he'll meet you by the lockers."

We walk as a group toward the school.

"Do you share any classes with Bailey today?"

Nicky nods. "I'm pretty sure I do."

"Good."

Her eyes move from me to Bailey. "Do you think Jamie might try and come to school?"

I shake my head. "No, but I don't want Bailey left on her own. Just because Jamie isn't here, doesn't mean one of his friends won't try anything."

A shrill laugh sounds over the chatter of students.

"And then there's Sofia."

Bailey stops. "I can't do this."

"You're not going to let that bitch send you running, are you?"

"She's going to try and start trouble."

I snort. "Sofia attaches herself to whatever guy she thinks will help her climb the ladder to being queen of the school. She's a Puck Bunny. There isn't a guy on the team who hasn't had his dick sucked by her."

"She hasn't sucked mine." Seven opens his locker.

"That's because she's scared of you."

"I prefer a more challenging prey. It's no fun if they're eager. I prefer a fight before she submits." He leans back and raises his voice. "Isn't that right, Cupcake?"

For a moment, I think Tamara is going to ignore him, but then she lifts her head and meets his gaze full-on.

"You are perverted." Her voice is soft and husky, but firm.

"Am I? You weren't saying that when your pussy was grinding on my face and you were begging for me to let you come."

Her cheeks turn bright pink. "That didn't happen. That is *never* going to happen."

"My bad. It must have been a dream I had. Funny, it seemed so real." He licks his lips. "I can still taste your frosting on my tongue."

Her lips twist. "You're disgusting." She spins away, grabs her books from her locker, slams the door and hurries away.

"Did you really eat her out?" Dom bumps my shoulder when he reaches us.

Seven smiles. "A gentleman never tells."

"You've literally just told the entire school you know what her pussy tastes like."

"Then why are you asking me a question you already know the answer to?"

Dom shakes his head. "You're impossible." He turns to Nicky. "Hey, gorgeous." He pulls her in for a kiss.

I hook my arm around Bailey's waist and tuck her into my side. "We have math together first."

"So does Sofia."

"Bug, you'll be fine. Just shoot her down if she starts anything. Give her a taste of that red headed temper I know you have lurking beneath those freckles and gorgeous eyes."

"You like my eyes?"

"I like everything about you." I lower my head until I can whisper in her ear. "Especially the way you come apart when I fuck you."

72
Bailey

"I'll see you later." Rush drops a kiss on my lips.

I nod, smile, and attempt to hide the fact I've been a ball of nerves since school started. As promised, he's been at my side all morning. But I haven't missed the unfriendly glares Sofia and her friends have given me, or the pitying looks from the other students.

Nicky grabs my hand. "Don't worry, I'll keep an eye on her."

She tugs me away from Rush. I give him one last look as she pulls me into the classroom. We take our seats at the back.

"Hey Bailey, have you heard from your brother lately?" Sofia calls from her seat. "Oops I forgot you're adopted, so Jamie isn't really related to you."

Ignoring her I pull out my books.

"That kind of explains a lot. Is that why you were so eager to see us making out?"

"Why can't you just leave her alone?" Nicky snaps.

"She's the freak. I'm just doing a public service here."

"Why don't you shut your mouth?" The words escape before I can stop them.

Her eyes widen, then her lips twist in a malicious smile. "What's the matter? You don't want everyone to know that you're obsessed with Jamie? And that's why he acted so crazy in the cafeteria. You wanted him for yourself. Even if you're not related by blood, that's kind of twisted."

"You have got to be fucking kidding me. Can you even hear yourself? You're so full of shit, the mushrooms are jealous."

"I saw how you acted around him. The jealousy."

"I've never been jealous of him or you in my life."

"You think you can win everyone over by playing the victim, but I know the truth. Rush will see it too eventually."

"You're the only one who can't see the truth. Maybe that's because you and Jamie are so alike. How many of the girls you hang out with are actually your friends? You like to use people for your own gain, just like he does."

Her cheeks turn red. "You're the one with the problem, not me."

I open my mouth to respond, but the teacher enters the room and I snap my mouth shut. Sofia flips her hair over her shoulder, and her friends snicker. Nicky rolls her eyes.

Why did I let Rush talk me into coming back?

Because I need to graduate..

I should have known Sofia would cause trouble on Jamie's behalf. If Mom ... *Shawna* was already packing, they might have left for California already.

Would it really happen that quickly?

I want to text my dad and ask, but I can't. With Rush distracting me last night, I forgot to charge the new phone. It's still back at his trailer. Once I have it charged, I need to contact my friends at Churchill Bradley, although I'm a little hurt no one has come to check up on me.

They can't leave the school unless it's a weekend with a free pass.

Jamie would have lied to them if they'd contacted him. I can only imagine what lies he's spread around.

Class begins and my focus shifts to the textbook in front of me. Time drags, the teacher drones on and on. When the bell finally rings, I give a sigh of relief.

I glance over at Seven's table, while I gather up my things. He's missed the entire class, and I wonder if he's with Tamara, since she's not present either.

I half expect Sofia to toss more comments at me now the teacher has left, but when I check where she is, she's intent on her phone.

"At least that's over. She won't try anything with Rush around for the rest of the day," Nicky says.

I drop my books into my bag, then pull it over my shoulder. "Yeah. I guess."

"Sofia will get bored when you don't react to her the way she wants."

"I just wish that she'd stop lying for Jamie."

"Jamie Linnett is so last week. By the end of *this* week, she'll be after one of the other hockey players."

I desperately want to believe that, but a tiny niggling doubt worms its way through me.

I'm just being paranoid. Sofia likes to stir trouble. She is desperate to be popular, and now Jamie can't give her that status, so maybe Nicky is right.

Nicky's phone pings and she fishes it out of her pocket as we walk out of the class. Her face pales.

I frown. "Is everything okay?"

Her eyes jerk to me, then back down to the screen. "Sofia forwarded me a video. I didn't even know she had my number."

"What is it?"

"Bee, I..."

Worriedly I look over her shoulder at her phone. There is a video playing. It takes me a second to recognize the location. Someone has cleaned out the old fire pit and flames lick hungrily over the wood in the middle of it.

"I don't think you should see this." Nicky tries to hide her cell from me. I take it from her.

A box appears. *My* shoe box. The one I'd hidden at the back of my closet.

"*No!*"

He must have been going through my stuff. I thought they were safe.

Nicky is talking to me but I don't hear what she's saying, my attention welded to the screen.

Jamie removes the lid from the box. Inside is every letter Rush has ever written me.

Frozen to the spot, I watch in horror as he takes out a handful and tosses them onto the fire.

No, no, no!

The paper blackens and curls, shrivels to ash and floats away. Tears blur my vision.

Rush's words.

His letters.

Our link.

Oh god. How could Jamie do that?

I need to get to the house. I need to stop him before he can destroy them all. Rush's letters are the only things I have in my room that are precious to me. I should *never* have left them behind.

I shove the cell back into Nicky's hand. "I have to go."

She stuffs it into her bag and runs after me. "Bee, you can't!"

"I need to stop him before he burns it all."

I shake off her hand when she grabs my arm.

"You don't understand how important they are to me."

Nicky's gaze searches mine. "Bee…"

"Aw, what's the matter Bailey? Something upset you?"

My back snaps straight at Sofia's words. I spin around and jab my finger into her chest.

"You bitch! You knew what he was going to do."

She arches an eyebrow. "I'm to tell you that you have fifteen minutes until another pile goes on the fire. That's how long he's spacing it out."

Nicky tries to stop me heading for the door. "Please, Bee, think about this before you do something stupid."

"He's already taken so much from me, I can't let him take those too."

73
Rush

My cell pings as I make my way to the lockers, so I can stash my books and go for lunch. I pull it out of my pocket as I walk, tapping through to the messages app.

Nicky: Bailey is trying to leave school to go and face Jamie. There's a video of him burning her stuff and she's really upset.

I frown down at it.

Me: Where is she right now?

The response comes through almost immediately.

Nicky: On her way to the entrance.

Me: Stall her. I'm on my way.

I toss my books into the locker, slam the door, stuff my cell back into my pocket and take off down the hallway. I intercept Bailey and Nicky just as they reach the main entrance. Wrapping my arms around her from behind, I lift Bailey off her feet.

"Hey, Bug. Where you going in such a hurry? I thought we had plans to meet for lunch?"

"Put me down!" She tries to prise my hands apart. When that doesn't work, she punches them. "Let me go, Rush! I have to get home."

"Why?" I tighten my hold on the girl wriggling around in my arms.

"He's burning them." Her voice is shrill.

"Burning what?"

"Your letters. He's burning them all! I have to stop him."

"You're not going to the house."

She redoubles her efforts to get free. I ignore her and move to one side, away from the flow of students moving in and out of the doors. Setting her on her feet, I cage her against the wall with my arms either side of her body. She spins around, and goes to duck beneath one. I catch her arm and tug her back.

"Talk to me."

She lifts her face, eyes brimming with tears. "Sofia sent a video to Nicky of Jamie burning all the letters you sent to me. She said he'll burn a bunch every fifteen minutes until I go home."

"Let them burn."

"No!"

I haul her back when she tries to escape again. "Bailey, they're just pieces of paper."

Her hands slam against my chest. "That's not true. They're more than that. You *know* they are!"

I catch her wrists and pull her arms up to loop around my neck and step closer. "Baby, listen to me. I can write you more letters. You don't need them anymore."

"Of course I do!"

"No, you don't." I lower my head and kiss her eyelids, the tip of her nose, her cheeks. "If you need letters, I'll write you one every single day until you have so many you don't know what to do with them. They're just words, ramblings of kids who didn't know who they were. That's changed now."

"But they helped me when I felt like no one understood me." The words are a broken whisper.

"You have me to do that now. I understand you like no one else. The same way you understand me. We don't need old letters to know that." I press a kiss to her lips. "He wants you to go there, Bug. Don't you see? Doing it plays right into his hands. Fuck him. Let him burn the letters. When he realizes you aren't running back to the house to stop him, he'll give up."

"They're pieces of you, of *us*, of our story."

"We'll write a new story. A better one." I run my nose along hers. "Those were just the prequel. This is the main event, baby."

She gives a little hiccuping laugh at that, and pulls a hand back to swipe over her eyes.

"Will you really write me a letter every day?"

"If that's what you want me to do." I kiss a path over her cheek, licking away the teardrops, until I reach her ear. "I'll write it on your skin in bed at night with my hands and my mouth. I'll bury our story into your body with my dick." My teeth close over her ear. "I'll burn it into your mind by hunting you through the woods in the dark and fucking you under the trees."

"Rush." Her head turns, mouth finding mine, and we kiss, tongues tangling. Her hands lift and her fingers slide through my hair. My hands find her ass and squeeze, pulling her into my body, and I'm giving serious thought to finding the closest restroom, when Seven's dry voice breaks us apart.

"When you're done tongue-fucking your girlfriend, I'd like to eat before I lose my appetite."

74
Bailey

HAND IN HAND, Rush and I walk back to the trailer park. It's been a long day. There's still an ache in my heart at the loss of the letters. They are a part of the past I'm never going to get back and it still hurts. But Rush is right though. We aren't the same kids who wrote those words. We've grown so much since he found the first one in my old room.

I have to look forward, not back. Jamie wants to hurt me. He used the thing I treasured most as a weapon, but he hasn't managed to take away the source of the words. The boy who holds my heart.

My fingers tighten around Rush's hand. "When did you say your grandma was coming home?"

He smiles. "Tomorrow."

"I could cook something to celebrate her return."

"You can cook?"

I bump my shoulder into his, at the surprise I hear in his tone.

"Hey, don't get too excited. I can't make anything fancy."

"I'm sure she'll love whatever you make." He pulls me to a stop. "And I know she'll love you."

My cheeks heat. "I hope so."

"When you blush, it makes your freckles stand out." He kisses the end of my nose.

I push him away. "I hate them."

"I think they're beautiful."

My heart flips over and I turn toward the trailer. "Come on or you'll be late for hockey practice and I need to get ready for my shift at the diner."

Rush walks after me. "About that…"

I stop and swing back around to him. "What?"

"You don't have a shift tonight."

My brow knots in a frown. "Of course I do."

He shakes his head. "Hank talked to Darla. She's moved the schedule around so you work longer on the weekends instead during the day."

"When did this happen?"

"He talked to her today."

"You did this without talking to me first?"

"Jamie is still at the house."

"So my life is on hold?" I snap.

"We just think it's safer for now. Once he's left Red Creek you can return to your original hours. It's not forever."

"He's not even at the school, but he's still trying to ruin my life."

Rush hauls me into his arms. "We're just trying to protect you baby."

I wrap my arms around him and bury my face in his chest. "I know."

"Anyway, as I was saying *before* you interrupted me. You don't have a shift tonight and *I* don't have practice. It's been moved to tomorrow morning, so I thought we could go out."

"Out?"

"Yeah. Me and you."

"Like ... on a date?"

His lips twitch. "Something like that. Go and get changed. Wear something warm."

That makes me frown. "Where are we going?"

He smiles. "You'll see." And I have to be content with that because he ignores everything I say until I've pulled on a clean pair of jeans, and one of his jersey's. He hands me a soft black hoodie, which I pull over my head, then leads me out to his bike.

I frown when we park outside the ice rink.

"What are we doing here?"

"I have a game tomorrow, and I want you there." He takes my hand and leads me to the entrance. "But I remember the last time you were here. I found you in the restroom, hyperventilating."

"Rush." I try to pull my hand free.

"No. Trust me, Bailey."

He pulls me through the doors and along the hallway to where the locker room is. It's silent when we walk inside. He stops outside a locker with the number '13' on it, and pulls it open. Reaching in, he takes out two hockey sticks.

I eye them nervously. He holds one out.

"Take it."

I shake my head.

"Baby, it's not a snake. It's made from a composite of fiberglass,wood, carbon fiber and kevlar." He props them against the front of his locker, then reaches inside again. This time he pulls out two pairs of skates. "Sit down."

"What are you doing?"

"We're going skating."

"No, I'm not doing that."

He ignores me, and pushes me onto the bench, then lowers himself to his knees in front of me and pulls off my sneakers.

"I think I got the right size." He pushes one of the skates onto my foot and laces it up, then repeats the action with the other. His grin is satisfied when he looks up at me. "There. Let me just put mine on."

"Rush."

"Nope. Don't want to hear it. You're a hockey girl, now. That means you can't be afraid of the game or our equipment."

While he talks, he pushes his feet into his own skates, then pulls me to my feet, and picks up the hockey sticks. I wobble. He laughs.

"I'll keep you upright. Come on."

It takes us way too long to walk out to the ice. There's no one there, and the lights are dim.

"Are we allowed to be in here?"

He taps his chest. "Hockey captain." He stops at the gap which leads onto the ice. "Ready?"

"No?"

His deep chuckle does things to me. Things I probably shouldn't be thinking about while we're standing next to the ice.

He lets go of my fingers, slides off the guards from the bottom of our skates, then straightens and steps out onto the ice. He skates backward a few feet, then holds out his hands.

"Come on, Little Rose. Come and play with me."

"I can't."

He makes it look so easy, so graceful, as he glides around then comes to a stop in front of me.

"Give me your hand."

"This is a bad idea."

"Hand."

I huff, but wrap my fingers around his, and gingerly step out onto the ice. My legs go in different directions. I shriek. Rush hauls me upright, laughing.

"Oh my god. I can't do it."

"Hold on to me."

His patience is incredible. He spends an hour just teaching me how to balance and skate in a straight line, slowly coaxing me away from the edge and into the center of the ice. Once we're there, he skates away, and comes back with the hockey sticks.

I swallow.

"Baby, trust me." He skates a circle around me, until he's standing at my back, then curves an arm around my waist and places one of the sticks in my hand. His fingers curve over mine.

"Close your eyes," he whispers next to my ear. "Let your fingers tell you how it feels in your grip." He moved our arms together, swinging the stick. "Feel it?"

"Rush, I don't think—"

"That's right. *Don't* think, just feel."

* * *

My eyes snap open and disorientation hits me hard. Light spills out from a little TV and the rest of the room is cloaked in shadows and darkness. It takes me a second to realize I'm sprawled out on the narrow couch in Rush's trailer. I must have fallen asleep, almost as soon as we got back from the ice rink.

Where is Rush? Did he go to bed and leave me here?

Voices from outside shift my attention toward the window. One sounds like Rush, but the other is feminine. I frown.

Sofia? That bitch better not be trying anything.

Muscles stiff, I grimace as I scramble up off the couch, and move to the door, and peer outside. My eyes widen at the scene that I find. Rush is on the ground and Zoey Travers is standing above him with a baseball bat in her hand, the end resting on his forehead.

"Where is Bailey?" She waves the tip threateningly above his face.

Behind her are Kendall, Faith and Zuri. All four of them are dressed from head to toe in black.

"What the hell is going on?" I run down the steps toward them.

Five sets of eyes snap my way.

Zoey's expression lights up, and a bright smile pulls her lips up. "Oh, hi Bee."

Rush rolls to his left, and climbs to his feet. "These crazy bitches fucking jumped me."

Zoey rests the bat over her shoulder. "Oh, you haven't seen

354

anything yet. Buckle up, baby."

I move in front of him. "What are you doing to my boyfriend?"

Kendall frowns. "Jamie told us that he's forcing you to have sex with him. We're here to rescue you."

Faith nods. "He also told Cooper that he smashed your phone so you couldn't talk to anyone. He *has* been passing on our messages, right?"

"We won't let him hurt you, Bee. We'll make sure he never does it again." Zoey's cold, hard gaze flicks from my face to the boy behind me. "Just give us ten minutes alone with him."

"Whoa. Zoey, notch the crazy down for a second." I put my hands out in a gesture of peace when she swings the bat menacingly from side to side. "Jamie isn't my brother."

Zuri blinks and her smile falters. "What?"

"I found out I'm adopted and Jamie has been making my life a misery because he found out before me. He blames me for everything. He … he hates me, and Rush is the one good thing I have right now, so please I'd really appreciate it if you didn't break his legs."

Faith tilts her head. "He's not forcing you to have sex with him?"

"No!"

Kendall clears her throat. "Well, this is awkward. I suppose you better introduce us."

Shoulders relaxing, I turn to the boy behind me. "Rush, these are my friends from Churchill Bradley Academy. Zoey Travers, Kendall Hale, Faith Watson, and Zuri Reed."

Rush eyes the four of them. "Who took me out with a leg sweep?"

"That would be me." Zoey lowers the bat. She grins.

I hug them one by one. "How did you get out of the Academy?"

Faith glances at Zoey. "Oh, it's not so hard, if you know how."

"I've missed you guys so much. Do you want to stay for pizza? We were going to order one. That's okay, right?" I glance at Rush and he nods.

Kendall pulls me into a tight hug. "Pizza sounds good and I want to know more about what happened with Jamie."

75

Rush

Bailey's arms are wrapped around me when my alarm goes off. I throw out a hand, groping around the floor and slap the screen of my phone until it stops making noise, then just lie there, face down, on the mattress.

It's game day.

It's also the day my gran comes home.

I need to get up, make sure everywhere is tidy, then head over to the barn for a last minute practice, before the game this afternoon. We're playing against the Churchill Bradley Crows again, only this time it's not a pre-season warm-up. This is the real deal. Which means it's not going to be anywhere near as friendly as the last time we faced off.

I roll onto my back, and reach down to untangle Bailey's body from around me.

"Hey, Bug." I shift onto my side, facing her, and brush her hair away from her face. "I need to get up and get ready for practice."

She mumbles something and burrows deeper under the sheets.

I laugh quietly. "Baby, come on. You need to wake up. You don't want to still be here when my gran gets home, do you?"

That gets her attention. Her eyelashes flutter, then her lids lift and she peers at me out of sleepy blue eyes.

"What time is it?"

"Seven."

She groans. "We didn't get to bed until *three*."

Her friends had stuck around for *hours*, catching up with Bailey, cursing Jamie, and generally making me wonder if all girls were psychotic. Or whether it was just CBA girls. Or maybe it was just the one.

Zoey Travers.

She'd kept the baseball bat resting against her knee the entire time she was here, and every time I caught her eye she'd tap it with one finger and smirk at me. She gave me total Harley Quinn vibes. Cute but fucking crazy. I pitied the guy she finally set her sights on, while at the same time thought he'd be in for one hell of a ride if he managed to actually tame her.

God fucking help him if he ever hurt her, though. If Zoey didn't kill him, her twin brother would.

Bailey moves beside me, her hand sliding down my chest and distracting me from my thoughts. Her lips press against my throat, and then she's on top of me, legs astride my hips, gloriously naked with her hair flowing over her shoulders. The early morning sun catches it through the gap in the curtains, turning it to a fiery halo around her face.

I curve my hands over her thighs and rock my hips up so my dick rubs against her pussy. Her breasts bounce with the movement. She makes a soft sound in her throat, lips curving up into a smile.

"You like that?" I repeat the action.

Her hands flatten against my chest and she leans forward. "I'd like it more if you were inside me."

"Me too, but I have a game today."

"So?" Her breasts rub against my chest when she lowers herself further so she can kiss me.

I move my hands to her waist and lift her off, then pin her beneath me.

"If I fuck you now, and then we lose the game this afternoon, it'll be because you exhausted me." I roll my hips again, making us both groan. "So, hold that thought and when we win, I'll take you into the woods and make you scream."

I suck her bottom lip between my teeth and bite down gently, while my hand finds her breast so I can pinch her nipple. Her arousal soaks my dick where it's pressed against her pussy. I reach down and grip it so I can rub it up and down, dipping the tip inside her and then withdrawing. Her back arches, as she tries to get me to go deeper. I laugh against her lips, and kiss across her jaw, so I can bite my way down her throat.

"I love seeing my teeth marks on your skin. Wear my jersey at practice this morning, but no bra, so I can see how hard your nipples are every time I look over."

I move lower down her body so I can lick a circle around one hard little peak before I suck it into my mouth. Her fingers find my hair, slide through and grip it tight. The stab of pain sends a jolt of lust right through me. I tug her nipple with my teeth, biting down, then soothe away the sting with my tongue.

"You want me to come and watch you practice?"

"What do you think all that time spent on the ice was for last night? You're my girl, Bailey. That means you come to every practice, every game. I need to know that you're comfortable there, otherwise I'll be distracted." I push a finger inside her, my thumb finding her clit. "Today, I want to know you're watching me, all wet and turned on, ready for my dick to slide right into this tight little pussy once it's over. No bra, no panties. That way you'll be focused on how turned on you are, and not what happened to you. I can come and play with you whenever I want throughout the day before the game." I add a second finger. "And then, afterward, when we win, I'll take you to the woods and chase you down like the prey that you are. I'll take my knife to your clothes and strip you naked, tie you to the nearest tree and devour you." A third finger slides inside and I scissor them in and out, while my thumb flicks against her clit. "I want you completely at my mercy, spread open, on display, tied up and helpless, ready to be fucked however I please."

She moans, her hips lifting in time to the thrust of my fingers.

"And then," I whisper as I slide further down the bed. "I'll drag my knife over your skin. I'll leave my mark, and make you bleed …" My tongue connects with her clit. "And after all that, my pretty Little Rose … I'll make you scream."

I lick her again, swirling my tongue around her clit, then lift my head. Her skin is flushed, nipples hard, and she's writhing against my fingers. Her breath leaves her in small, panting moans, and as much as my dick is screaming at me to fuck her, I force myself to pull my fingers free from her body, and roll away.

I'm outside the door of the bedroom when she realizes I've gone.

"Rush?"

"I want you to stay just like that. On the edge all day. Whenever you feel the need to come start to ease, get those fingers on that pretty little pussy and bring yourself back to the edge. Do not *fucking* come, though. That's *mine* to do. If I find out you've ignored me, I'm going to add spanking to the list of things I've got in store for you later."

Her curses follow me into the bathroom, and I jerk myself off to the sound of them.

When I come out, she's wearing a pair of black yoga pants and my jersey and sitting on the couch. I throw on some sweatpants and a T-shirt, then walk over to stand in front of her.

"Lift your top up."

She frowns at me. "Why?"

"I want to see if you did as you're told."

Glaring, she slowly lifts her top to bare her breasts. I reach out and pinch each nipple. "Good girl. Now pull your pants down."

"Rush!"

Taking hold of the waistband, I drag the yoga pants down over her hips until I can see her pussy. Using two fingers, I part the plump lips and flick her clit. She flinches.

"Sensitive?"

"Yes!"

I do it again. "Good. Keep it that way. Nice and wet, so I can do this whenever I want." I stroke my fingers over her clit and then shove them inside her, giving two or three rough pumps before pulling them free and pressing them against her lips. "Lick them clean."

Her tongue snakes out over my fingers, lapping up the taste of her arousal. My dick hardens.

"Good girl. Okay, let's go."

"Wh-what?"

"I have to be at practice for nine." I palm her pussy and squeeze. "I expect there to be a wet patch on these pants by nine-thirty."

My gaze skims over the stands at the few spectators who have gathered to watch the pregame practice. Rush walked me to the seats, kissed me to the sounds of his teammates laughing and hollering, then walked away, leaving me wet and breathless. There's a needy ache between my legs and no matter how I'd tempted him he'd refused to fuck me. I want to touch myself and find release, but the promise he made to take me to the woods later keeps me from doing so.

I want him to chase me.

To hunt me down.

I need to feel the bite of his knife as he fucks me.

It will give me more pleasure than a few moments release if I get myself off.

"Hey Bee, over here." Nicky calls as she waves from further down the row.

I walk over to her, see a flash of red, and turn my head just as Sofia walks past on the opposite side of the rink.

"What's *she* doing here?"

My friend's gaze swings across the ice. "I don't know. Maybe she hooked up with someone new?"

The girl in question glances over at us, the smirk on her glossy red lips is clear. If she's here to weave more lies or to try and take Rush from me, I'm ready for her. Jamie might think that he's clever, but after the chat I had with my Churchill Bradley friends last night, he'll soon find his connections severed at the Academy.

Zoey will tell Kellan. No one will want to associate with him once she does. I doubt very much that Cooper will continue lending him money when he finds out.

My attention is drawn over to the players as they skate out onto the ice. Rush's gaze searches the stands until it locks with mine. I squirm in my seat as I recall his words from earlier.

I want you to stay just like that. On the edge all day. Whenever you feel the need to come start to ease, get those fingers on that pretty little pussy and bring yourself back to the edge. Do not fucking come, though. That's mine to do. If I find out you've ignored me, I'm going to add spanking to the list of things I've got in store for you later.

Why do I find the idea of him spanking me exciting? Maybe it's the thought of the pain? Would it really hurt?

Heat pools low in my stomach at the thought. I press my thighs together, attempting to ease the throb between my legs, but it only makes me wetter. His teasing has left me on edge. All I need is his tongue or fingers to finish the job he started this morning, while he growls dirty words in my ear and strokes my skin with his knife.

Nicky nudges me. "Are you okay?"

I nod.

"Just ignore her."

"Who?"

She frowns. "Sofia."

That girl is the furthest thing from my thoughts at the moment, but I'm not about to admit that the only thing I'm thinking about is Rush fucking me after the game.

A whistle blows, and the players skate to the center of the ice, where their coach waits.

I try to pay attention to the practice, but I can't stop fantasizing about my boyfriend. I chew on my bottom lip as Rush glides around the ice. He's the only one who knows I'm naked under the jersey and yoga pants I'm wearing. I recall how good it had felt as he'd slipped the tip of his dick inside me earlier, and fresh wetness soaks my thighs.

Win or lose I'll have him inside me after the game tonight. I'll get my orgasm. But that's hours away ... I stand up.

"Bee?"

"I need to go to the bathroom."

I leave her and head for the ladies' restroom. The second I'm inside one of the locked stalls, I push my hand down beneath the waistband of my yoga pants, and drag my fingers through my wetness. Eyes closed, I imagine Rush covering my pussy with his mouth. I stroke a finger over my clit. A moan leaves my lips as pleasure shivers through me.

Can I really wait until the end of the game to come? He won't know if I give myself an orgasm ... right?

A fantasy unfolds in my head.

Rush is on his knees before me as he nibbles and teases me with his tongue. I fist a handful of his dark hair, and his hands grip my thighs to keep me in place. His tongue pushes inside me.

I slide my fingers into my pussy and imagine it's Rush's dick I can feel. It feels good, but it's not enough.

The chime of an incoming call breaks my concentration. Swearing under my breath, I scramble to pull my phone out of my pocket. I swipe my finger over the screen and see Rush's number. As soon as I tap to answer the call, it stops ringing, and a message flashes up.

Rush: Open the door.

My lips part.

Rush: Come on, Little Rose. I know you're in there.

My gaze darts up to the locked door, then back to my screen.

No way.

Biting my lips, I warily slide back the bolt. When the door swings open, I come face to face with my boyfriend. He's still wearing his hockey gear, face slick with sweat.

He arches an eyebrow. "Did you make yourself come?"

My cheeks grow hot. "N-no."

"Because you're my good girl or because you've just been caught?"

I contemplate lying, but the smirk on his face stops me. "It's not my fault you left me so horny! I want your tongue on my pussy."

The corner of his mouth quirks.

He knows *exactly* how I feel.

L. ANN & CLAIRE MARTA

77

Rush

Tipping her chin up, I capture her lips with mine, slipping my tongue into her mouth to stroke along hers. My other hand lowers to find her pussy, wet and eager for my touch. Her hips rock forward, rubbing her clit against my fingertips, and she moans into my mouth.

"Want to come, baby?"

"So much," she whispers.

I press another kiss to her lips, and step away. "Keep it that way. Fix your clothes. Let's go. I need to get back onto the ice."

"Rush!"

I smile. "Sorry, Bug. I told you that you're going to have to wait." I reach out and wrap my fingers around her throat, pull her toward me, and kiss her hard, sinking my teeth into her bottom lip. "Now be a good girl, and come and watch me practice."

She glares at me, but straightens her clothes. Once she's

presentable, I take her hand and lead her out of the stall. When she moves toward the sink, I stop her.

"Oh no. You came in here to get yourself off, thinking I wouldn't catch you. Now you can sit with your friend, knowing that at any moment she might catch the scent of your pretty little pussy. No washing your hands. You can smell yourself on your fingers while you watch me."

I smirk at her shocked gasp. "Actions have consequences, baby." And with that, I drag her back out and to her seat. I steal another quick kiss, then step back onto the ice.

While keeping her on the edge, teasing her, making her hot and wet is fun, it's not the real reason I'm doing it. I'm purposely keeping her mind on me, on sex, on *coming* to *stop* her thinking about where she is, what she's surrounded by, the memory of what Jamie Fucking Linnett did to her with a hockey stick.

"Stop fooling around, and get your head in the game," Coach snaps.

"Sorry, Coach." I take my position on the ice and spend the next fifteen minutes reminding him why I'm the center *and* the captain of the Red Creek Ravens.

"Okay, come over here!" Coach waves us to the center of the ice, and we form a huddle around him. "I don't need to tell you that the game today is going to be tough. You need to be at the peak of your performance. The Crows will not go down without a fight, not after the last time you faced off. So I want you to focus on that. Form two lines." He calls out names, dividing us into two teams. "We're going to keep this short, but I want a fifteen minute game. Behave like the other team is the Crows, and work your asses off to win!" He blows his whistle and the rink immediately turns into a battleground.

Exhilaration courses through my veins as I skate up and down the ice, anticipating what play each person will make and making sure I'm right where I need to be when the puck comes sailing in my direction.

Each team member has pushed themselves to the limit, and we're all panting, slick with sweat, and ready for the game to be over, when there's a shout from off to the side somewhere.

I turn my head, frowning. It sounded like a girl. A girl *screaming*. The moment of distraction costs me, and Bellamy crashes into me, sending us both to the ground. The impact knocks the air out of my lungs, and it takes a second or two for me to catch my breath. When I do, I take the hand Bellamy is holding out and let him haul me to my feet.

"What were you looking at?" he asks.

I shake my head. "Not sure. Thought I heard—"

My eyes zero in on red hair and pale features moving slowly along the edge of the ice, then shifts to the taller person beside her.

"Is that—"

"What the fuck is he doing here?" Seven snaps from behind me.

"I guess that's why Sofia came."

The three of us watch as the girl in question rounds the end of the rink and moves toward the small cluster of friends and fans watching us practice. The boy beside her keeps pace, his head lowered. From where I stand, I can't tell if he's talking to Sofia, but she nods and points to where Bailey is sitting with Nicky. Neither girl is paying attention, their eyes on us.

The hairs rise on the back of my neck, and I pull off my gloves, and unbuckle my helmet.

"If that fucker is here to start shit." I toss my helmet to the ice and skate across, calling Bailey's name.

And then three things happen all at once.

Sofia screams my name. I turn my head just as Jamie shoves her forward and lifts his arm.

"Rush, run!" Sofia's head snaps sideways as Jamie backhands her.

And then there's a noise, almost like the sound of a car backfiring. Which makes no sense. We wouldn't be able to hear that from here.

The sound is repeated.

Once …

Twice …

The plexiglass screen above the boards closest to me crack … And then the screaming starts.

78

Bailey

"Rush, *run!*"

I turn my head at the screamed words. My gaze latches onto Sofia, and my heart stops. *Jamie* is with her.

What's he doing here?

My stomach drops when she twists away from him, and tries to run. He hauls her back by her hair and backhands her, sending her to the floor.

What the hell?

Everything seems to happen in slow motion after that. Jamie raises his hand, and for a split second, my brain doesn't register what he's holding.

No. No this can't be real. Jamie would never do this.

It's only when the first shot rings out that horror hits me. The plexiglass that's supposed to protect spectators from stray hockey pucks shakes, and fine lines spread out across it. My eyes focus on the bullet stuck in the center of the pattern, and my hand covers my lips to muffle my scream.

The gun swings away from the rink and toward where I'm sitting. Screams erupt around us.

A second shot goes off.

Then a third.

The small group of friends, girlfriends, and family members seated nearby all lurch to their feet.

"Gun! He has a gun!" One of them shouts and points to where Jamie is stalking along the path between the boards and the row of seats we're on.

I exchange horrified glances with Nicky.

"Bailey!" Jamie shouts.

"Oh god," Nicky whispers. "He's coming this way. We have to run."

She reaches for my hand. I shake my head. "What about Rush and the other guys?"

"Bailey, he's not here for *them*. Look!" She points. I follow the direction of her finger. Jamie is coming straight at us, jaw set, gun aimed in our direction. "We *need* to run."

We make it to the steps which lead up between the stands and to one of the exits, but instead of following Nicky, I turn toward the ice.

"What are you doing?" She grabs my arm and tries to haul me up the steps.

I pull away, frantically searching for Rush. Just as I spot him, my view is blocked.

"No. Oh no no no," Nicky whispers beside me.

"Jamie … " I breathe his name.

His eyes are cold, hard, and empty of emotion. Instead of answering me, he lifts the gun. Something hits me from the left, and I stumble, just as gunfire rings out. I start to turn, only for Nicky to slam into me. The weight of her knocks me off my feet and we both crash to the floor.

"Nicky!"

She doesn't speak, her body slumped over mine. I shake her.

"Nicky? Oh my god, please answer me. Nicky!" My voice becomes more frantic with each word.

A shadow falls over me.

Oh, God.

"Jamie … please. You don't have to do this."

He doesn't reply. There's not a flicker of guilt or remorse in his eyes as he stares down at me.

"Help! Somebody, *please!*" The words leave me on a broken shriek.

Reaching down, he grasps the back of Nicky's shirt and throws her to one side, then levels the gun at me.

79
Rush

THE SECOND BAILEY falls to the ground, I lose all sense of reason. I don't know if anyone else keeps up with me, but I'm across the ice, through the gate, and launching myself at Jamie between one breath and the next.

We go down in a tangle of limbs ... *too many* limbs, and my vision clears enough to acknowledge Seven, Dom, Levi, and Bellamy are either side of me. I make a grab for the gun, but Jamie twists beneath me, and brings it up between us. Another hand shoves it sideways just as he squeezes the trigger, and the bullet flies so close, I feel the burn of its passing against my bicep. There's a grunt to my left, and then Seven surges forward, fingers tangling into Jamie's hair. He slams the other boy's head into the floor, curses spilling from between gritted teeth. I go for the gun again, but my hands are slick with sweat and I can't get a decent grip on it.

Pain explodes over my ribs, and I double over, Jamie rolling above me to straddle my hips and the hand holding the gun comes down to point between my eyes. My heart stops. And for a second … a minute … a year … *a fucking lifetime* … I see everything I've done flash in front of my eyes.

Moving to Red Creek. Finding Bailey's first letter. Burying her stray cat. Losing our home. Losing my mom.

Hurting Bailey … Kissing Bailey … Fucking Bailey … *Loving* Bailey.

Then Dom is there, body slamming into Jamie, and they both go sideways, rolling over the floor, through the gate and onto the ice. Seven hauls me to my feet and we take off, after our friend, with Bellamy and Levi on our heels.

A shot rings out, and then another one and both boys go still.

"Dom!" All three of us shout his name at the same time, and we fly across the ice and drop to our knees.

Seven rolls Dom off Jamie, and our friend falls onto his back, head lolling sideways. There's a red stain spreading across the shoulder of his jersey. He presses two fingers to Dom's throat, then twists to find me, while Bellamy checks Jamie. Levi kicks the gun across the ice.

"He's breathing." Seven's voice is relieved.

"This fucking asshole is—"

I don't wait to hear the rest of Bellamy's words, turning away to search for Bailey.

Where the fuck is she?

I can't see her amongst the people hurrying back and forth.

Students, fans, friends, and people in uniforms—police and EMTs, I think.

"Bailey?" My roar echoes around the rink. "*Bailey?*"

Someone grabs my arm, and I twist, intent on punching whoever it is.

"Take a breath, son." Coach's voice cuts through my panic. "She's safe. Let me look at your arm."

"I need to see Bailey."

"In a minute. The police are here, and there's an ambulance outside. You're bleeding."

I shake him off. "Where the fuck is Bailey?"

"I'm here." The sound of the small voice to my right, trembling and breathy, makes my vision dim.

I fight against the blackness threatening to drag me down, and reach out. "Come here."

And then she's in my arms, her face pressing into my chest. I can feel her heart hammering, hear her shaky breaths.

But it doesn't matter because it means she's alive. And that's all I care about.

ARMS WRAPPED AROUND my middle, head lowered so all I can see are my feet, I sit still on the plastic chair in the hallway. No matter how much I try to stop them, I can't stop the tremors that roll through me.

The doctor checked me over a little while ago, confirming all I have are a few scrapes and bruises, and he left me here with instructions to wait until someone came to speak to me, before hurrying to the next person.

I can't stop the images of what happened from playing over and over in my head. The look on Jamie's face is burned into my brain.

How could this have happened? Where did he get the gun?

Is this my fault? Did he come to the rink looking for me? Nicky got shot because she was with me. How many other people have been hurt because of me?

Slowly I lift my hands to stare at them. They're shaking, blood staining my palms and fingers.

My friend's blood.

They carried her out on a stretcher. Her eyes were closed, lips parted. *Was she breathing? I couldn't see her breathing.*

I rub my palms frantically against my pants, trying to wipe away the blood. It won't come off.

There had been so much blood.

"Bailey?"

My head snaps up at the gruff voice.

Hank is standing near the doors, watching me. "Is that blood? Shit, why aren't you with a doctor?"

At the sound of his voice, my bottom lip wobbles, and the tears I've been holding back fall free. "It's not mine." My voice shakes. "It's Nicky's blood. I couldn't stop it. I couldn't stop him."

In three steps he's in front of me. He crouches and takes both my hands in his. "Jesus, your hands are like ice." He rubs his hands over mine. "You're in shock."

"It's my fault."

"No, it's not."

"Jamie came after me."

His arms wrap around my shoulders, he pulls me down into his embrace. "You are not responsible for this. Do you hear me, Bailey? That boy did this, not you."

I cling tightly to him, sobbing against his chest. "H-he hurt them."

He rocks me gently. "It's going to be alright."

Will it? I don't believe him.

Tears fall until my eyes burn. Until I have no more left to give.

And when they stop, and my sobs turn to hiccups, he scoops me up and sits on the seat with me cradled in his lap. One of his hands strokes my back.

I'm tired, scared, and confused. Ear pressed to his chest, the slow beat of his heart calms the rapid rhythm of mine. The problem with that, is with relaxation comes questions. Questions I *need* the answers to.

Sucking in a deep, shuddering breath, I sit up. "Can you see if you can find anything out about my friends, please?"

He loosens his hold on me. "I can see what I can do. Wait here."

He sets me on my feet and stands, then turns and guides me back onto the chair. I'm too exhausted and shaken to argue. Tipping my head back against the wall, I close my eyes.

Please let everyone be okay.

"Oh my god, Bailey?"

My eyes snap open. "Daddy?"

"Oh, sweetheart." He's coming toward me at a quick pace. Mom is just behind him, just as pale faced.

"Are you okay?" He runs his hands over my head and hair then his attention drops to the blood stained jersey I'm wearing. "Are you hurt?"

I shake my head. "It's just some bruises."

"Where's Jamie?"

My gaze shifts to my mother. "What?"

"The phone call said both of you were here. Is he okay? Have you seen him?"

"I don't know."

"What do you mean, you *don't* know? Were you separated? What happened? All the information we received was so confusing. They said someone had a gun, and was shooting at the hockey team."

"Mom …" I lick my lips. "Mom, it was Jamie. He had the gun."

Dad gasps. "*What?*"

"H-he shot people." I look at the floor.

"No." My mom's voice is sharp. "No, my baby wouldn't do that."

"There were witnesses. He shot my friend. He tried to shoot *me*."

"Not my Jamie."

"But where did he get the gun from?" Dad's confusion sounds in his voice.

Mom makes a strangled sound. I lift my eyes to find her. Her face is white, fingers pressed to her lips. "Kelvin …"

My dad's head swings toward her, and whatever he sees in her face makes him rock back.

"Shawna, no." His voice is soft. "Tell me you didn't …"

"We needed something for protection. This town isn't the safest place to live, you know that. But it was locked away, Kelvin. I swear it was."

My brain sluggishly tries to connect what she's saying, and when I finally figure it out, shock ripples through me. "The gun was *yours?*"

She ignores me, eyes on Dad. "Jamie can't have it. It's safely locked away in a metal box under our bed. There's a thumbprint code. There's no way he could have gotten into it." She sways.

"What is it?" Dad grips her arm. "Shawna, *what?*"

"He told me it was for school. Oh god …" Her eyes close. "He said they were doing forensics and needed to take fingerprints. He had me press my thumb against a glass, and dusted it, then used tape to lift the print."

Movement to the side brings my head around. Hank is walking toward us, his expression is grim, lips pressed tightly together. When his eyes meet mine, I can tell something is wrong.

"I couldn't find much out, but I know that Nicky has gone—"

I blank out the rest of his words. I don't want to hear it. I don't want to hear that my friend is dead.

81

Rush

"Stop fussing. I'm fine." I try not to snap the words, but judging by the look on the nurse's face, I fail.

"If you were fine, you wouldn't be sitting here while I stitch up your arm."

"I've had worse injuries playing hockey." Bickering with the doctor keeps my mind off what happened at the barn. I don't want to think about how close we all came to being killed. How close *Bailey* came to being killed.

My throat closes, eyesight swimming in and out, and I suck in a deep breath through my nose, blow it out through my mouth, then sit up straight.

"How's Dom and Seven?"

"Seven is okay. Just a few bruises from the fight. Dom is in surgery."

Tension zips up my spine. "He's going to be okay though, right?"

"The bullet lodged in his shoulder. They're operating to remove it."

"Fuck."

"Okay, there. All done." She takes a step away and admires her handiwork. "Keep it dry and covered for at least twenty-four hours, after that you can shower, but be careful. Don't get it too wet. No swimming until the sutures have been removed."

"Yes, ma'am. Can I see my friends now?" What I really mean is can I see Bailey now.

I hop off the bed, and sway. The doctor catches my uninjured arm. "Steady, Rush. You're not quite ready to go wandering around. Sit back down. Your grandmother is on her way."

"Gran?" I frown, and glance at the wall clock. It's twelve-fifteen. "How long have we been here?"

"An hour."

An *hour* has passed? There's a part of me that knows I'm in shock, no matter how much I try to deny it. That my unawareness of how much time has passed is part of my reaction to what has happened. And *that* thought takes me way too close to facing what we've been through. I shake my head.

"Can I at least see Bailey?"

"Let me go and check if she's been released yet."

She leaves me alone, and I pluck at my hockey pants. The vague thought that I'm glad they're black and won't show up any blood goes through my mind, and nausea rises again.

"Hey." *Not* the female voice I wanted to hear, but it's a welcome one all the same.

"Seven."

We meet in the middle of the room, stare at each other for a full second, then wrap our arms around each other.

"What the fuck?" His voice is a whisper. I've never heard my best friend sound so shaken before.

"I don't know." My voice is just as hoarse. "I don't fucking know." We're both shaking, clutching at each other. I think if one of us lets go right now, we'd both fall to the ground.

"He shot Dom."

"I know."

"He fucking shot at you."

"I know." It's all I can say.

"If Sofia hadn't warned you ..." His grip on my arms tighten. I hiss as pain shoots down my left arm, but don't pull away. "That first shot was aimed at you, Rush."

"But he missed. He didn't shoot me." Well, not completely. He grazed my arm when we fought later.

We fall silent, and just stand there, holding on to each other, and that's when my gran walks in.

"Rush?" Her voice is thin, scared, and shaking. "Seven! Boys, are you okay?" She dashes over and wraps her arms around the both of us.

"Gran." I turn in her embrace and bury my face against her shoulder. Seven does the same. And we both cling to the older woman. "Fuck. Gran, he tried to kill everyone. He tried to—"

"Hush." She strokes a hand through my hair. "It's okay, honey. It's okay."

But it isn't okay. I don't think it'll be okay ever again.

82

Bailey

"Oh my god, she's dead." My shoulders shake, eyes burning with fresh tears.

Nicky is gone. She saved my life and Jamie killed her. Where's Rush? I need to see him.

Dad pulls me up from my seat and wraps his arms tightly around me in a fierce hug.

Hank shakes his head. "No, no, you didn't listen to me. She's been airlifted to another hospital."

The tears that swim in my eyes distort my vision and I have to blink furiously to clear it. "Air-airlifted?"

He nods. "She's alive, but in critical condition. They don't think they have the facilities here to give her the best care."

"What about Jamie? Is there any news on what happened?" Mom's voice is anxious.

Hank's gaze swings her way, his face stony. "I'm sorry. I didn't ask."

"Is there any way you could find out?"

"I'm afraid not. I don't work here."

"You're not an orderly?"

"No ma'am, I'm here for Bailey."

"You know *Bailey?*"

"Hank works at the diner with Bee." Dad says. "He also lives at the trailer park near Rush Carter." He gives Hank a tired smile. "Thank you for being there for her."

Hank nods. "You're welcome."

I rub a hand over my face. Now isn't the right time to introduce who Hank *really* is to them. A nurse appears through a door, a frown on her face, looking up and down the hallway.

Mom hurries over to her. "Excuse me, my son was brought in from the ice rink. Could you find out what happened to him?"

"Of course. What's his name?"

"Jamie. Jamie Linnett."

"Let me find the doctor who saw him. Wait here, please." She turns and disappears back the way she came, and returns half a minute later with a male doctor.

"Mrs Linnett?"

My mom nods. "I'm looking for my son."

"Why don't we go through here?" He touches her arm. "Do you have anyone else with you?"

"Kelvin?" Her head turns to find my dad.

I untangle myself from his arms. "Go and find out how he is."

"Bailey—"

"I know, Daddy." I smile. "He's still your son."

"I'll stay with her." Hank steps up beside me.

Dad hesitates for a second longer, then follows the doctor as he leads them into a room.

"W-what?" Mom's cry reaches us a moment later. "No. That can't be right."

I look at Hank.

"Jamie's dead," he says softly. "It wasn't my place to tell her. He died at the scene. They think when there was a scramble for the gun, it went off. The bullet went straight into his heart, killing him instantly."

Jamie is dead?

Pain doubles me over. My brother is dead.

I shake my head, memories of him flashing through my mind. Memories of laughter, of bickering, of fooling around on hot summer days. Memories of joining Churchill Bradley together, sharing confessions of homesickness.

And then later of the arguments we had. The fights. The slow descent into anger and hatred.

Sobs wrack my body. He hated me, but I *never* hated him. He was my brother. It didn't matter if we didn't really have the same parents. He *was* my brother, and I *loved* him.

"I'm sorry, Miss Linnett?" A gentle voice breaks through my tears.

I sniff, wipe my eyes and seek out the source of the voice. A nurse is standing in front of me.

"Bailey?"

I nod.

She smiles. "There's a boy who's very insistent on seeing you.

Would you follow me?" She looks at Hank. "You owe me another date, Hank Hicks."

He drops a kiss on her cheek. "You got it, sweetheart."

83
Rush

"No!" I SURGE up, legs tangling in the sheets, and almost faceplant the wall. "Fuck."

My hand slaps against the side of the trailer and I shove myself back to the center of the bed. My heart is racing, mouth dry, and the sound of the gunshot is still ringing in my ears. I roll onto my back, staring up at the ceiling, and will my heartbeat to slow down to 'not about to have a heart attack' levels. When I can't hear it thundering in my ears, I slowly ease up into a sitting position.

It's been three days since the shooting. Three days of being questioned by the police, by a therapist the school brought in, by reporters who have set up camp all around town. I've reached the point where I don't leave the trailer in case a microphone is thrust into my face, and my only communication with my friends is via cell phone, while they also hide away.

But today … Today I'm determined to go outside. To breathe in some fresh air. To prove to myself that my life isn't over. It's that or buy vodka and block out the world in a way that has proven to be effective.

My cell vibrates, and I reach down to pick it up.

Seven: Anyone awake?

Me: Yeah.

Bellamy: Yeah, me too.

Levi: I'm here.

There's no response from Riley or Dom in the group chat. But that's not a surprise. Riley's parents have taken him out of town, away from the media circus. And Dom is still in the hospital. I'm not even sure he has his cell phone. My gran is in contact with his parents daily, so we know he's alive, but I want to speak to him myself and make sure.

So today I'm also going to pay *him* a visit and not the nearest liquor store.

Me: Still meeting me at the hospital later?

All three reply with an affirmative.

Bellamy: How's Bailey?

Me: Hard to say. We've talked on the phone, but haven't been able to see each other since

I hit send without finishing the sentence.

That's something else I plan to do today. Convince Hank to let me see Bailey. Both he and my gran have forced us to stay apart for a couple of days while the authorities went through what had happened. They both said it was better that way, so what happened to us both didn't merge together and become confusing when we had to explain.

I understood it, but I didn't like it. I needed to see her and make sure for myself that she was okay. Reliving what had happened by recounting it—first to the hospital, then to the police, and then again to the school therapist had caused my mind to spin in loops, questioning whether the series of events which caused Jamie to fall off the rails was, in some way, my fault. I am sure Bailey feels the same. It also makes me desperate to reach for a bottle of vodka. I'm scared I won't be able to resist. I need a distraction.

I need *her*.

I navigate over to my chat conversation with her.

Me: Hey Bug. Are you awake?

Just like the boys in the group chat, she replies immediately.

Bug: Can't sleep. You?

Me: Same.

An idea comes to me. One so obvious that I can't believe I haven't thought about it sooner.

Twisting around on the mattress, I ease open the window above my bed, and climb out.

It's dark outside—too late for people to still be moving around, but too early for the sun to rise, which means no one will see me creep across to the trailer next to mine and tap softly on the window.

The curtain twitches to one side, and then the window is sliding up and Bailey's head pops through the gap.

"What are you doing?" she whispers.

"Come out here."

I reach up to steady her and she climbs through the window and drops to her feet in front of me. We stand, a foot apart, and stare at each other. Her red hair is a messy tangle around her face. She's wearing thick socks, pajama shorts, and a tank top. I've never seen anything so fucking beautiful in my life.

The silence between us lengthens, stretches, until she catches her bottom lip between her teeth. The action breaks my frozen state, and I take her hand, linking our fingers together, and draw her around the back of the trailer, where my gran keeps a small deck area, complete with table and chairs. I guide Bailey to one of the chairs and wait for her to sit down, then lower myself to my knees in front of her.

"What are you doing?" She repeats her earlier question.

I lean forward and rest my head across her legs.

"I miss you. Talking on the phone isn't the same. I wanted to see you." My lips brush against her knee with every word. "I *needed* to see you."

Her fingers slide through my hair, and at her touch, something inside me eases.

"Did I drive him to it, Bug? Was it my fault?" It isn't what I planned to say, but the words left me before I could stop them. "I keep wondering if it was something I did. Did the clashes we had break something inside him?"

"No. No!"

The fingers in my hair curl, and she tugs on the strands until I lift my head. She palms my cheeks.

"It's not your fault, Rush. Not yours. Not mine."

THE VULNERABILITY SWIMMING in his gaze tugs at my heart. "Jamie was out of control. He has been since we moved here. Nothing we said or did would have changed his actions."

He closes his eyes and swallows hard. "If I'd only—"

"No." I gently stroke his cheek. "He was set on a path of destruction. Maybe he just couldn't cope with the loss of everything we had before, or maybe it ran deeper."

"You think he was unstable?"

I shrug, feigning a casualness I don't feel, but I think it's something Rush needs. There's something about him. An edginess that worries me.

"He was always one of the golden boys at Churchill Bradley Academy. Once we were settled and had our own friends. We didn't hang out much, unless we were at home. I thought he was okay.

Maybe I was wrong. Being the best at everything was something that was an obsession for him once he became friends with Cooper, and Kellan and the others. When my dad lost everything, it took all that away from him. I guess he just couldn't cope."

Rush rubs his cheek against my palm. "When did you become so wise?"

A small smile curves my lips. "I'm not. I've been spending the last few days blaming myself too."

"Bug—"

"No. Let me finish. I've been going crazy, repeating everything in my head, trying to think of all the things I could have done differently to prevent what happened. How I could have fixed things. Could I have been a better sister? Should I have taken time to listen to him more? I've cried myself to sleep every night over it." I release a long breath. "But Hank has been the voice of reason the last few days. We are *not* responsible for Jamie. We didn't put the gun in his hand."

"I don't know if I can believe that." His voice is loaded with guilt.

"I know, but maybe if we repeat it enough, we will." I cup the back of his head and pull him closer, so I can rest my forehead against his.

"I want a drink." The confession falls from his lips. He closes his eyes and turns his head away. "It's eating at me. The need to get drunk and block everything out. I'm not sure I can beat it, Bailey," he whispers.

I swallow hard. "What do you need me to do?"

He shakes his head. "I don't … I don't know. Don't let me?" He gives a half laugh. "Distract me?"

I lean forward and capture his lips with mine. "I love you, Rush."

85
Rush

I TAKE ONE last look at my reflection in the mirror on my grandmother's bedroom wall, straighten the black tie around my neck, then turn away.

"Are you sure about this?" Gran asks when I step into the living room.

I nod. "I'm not letting Bailey go alone."

"She won't—"

"I *know*. Hank will be there. Her dad, as well. But they're not *me*. She needs *me* there." I pick up the black jacket from the back of the couch and slip it on. "Plus, I think going will be cathartic. That probably sounds weird. It's the funeral of the guy who tried to fucking kill us but …" I shrug. "I dunno, Gran. It just feels like the right thing to do."

"Would you like me to come with you?"

I shake my head. "No. I mean … you can go, if you like. They're holding the funeral at St. Jude's." I name the town's only church. "I'm sure other people from the town will be there. Or, maybe they won't. We weren't the only people at the barn." I give another headshake. "Anyway, I need to do this."

"What about Shawna Linnett?"

"Bailey's dad said she's not going to be there. She had a breakdown when she was told Jamie was dead. The doctors have prescribed something for her, but Kelvin said there's no way she could handle the funeral in her current state of mind."

I almost pitied the woman. She's been a bitch to Bailey *and* to me, but I still don't think she deserved to lose her son.

"There's nothing worse than outliving your children." Gran's voice is soft.

Our gazes connect and lock. She's thinking about my mom. I cross the room and gather her into my arms.

"She'd be so very proud of you, Rush."

I kiss the top of her head. "Thanks, Gran. I think she'd have been very disappointed in me for a while there, though." My voice is wry.

We stand together for a moment. I don't know what she's thinking, but my thoughts are with my mom. The happy days instead of the bad ones. It's been a long time since I thought about her smiles, her laughter, the sound of her humming while she baked. And, for the first time, the memories of her don't hurt. They make me smile.

Dropping my arms, I straighten and step back.

"I should go. Hank is driving us both to the church."

She reaches up to kiss my cheek.

"I love you, Rush. You're a good boy."

***

There are more people milling around outside the church than I thought there would be. I help Bailey out of the pickup, and she holds tight to my hand as we walk along the path. Two figures in dark suits break away from the small group to one side of the entrance and come toward us.

Kellan and Zoey Travers. The second they reach us, Zoey wraps Bailey into her arms and draws her away, leading her toward the other girls who have detached themselves from the waiting group, whispering quietly. Kellan looks at me. For once, that ever-present grin isn't smothered across his face.

"Rush." His voice is quiet, serious.

"I understand why Zoey is here, but why are you?"

He turns to look at the church. "Jamie was my friend." He holds up a hand when I start to protest. "No, hear me out. The Jamie *I* knew, when he was at school with us, isn't the one you knew. Sure, he had his moments of assholeness, but don't we all? I'm not here to mourn the bastard who shot up the rink. I'm here to mourn the friend I spent five years at school with. So are the others." He waves a hand behind him, and I focus on the small cluster of CBA students. "But, if that's going to be a problem, we'll leave. No harm, no foul." He faces me again. "We might be opponents on the ice." A small smile ghosts over his lips. "And occasionally face off in the woods. But I think, in different circumstances, we could be friends." He holds out a hand. I take it and we shake. "You'd make a good Monster, Rush."

It's an odd thing to say, but I take it as the compliment he seems to think it is. Together we walk across to the rest of his group. Cooper steps forward.

"I'm sorry, man. If I'd known—" He shakes his head. "He just didn't act any different whenever I saw him, you know?"

"It's not your fault. It's not anyone's fault." I repeat Bailey's words to him. "No one could have predicted what he did."

"But if I hadn't loaned him money, he might have come to terms with his situation sooner."

"You don't know that. If we go down the blame path, then we could blame his dad for bad financial decisions, his mom for the way she babied him. Maybe a teacher was mean to him. Maybe our coach should have pandered to him." I shake my head. "If that was the case, then we'd all be fucking bouncing off the walls insane."

His sigh is heavy. "I guess you're right."

"I think everyone is going inside." Kellan says. "Are any of your friends here?"

"Seven and the others refused to come. Dom is still in the hospital."

He pats my shoulder. "Then for today, you're one of us."

ZOEY SQUEEZES MY arm, leading me toward my cluster of friends. They look out of place outside the small church, dressed in fashionable black dresses. To our right, a wall runs around the graveyard, over which trees loom.

I check back to see where Rush is. He's standing with Kellan and Cooper, and I worry that there might be trouble. There's so much rivalry between the schools. I hope they don't bring it here today. I'm surprised to see so many kids from Churchill Bradley. I shouldn't be, Jamie was popular, but with everything he's done, I didn't expect them to show up. I guess they all remember the boy he'd once been. The kid with the charming smile who'd grown up amongst them.

"Bee." Kendall throws her arms around me and hugs me fiercely.

It's the first time I've been able to see them since the shooting. We've been constantly texting and calling each other, but they hadn't been able to get a pass from school. Seeing them makes the reason we're here all the more real.

Faith hugs me next. "I'm so sorry."

"Thanks for being here." My voice is low, absent of emotion.

Zuri gives me a worried look. "Are you okay?"

Zoey rolls her eyes. "Of course she's not okay."

No, I'm not. I'm frightened that if I loosen my grip on my emotions, I'll fall apart. Shatter like a fragile piece of glass.

This shouldn't be happening. Jamie shouldn't be dead.

I can't stop thinking about the boy I grew up with. My little brother. All the games we played. The laughter we shared.

Gone. It's all gone.

"Where's your mom?" Faith asks.

I swallow around the lump in my throat. "Dad thought it was best if she didn't come today."

Kendall curves her arms around my shoulders. "Have you spoken to him this morning?"

I shake my head.

Things have been strained between us over the past couple of weeks. I don't *think* he blames me for what happened with Jamie but there's a distance between us that wasn't there before. Maybe I'm imagining it but I'm grateful I have Hank and Rush to lean on right now.

My gaze moves over the people outside the church. Only one or two faces from Red Creek High stand out. None of Rush's friends are here. Daryl and Adam are standing near the doors.

Across the street from the church is another matter. There are small groups of local people, school students, hockey players. As soon as they make eye contact with me, they turn away and whisper to each other.

"Ignore them." Zoey advises. "They're nothing but vultures looking for gossip."

I nod, absently. She means well, and Hank has tried to keep me away from social media and news reports, but I've seen the things that have been posted about my family. No one in town is going to forgive Jamie for what he did. And because he's not here, they'll target their anger and grief at the family members who survived him.

"It's time." Zoey turns me toward the church.

The others fall into step around me. When we reach the heavy oak doors, Rush is waiting there with Kellan.

With a solemn expression he takes my hand, and escorts me inside. The stained-glass windows throw rich color across the stone floor as we move to the front to take our seats. My dad stands when I approach and takes my other hand. He leans in to kiss my cheek.

"I'm glad you came," he whispers.

87
Rush

THERE ARE NEWS vans outside the church when we exit, and the boys from CBA form a line in front of me and Bailey, blocking her from their view. Kellan drops back to walk beside me, while Zoey moves to Bailey's other side, with the rest of her friends fanning out behind us.

"Can I give you a ride somewhere?" Kellan asks in a low voice. "They'll be watching for Bailey and her dad, so they won't pay much attention to a bunch of snobby kids from the local private school."

I glance at Bailey. "Do you want to come back to my place? Hank's at work, I think."

She nods.

"If you could drop us at the trailer park, that'd be helpful."

"Not a problem. My car's the black one." He jerks his chin toward the black sports car parked at an angle on the grass, then touches Cooper on the shoulder. "Cause a distraction."

Cooper inclines his head and peels away from the group, taking three other boys with him. Kellan smiles at me.

"Wait for it …"

Almost as soon as he stops speaking, there's a shout followed by laughter, and then yelling.

"Get in the car."

The lights flash, and he pulls open the back passenger door. I push Bailey in, then join her in the back seat. Kellan is in the driver's seat seconds later. He wastes no time starting the engine, and slams his foot on the accelerator. The car takes off with a squeal of tires and the smell of burning rubber.

"What did they do?" Bailey asks.

Kellan laughs. "Who cares as long as they don't get caught?"

At the speed he's driving, it takes less than five minutes to reach the trailer park.

"Here will do." I lean forward and point to a spot near the entrance.

He brings the car to a stop, then twists in his seat. "It's nothing to be ashamed of, you know."

"What isn't?"

"Living here. Some of the richest people in the world started out in poverty."

"Thanks, but I don't need a pep talk from you."

That ever-ready smile curls his lips up. "That go-getter attitude will take you far."

"Fuck off, Travers." I throw open the door and climb out.

The driver's window slides down and he leans out. "You're welcome for the ride." His smile drops away, and he cuts a quick glance at Bailey when she climbs out and turns to face the trailer park. "If you'll take some advice …" His voice lowers and turns serious. "I'd find something to occupy her mind for a few hours. The come-down after something like this is fucking hard. So go find a way to boost her serotonin levels, or take some uppers. Because, trust me, the crash is going to be fucking hard otherwise."

He doesn't wait to hear a reply, taking off down the road, his hand waving out of the window as he goes. I turn slowly, my eyes searching out Bailey. She's standing by the entrance, arms wrapped around her waist, staring off into the distance.

Kellan's words roll around my head, and I check the time on my cell, glance at the sky, then move to stand beside her.

"Hey." I slide my arm around her and pull her into my side. "What do you say we go for a ride?"

She blinks, and turns her head to look at me. "A ride?"

"Yeah. Clear our heads. It's been a heavy afternoon." I guide her forward, and we walk to my trailer, where the door is open and my gran is sitting on the small table outside, chatting with some of her friends.

"Wait here," I tell Bailey, drop my arm and go over to my gran. "I'm taking Bailey for a ride."

She reaches out and pats my arm. "That's a good idea, sweetheart. Get some fresh air. Just be careful."

I nod. "We will. I just need to grab something from indoors." I jog up the steps and inside, rummage around the boxes stacked near the end of my bed, stuff a few things into a backpack, then head back outside. "Let's go."

I unchain my bike, put the helmet on Bailey's head, then climb on. Her arms wrap around my waist from behind. I pat the hands holding onto the front of my shirt. "Ready?"

She nods against my back. I fire up the engine, and take us both out of the trailer park.

A HAND TOUCHES mine. "Bailey?"

I blink, looking around. We're no longer in town. The bike has stopped, and Rush has one leg braced against the ground.

How long has my mind been drifting?

The sky has turned into a light dusky purple. Trees stretch around us in every direction, and it doesn't take much to recognize the clearing Rush has brought me to. I climb off from behind him, and remove the helmet.

Rush kicks the kickstand into place, swings his leg over the bike, and straightens. He takes the helmet from my hands, and hooks it over the handlebars, then turns to face me, head tilting.

"You ready?"

"For what?"

He moves to stand in front of me, his gaze searching my face for a moment. "I thought we could play a new game."

"We are?"

"You're going to hunt me this time."

"*Me?*"

He nods. "If you can catch me, I'm all yours to do with as you please."

"But—"

His finger presses against my lips. "Don't overthink it. Yes or no. Do you want to play?"

"But you're faster than me."

He smiles, wraps an arm around my waist and pulls me in so he can brush his lips over mine. "You're not scared of the Big Bad Wolf, are you?"

"No."

"Good." He lets go of me, takes his bag off his shoulder and reaches inside. "Here."

My eyes lock onto the switchblade he holds out to me. "Rush?"

"Hunt me."

"But—"

He takes my hand and presses the handle into my palm. I close my fingers around its solid length.

"You're in control here tonight. This is *your* game. Your rules. Not mine."

Eyes on his, my heart thuds wildly in my chest. He wants me to chase him through the woods. Hunt him down like an animal. A spark of desire ignites inside me and I lick my lips.

The idea shouldn't excite me, but it does.

He reaches out and brushes his thumb across my chin. "You're the hunter tonight."

He drops his hand and backs away. His gaze holds mine for one brief moment before he turns and heads off into the trees. The second he vanishes I look down at the knife in my hand. A strange sense of anticipation buzzes through me at the knowledge of being the pursuer.

Is this what he felt when he hunted me?

89

Rush

I MOVE THROUGH the trees, keeping pace with Bailey. Not that she can see me. Her gaze is focused straight ahead, and she's not looking at what might be happening to either side of her.

"Hunters should always be aware of their surroundings, Little Rose."

She stops, her head swinging from left to right when I speak. I lean against a tree, just out of view.

"Maybe you're not a wolf, after all. Maybe you're just a sheep in wolf's clothing."

Her fingers clench around the knife, and a scowl pulls her brows together. "I can hunt you."

"Prove it." I step out, so she can see where I am. "Come and catch me."

She turns toward me. I hike an eyebrow and back away slowly, until I'm out of view again. Predictably, she walks to the spot I'd been standing and keeps going in a straight line. I shake my head. The girl has no hunting skills at all. I wait until she's a few feet ahead of me, then move onto the path behind her.

I follow her, step for step, as she creeps through the trees, not once checking behind her. When we reach a clearing, she steps out into it while I remain where I am, waiting to see what she does.

She calls my name softly, and turns in a slow circle. "Rush? Are you here?"

When her back is to me, I move. I come out of the trees at speed, grab her around the waist and pin her against the nearest tree. Dipping my head, I press my chest against her back and put my lips to her ear.

"A wolf doesn't call for its prey, Little Rose. It *takes* what it wants." My teeth sink into the lobe of her ear. "It stalks and watches for weakness, and then it strikes." I drop one hand and squeeze her ass. "And when it sees the right moment ..." I drag my tongue down her throat and bite the curve of her shoulder. "That's when it strikes."

When her neck arches, I release my hold on her.

"Last chance, Little Rose. Otherwise, the hunter will become the hunted." I spin her to face me, cover the hand holding the knife with mine and lift it so the blade is between us. "If you want me, come and get me."

I take a step backward, then another, my gaze locked on hers. "What's the matter? You afraid? Think you can't do it?"

Something kindles in her eyes at my taunt, a fire I've not seen there for days. The fingers wrapped around the blade flex, and she launches herself forward. There's a quick flash of silver, then the knife is pressed against my throat, just beneath my jaw.

"Maybe I was waiting for you to show your weakness," she whispers.

"Is that so? And what is it?"

"*Me.*" She reaches up and sucks my bottom lip into her mouth, nipping sharply before pulling away. "Now back up." The knife tip digs into my skin and I do as she says, moving carefully until my back hits a tree. She pats my cheek with her free hand. "That's a good boy."

Her fingers toy with the buttons on my shirt, and she gazes up at me from beneath her lashes, dragging the blade down my throat, along the collar of my shirt and then she slices through the thread holding the first button in place. It falls to the ground. A second one follows it, then a third. The shirt parts, and she nudges it aside with the knife tip, dragging it over my chest until she bares my nipple. One corner of her mouth curls up, and her tongue peeks out from between her lips.

The blade circles my nipple. I tip my head back against the tree, and close my eyes.

"What are you going to do with me now that you've caught me, Little Rose?" My voice is rough.

Something wet laps over my nipple, and then there's a sharp sting of pain.

"I'm going to make you bleed … the same way you did me." Her teeth close over my nipple and she bites down.

"Fuck." The word leaves my mouth in a groan, feeling the pull as she sucks on it right down to my dick.

"Open your pants." The blade is on my other nipple now, following the same circle.

My hand falls to the belt around my hips and I unbuckle it and slide it off, then lower my zipper.

"Push them down. Underwear, too."

I shove both down my legs. She steps back and her gaze drops down to where my dick is straining upward, precum already beading the tip. She licks her lips.

"Touch yourself."

I reach down and wrap my fingers around my dick.

"Good boy. Now stroke it."

Her eyes don't move from my dick, tracking the steady movement of my hand as it moves, pumping slowly up and down.

"Faster."

I increase the speed, my teeth clenching. Her watching me pleasure myself amplifies the sensation, taking me from zero to sixty in seconds.

"Does it feel good?"

"You know it does."

"Do you want to come?"

"Yes."

"Too bad. Slow down, and open your eyes. Look at me."

I force my eyes to open and search her out. She's perched on a tree stump, watching me, eyes bright, nipples clearly outlined through her shirt. I wonder if her panties are wet, and have to control the urge to end this game and take over. I promised her control. I have to see this out to the end.

"Get naked."

I strip out of my ruined shirt, toe off my shoes, then kick out of my pants and underwear, until I'm standing completely naked in front of her.

"Turn in a slow circle. Show me your body."

I feel like a fucking piece of meat. Is this how she felt when I was tormenting her, when I was using her, when I was fucking with her?

I move away from the tree and turn, presenting her with my back.

"I didn't tell you to stop stroking your dick. Keep fucking your hand, and turn back to face me."

I grit my teeth, and face her. My body is almost vibrating with the need to come.

"Bailey." Her name is a growl.

"Get on your hands and knees and crawl to me."

I narrow my eyes. She arches an eyebrow.

I drop to my hands and knees and crawl across the ground to where she's perched on the fucking tree stump like it's a throne and she's the fucking queen of the forest. When I reach her, she pats my head.

Pats. My. Fucking. Head.

"Good boy. Now sit back on your heels and open your legs. Go back to stroking your dick."

I can feel the muscle popping in my jaw when I do as she says. I'm almost at the limits of my control. If I don't come soon, I'm not going to be responsible for my actions.

She hops off the stump and comes to stand in front of me. With slow movements, she draws her skirt up her thighs, until her panties are on show. She steps between my legs, slips her foot out of a shoe and places it on my thigh.

"Kiss me."

I start to stand. She presses down on my thigh. "Not the lips on my mouth." Her fingers hook into her panties and she pulls them down. "Here."

I don't need telling twice. I let go of my dick, grab her thighs and pull her pussy against my mouth. My tongue pushes between the plump lips to search out her clit. She tugs my hair.

"Bad boy. I said kiss, not lick." Her voice is breathy. "Tell me you're sorry."

I press a kiss to her hip, another to her thigh, then a third on her pussy. "I'm very sorry." I don't *sound* sorry. I sound fucking feral.

She pats my head again. I snap my teeth together to stop myself from growling at her.

"Is my Big Bad Wolf hungry? Does he want to eat?"

My fingers tighten around my dick.

Fucking *eat*?

I want to devour her until her throat is hoarse from the screaming.

Her fingers run through my hair. "Ask to eat my pussy like a good boy."

I clench my jaw and tip my head back to look her dead in the eye. "May I please have the pleasure of eating your pussy, Bailey?"

She pouts, her finger toying with the front of her shirt.

"I think you can do better than that." Her legs widen a little, changing the direction of my gaze, and giving me a quick glimpse of wet, pink flesh.

"Fuck this." I surge to my feet, tear the front of her shirt open and toss her onto her back, then come down on top of her. My hand slides between her thighs, and I shove two fingers inside her. "This pussy belongs to me. It's *mine*. If I want to fucking eat it, I *will*. If I want to fuck it, I'll do that, too."

I drag down her bra, and bite a nipple. "These are mine. If I want to bite them and suck them, I will. If I want to mark them …" I suck hard on the soft underside of her breast. "I *fucking* will."

Her nails rake down my back, and she arches up against the fingers thrusting in and out of her in a furious rhythm.

"If I want you to come," I growl. "I'll make you fucking come." I pull my fingers free, and push her legs apart, kneel between her thighs and press my dick against her pussy. I use my thumbs to spread her open, displaying her clit, and flick it with one finger.

"Whose pussy is this?"

"Yours."

"Whose dick do you want?" I pinch her clit.

"*Yours*." The word ends on a gasp when I slam into her.

"And don't you fucking forget it."

L. ANN & CLAIRE MARTA

90

Bailey

Rush takes my mouth in a savage kiss. He's out of control and I love every second of it. Taunting and teasing him has been a delicious kind of payback after what he did to me for months, but *nothing* was going to stop me from having him fuck me out here under the trees.

He rides me hard and fast. There's nothing but him. Us. My wolf who's set on taking what's his. What's always been his.

His hand tangles in my hair and pulls my head back. His teeth bite down on the side of my neck, and my eyes roll back.

"Rush!" I cry out, arching up into him.

His grip on my hair tightens, the fingers of his other hand circle my throat. The action only builds my excitement.

"That's it. Take my dick." He grinds himself into my pussy. "I'm the only one who will give you what you need."

I clutch at his shoulders, his back, dig my nails into his ass to pull him deeper. I'm just as hungry for him as he is for me. He reaches down between our joined bodies, finds my clit and pinches it.

The pain is enough to send me shooting toward the stars and I come ... *hard*, screaming into his mouth as my body jerks beneath his, my nails clawing at his skin. He groans, swearing furiously, as he slams into me, over and over.

Violent shivers wreck my body, and I float back to earth, while his movements slow until he shudders, and collapses on top of me. The only sounds I can hear are our heavy breathing. My heart is throwing itself against my ribs, and I can feel his doing the same.

I run my hands through his hair. "I love you."

His lips curve against my throat. "I love you, Little Rose."

Tightening my grip in his hair, I pull his head up and kiss him. His teeth close over my bottom lip, and he tugs it, nipping gently. The small stab of hurt makes me twitch and clench around his dick. He chuckles and runs his nose along mine.

"Greedy prey." He presses lazy kisses over my lips, my cheeks, the tip of my nose, and the unbearable gentleness of the action smashes through the final blocks of ice that have been protecting me.

Sorrow and grief crash over me. Tears fill my eyes, and spill over before I can stop them. Rush's tongue catches one, then another.

"That's it, baby. Let it all out now."

The soft growl is my undoing. A sob rips from my throat, and the pain of loss overtakes me. I cling to him, mourning the loss of the brother I'd lost. For the family that's been destroyed.

"It's going to hurt," he whispers. "But you're strong enough to face it." His thumb sweeps away another tear. "That's what you taught me, baby. It's okay to grieve. It's okay."

I lose track of how long we lay there in the dirt, Rush's weight holding me secure in the storm of grief, but eventually the tears slow to a stop.

I sniff. "I'm sorry."

"You have nothing to be sorry about. You *never* have to apologize for what you're feeling." His mouth finds mine again. "I love you, Bailey." He presses his forehead to mine. "Let's go home."

***

Hank is sitting on the step of his trailer when we return.

"You two okay?" he asks when we reach him.

Rush nods. "We will be."

His attention leaves the boy at my side. "I have something for you."

"*Me*?"

"Kelvin dropped it off earlier. Said you'd want it." He twists on the steps, reaches into the doorway of the trailer and lifts out a shoebox.

I press my hands over my mouth.

Rush steps forward to take it from him. "Isn't this—"

"Your letters." I whisper shakily.

"But I thought Jamie destroyed them all."

Hank rises from the step. "Kelvin said he stopped him before he could burn them all."

Tucking the box under one arm, Rush takes my hand. "Come on."

I let him lead me through the trailer park toward a cluster of empty picnic tables. He places the box onto the table, and pulls me down to sit beside him. I'm scared to open the lid. I don't want to see how many letters Jamie destroyed.

"Did you ever read the end of the book I sent you? The one you took to Churchill Bradley?"

I shake my head. He smiles, sorts through the letters, then frowns.

"Where did you find this?" He takes out a leather wrist wrap and turns it over, finding the branded initials on the inside.

I attempt to smile. "You left it in the closet when you moved out. It's how I figured out who you are."

He strokes his finger over the worn lettering. "My dad got it made for me a couple of years ago. I thought I'd lost it for good." He reaches for my hand, lifts it, and snaps the wrap around my wrist. "It's yours now."

He reaches back into the box and takes out the small book. I watch with a weird sense of anticipation while he flips through the pages until he gets to the back, then places the book on the table and turns it toward me.

"Read it."

His tone of voice, his *wolf* voice, refuses to be denied, and my gaze lowers to the words on the paper.

Hey, Bug.

I hope this book has helped. I didn't want you to feel alone at the Academy. I promise I won't ever stop writing to you, but I hope you have found some friends.

I thought maybe we could make a promise to each other. Would you meet up with me the day after graduation? There's a diner in Red Creek. Darla's. We could go for milkshakes.

I glance up to find Rush. There's a smile playing around his lips.

"You wanted to meet me at Darla's when we graduated?"

"I told you. You've always been my girl. I wasn't prepared to wait any longer than that to claim you."

If this boy didn't already have my heart, he would now.

We've been bound together longer than I realized.

Our hearts and lives have been woven together through ink and paper since we were eight years old.

THE END

(for now ... well, until Seven's book where we'll see more of Rush and Bailey, as well as what Seven is up to ...)

We know ... there's no epilogue fast-forwarding years into the future. We haven't forgotten. We promise, you'll see how everyone's lives turn ... just not quite yet.

Please stick wtih us ;)

The Red Creek Ravens return in Dirty Snipe (Seven's story) - https://books2read.com/dirtysnipe

If you enjoyed Broken Puck, we would love it if you could leave us a review on Amazon or GoodReads.

AUTHORS NOTE

Thanks must go to our ever-patient (not) Alpha reading team, who waited quietly for each new chapter to drop; Tee for her borderline obsessiveness over making sure the finished books were as error-free as humanly possible; and to everyone who didn't even look surprised when we announced we wanted to write a bully hockey romance.
It seems we were the only ones who were surprised by the idea.

We hope you enjoyed Rush and Bailey's story. We know we haven't added an epilogue yet, but things need to happen in the upcoming books before we show how their lives turned out.

Trust us.

You know it'll all be fine ....

L. Ann - https://facebook.com/lannauthor

Claire Marta - https://facebook.com/clairemartabooks

You can also join their active reader groups:-

L. Ann's Literati - https://facebook.com/groups/lannsliterati

Claire's Liquor & Lust - https://facebook.com/groups/clairesliquorandlust

You can find more books by L. Ann and Claire Marta on Amazon in paperback, ebook and audio.

Printed in Great Britain
by Amazon